THE FERRYMAN'S KNIGHT

SEAN MOONEY

For Kim: You enjoyed Persephone as a minor character so much, I made her the main character in her own story.

CHAPTER ONE

On this bright, crisp spring morning, I find myself at a fish market because the man with the fire in his eyes told me to do so. I linger, frozen in the moment, as my senses enjoy the symphony of sound and motion. Ships made for war with the sea creaking in the near distance. The smell of the marsh. The distinctive odor of mucked water. The scent of freshly caught fish resting in open crates and baskets. The crowd's murmur bubbles just under the hawking voices of the fishmongers calling from their stands, shacks, and stalls. Being here, I can't help but think of my childhood. Like my Patron, my father had angry eyes, and I often did as he told me. Like his crew, I feared those eyes that could be quietly supportive or silently demanding. However, in contrast to his crew, I was also privy to my father's kind and loving heart, mind, and arms. His absence was always dearly felt, and his homecomings were always a time of celebration. As a child, I often found myself at the seaside market or along the docks first thing in the morning, either standing with my mother to see him off or hiding in wait for his return.

But this isn't 1210; I'm not six years old or in Marseille's Old Port. This is 1761, I'm an agent for my Patron, and I'm in London's Billingsgate. My mind snaps me back to the present in time to sidestep as a cart, piled high with empty baskets, is pushed down the lane toward me by a sullen-looking young man. His sudden appearance happened as my mind drifted – *no coincidences*. I observe him, glimpsing the details of his life in a few steps. His graying trousers and shirt are typical of a laborer and, indeed, not a sailor with that pale skin. A new worsted cap pulled low over his eyes – it's something a mother would make as a birthday present. One wonders if she thought to give him such a gift to help hide the dark circles under his eyes. His hands and feet are what draw my attention. Long slender fingers, nails trim and clean, and although he's pushing a cart, his grip is light. His shoes, scuffed, not new, but maintained. The soft leather makes almost no sound as he takes his steps. Slender fingers, light of touch and step, making no eye contact but plenty of glancing around. A thief in the night. Given his lackluster expression, I guess he prefers his midnight roving to his day job.

Of interest, but I get no sense of urgency. A task is at hand; my Patron has set my course, and I know to follow the signs until all is revealed. After a few steps, I knew this young man not to be my reason for being here. I continue to follow him, though. It's easy enough, even to hide from someone who is trying to notice everything within arm's reach without being noticed himself. The crowd works in both our favors. Attentions are diverted, split, and occupied by the displays of goods, deals, and haggling. I barely need to tap my will as I weave through the crowd a few paces behind the cart pusher, a shadow in the eyes of any who notice – there and then gone again. I start to wonder about his destination as we pass by many of the stalls in the jumble of sellers, but the next moment, he begins to slow. He stops at a row of shacks behind a semi-circle of three tables busy with the morning trade, his way forward blocked. A gentleman in tan breeches, well-polished buckled shoes, and an expensive vest and coat is jabbing a cane into the chest of another gentleman wearing an apron mottled with fish blood.

"Excuse me, sir." The young man addresses the well-dressed man. "Begging your pardon, could I get through here? Thank ye."

I note the formal deference but also that he could have gone around the two men, and I think the scowl on the face of the well-dressed man suggests he knows this too. Without a word, however, the well-dressed man takes a step back, allowing the cart to pass. The cane immediately comes up and nudges the pile of baskets atop the cart, sending them toppling into the lane. With a satisfied smirk, the well-dressed gentleman returns to prodding the man with the apron. The young man plays at quiet annoyance, but I see the twitch of his fingers and the slight rise at the corners of his mouth. As he scrambles to collect his baskets, I watch him brush against the well-dressed man and come away with something shiny. It all happens quickly enough that I almost don't notice. I'm impressed. The young man continues on his way, calling out as he approaches a shack, "I've got your order, Mister

Stanwix." He deposits a few baskets at the last shack in this row.

A man I assume to be Mister Stanwix exits his prep shack and examines the baskets. Mister Stanwix is a brick wall of a man. A mighty beard hides most of his face. He and the young man begin to chat, interrupted as the well-dressed man pushes between them. "Out of my way," he snarls. Mister Stanwix tips his nonexistent hat while the young man flashes a rude gesture at the well-dressed man's back. I slip around the shack and follow the well-dressed man. I don't typically interfere with humans outside of my task, but there have been times when I've been tempted to bend that rule over the years. As I watch him sneer at the mud accumulating on his shoes with each step, I picture myself walking up next to him and giving him a nudge to tip him over. He wouldn't even know it was me. I would make sure of that. Besides, he's too distracted by the ruin of his fancy apparel — it would be no effort at all. I'm within an arm's reach as he turns onto more solid paving.

The gentle ringing of a handbell brings me to a stop. It's not a sound I hear, so much as feel tingling in my

mind. I glance around; something
flickers in the corner of my eye.
Something familiar. A man, tall and
thin, yet broad of shoulder, standing
with a hunch – his posture reminiscent
of a shepherd's crook. He's dressed in
wide ankle-length trousers and a linen
shirt partially hidden under a woolen
hip-length dark blue jacket. Balding
gray hair circles his head, and his
eyes are intent on me. Eyes with pupils
of fire. His appearance has shifted
over the many years, but I know my
Patron. And, just as quickly as I spot
him, he's gone. I continue to look
north, up King's Road into the borough
proper. I catch a hint of a scream and
then a woman dashing out of an alley. A
man quickly approaches her side;
consoling hands are set upon her
shoulders. Something has upset their
morning constitutional. I abandon the
well-dressed man and walk to the edge
of the wharf area. The couple has moved
off, but I see a small cluster of
humans in the alley the woman had found
upsetting. The crowd, consisting of two
sailors and an elderly woman of modest
means with a small basket hanging from
the crook of her arm, lingers outside
an alley door. Their bodies shift back
and forth, trying to see through a

doorway. I add my eyes to those gathered at the threshold.

The door frame appears undamaged, and so too the door itself – kept wide open by one of the sailors so as not to block the view of the bloody mess about ten feet in front of the door. The room beyond appears to be a small storage chamber. Stacked crates and barrels, shelves with burlap sacks, and a brick staircase up to a closed door along the back wall. The door at the top of the stairs suddenly opens, and a young city watch guard steps through.

"Nothing, Charles. They make chairs upstairs, and no one saw or heard anything," he calls down into the room.

Stepping out from behind some of the shelves is the other watchman, spear at the ready. "Same, James. Nothing down here. The room is clear," Charles says, a hint of disappointment in his voice. "Did you move the body?"

"No."

"Well, why not?" Charles sets his spear down as he kneels next to the body.

I hear a rush of footfalls; it's a man, perhaps thirty or so years of age, fit in his youth based on his run – though less so these days - black waistcoat, clean shirt, but ink stains upon his fingers. He comes in behind me and is about to say something as an expression of confusion passes over his face. I've been told it's like sudden dizziness when my will is exerted to filter a person's perception. He blinks and moves around me as if not seeing me. "I'm glad I ran." He huffs. "I was afraid I would miss it."

The guards look up at his voice and sigh.

"Got something for me, lads?" the new man asks, hardly hiding his excitement.

"William," Charles mutters with a sneer. "I'm beginning to think witchcraft."

James crosses himself.

"Come now, Charles, let's not say such things." William pretends to be offended.

"Yet you seem to have an uncanny ability to find such atrocity." Charles stands, taking up his spear.

A tense but silent tete-a-tete passes between Charles and William before William concedes with a step back and a smirk. "No witchcraft, my friend, just open ears and open eyes. This is a dangerous part of town; things are always turning up. And as for this, well, just down the lane, there is a pair of chirping birds pouring out their terrified little hearts to any who would listen."

I can see Charles working his jaw. "You lot," he shouts, "enough of this standing around. Off with you." He waves away the two sailors.

I look, the woman with the basket is gone — and I hadn't noticed. *Curious.* It will have to wait. I take the opportunity to follow behind William, his movement masking my own. As long as I can find a quiet corner, no eyes should be the wiser of me. It's easy enough to find a shadow beside a few stacked crates and lean in against a shelf. Invisibility would be better, but that's magic and not a skill I'm particularly adept at. Besides, magic leaves a trail, a scent that can be followed or discovered, while altering perception is a more precise and subtle manipulation. I prefer precise. Direct. Many of my brothers and sisters employ subversion and subterfuge as their primary tactics. "Give me a fight, and let's be done," I mutter. My breath catches as I see all three of their heads turn. My heart stops. They see me, or perhaps just a shimmer. I watch their faces trying to understand the sudden appearance of a tall, pale-eyed, black-haired woman dressed in a red and green bodice and matching quilted skirt. Excuses pile up in my mind, but before I can choose one, the moment passes - I'm able to shift their perception once more, and they're back to staring at the body.

"Help me with him." Charles sets his spear down and waves over James. There's a wet sucking sound as the body is rolled over. The ghastly outline of a torso remains in the pool of blood surrounding the body, which was so recently a man. I can properly see his injuries now that he's on his back. Most of the blood seems to have poured forth from the wound to his face - and by that, I mean by the caving in of his face.

"He's cold and stiff. Died during the night, I suppose." James cringes and looks away from the mangled face.

"Well, alright then." Charles gets to his feet. "Let's leave him for the night watch then."

"What? Leave him all day?" James says incredulously. "It's not winter out there. In an hour, you'll smell him all the way down to the docks."

Charles grumbles and sighs. "Fine. We'll get the Constable and call the wagon. But that's a lot of back and forth, and I'll not be doing that."

This time James sighs and gets to his feet. "I'll notify the Constable. What do I tell him?"

"We've got a… sailor, be my guess. Died during the night."

"More than that, I think." William, who had been silently taking in the scene, speaks up. "Any papers?"

Charles nods to James, who reluctantly gets close enough to the body to sort through the pockets. "Nothing. No papers. No bag. Nothing." He swiftly backs away.

Charles grunts. "Well then, you tell the Constable we have an unknown sailor. Dead."

"Murdered, I think." William nudges the leg of the deceased.

There's a moment of silent thought as they all contemplate the body.

"Cudgel, maybe?" James says.

Charles shakes his head. "The face is all torn up. No. A brick. Got his face smashed in by someone with a brick."

"Or a fist," William and I say at the same time. He jumps at my voice and scans the room. "You gave this place a look, right?" I see Charles and James follow his eyes around the room. I resist the urge to move deeper into the shadows. I hold my breath.

And then Charles chuckles. "It was just an echo. You're very jittery for a man who willingly lingers around danger." Charles chuckles again and nods to James. "Brick to the face. Some disagreement turned violent, ending with a brick to the face. The body was dragged in here. That's what you tell the Constable."

James gives a brisk nod and leaves.

"It's not what happened, though," William steps up beside Charles and points at the neck and the edges of the facial injuries. "Are those puncture marks? And look at this bruising. I've seen enough fisticuffs to recognize a punch."

Charles shrugs. "They fought, and *then* he got a brick to the face." He turns away and steps toward the door.

I can tell from William's expression that the explanation doesn't sit too well with him. But then he smiles. "Crusher strikes again."

Charles grunts from where he stands at the door and turns around. "You know a few others like this?"

I don't know if Charles picks up on this, but William is about to lie.

"Nope. But, `Crusher Strikes
Again´ makes for a better headline."

CHAPTER TWO

I watch as Charles pushes William from the room. The watchman takes up a position outside the door to the alley to await the return of James and the body cart. Thankfully, he hadn't taken the primary light source before leaving. The torch, set in a sconce by the stairs to the upper level, still burns, and other than some diffused light coming in from the open door to the alley, it remains my only way to see everything the city watch had missed. A storage room for certain, divided unevenly by a few floor-to-ceiling shelves, but no piles of the wood or barrels of nails I'm assuming chair makers would require daily. Instead, I see a line of dust-covered books on a shelf at the bottom of the stairs. A few canisters of oil. Several boxes of broken parts. The room is mainly occupied by burlap sacks filled with sawdust and discarded pieces of wood. There is a market for such waste among other merchants and even common citizens. But there's a stillness to the room, as if it is seldom entered. The air recently moved, yet

unmistakably stale. This smart use of
the business castoff as an extra source
of income may not be the work of the
man in charge. I think someone has been
stashing this material away and selling
it on the side as they can.

I next examine the door to the
alley, which has been partially pulled
closed. No boot marks on the wood. No
fresh scuffs to the wood frame. No
fresh scratches on the lock. No forced
entry. Whoever this person was and
whatever he was doing here, someone let
him in. "Or you had a key, and it,
along with all the rest of your
identification, was taken from you."

I return to the body as I complete
my pass around the room. With Charles
outside the room and turned away from
the door, I'm a little freer with my
movements as I examine the corpse
closely. My eyes linger on the puncture
marks at first. There is a faint
outline around the wound, almost as if
the poor fellow was bitten, but the
line is smooth. My guess is a weapon of
some sort with two prongs. "Something
that didn't leave even a trickle of
blood. Curious." My attention shifts to
the face. "Interesting that William
could so easily tell damage done by a
fist versus a cudgel." That aside, even

from across the room, I could tell this attack was swift and brutal. "Something strong and fast." There are ways to detect my brothers and sisters. We walk in magic, steeped in it, in fact. We leave wakes in the fabric of reality wherever we go. And yet, besides my gut, I sense none of that residual energy. "There are ways to mask ourselves, even from each other…" I mutter and shift my attention.

There are no drag marks on the soles of the man's shoes or the ground. He's dressed as a sailor, and his tanned complexion would suggest many hours in unshaded sunlight. Yet, his hands – I reach down and turn over his left and then his right hand. They've seen some hard work, but not nearly enough if he is a sailor. "Could be new to the sea," I say to myself. His clothing isn't new; much like his hands, there's wear, just not enough to convince me this man has spent years on the ocean. And something else about his attire is tugging at my attention. "The guards moved him, but…" I stand up and step back. "His shirt is crumpled." I click my teeth together as I think – and then stop abruptly. "He looks like he's been grabbed." I stand astride him and lurch forward as if being tugged.

"If he had been pulled forward, then,"
I noticed something the position of the
arms had been hiding. There's a fresh
gouge in the stone floor. Something
heavy had recently struck the spot,
chipping away some of the foundation.

I scan the room, keeping my
attention on the floor. "There." In the
corner of the room is a stack of crates
and a small wooden box at the base of
those crates. I step over to it,
observing it as fully as possible
before laying a single finger on it.
It's perhaps slightly bigger than the
palm of my hand. The wood is aged gray,
though there are places where the
yellow of the original color can be
seen. The paneling is dried and cracked
in places, with the corners of the box
capped in silvery metal. The lock,
crafted in the likeness of a bronzed
leaf, has three symbols I don't
recognize arranged in a circle. More
eye-catching is that the lock remains
open.

I'm cautious as my fingers reach
out for the box. I flinch as my
fingertips graze the lid – it's cold.
Not freezing, but well below room
temperature. I slide my fingers along
the contours, feeling the grain of the
wood made rough with age, and find it's

not just the lid that is cold. I sense
no traps and pick up the box. "Ugh," I
grunt as I pick it up. The only metal I
see are the corner caps, but the box is
heavy enough to be made from lead.
"Now, let's find out what was worth
murdering for." The tiny hinges give
the slightest squeak as I lift the lid.
The box is empty. There's a small slit
in the middle of the interior,
reminding me of a man I met once in
Venice. He was from the East and sold
decorative coin boxes. Just in case, I
give the box a little shake. Nothing
rattles. "Too easy, I suppose."
Whatever was inside is missing, but I'm
sure there's magic here. I turn the box
over in my hands. Other than the three
symbols on the front, no markings or
blood stains exist. I have no idea what
this item is, but I'm sure it's not the
murder weapon. A yawn from Charles
momentarily draws my attention,
reminding me that my time is not
indefinite.

I circle the body with one last
examination. "The dead man knew his
attacker," I mutter to myself, "Or, at
the very least, was not threatened by
his attacker. They had agreed to meet
here, knowing it was a place where they
could conduct their business

uninterrupted. They knew this because one of them had a key. After all, they were given a key by whoever filled this room with bags of sawdust. Which means -" I glance up the stairs as I slip the box into the leather satchel hanging off my shoulder.

The door at the top of the brick staircase is unlocked. I step through into a narrow and short hallway. It's dark, making the room the hallway connects with seem even brighter. Several large windows allow in the light of the day. I linger in the hallway at the threshold to the workroom. I see craftsmen working with drills, hammers, chisels – every tool of the trade to assemble chairs. *And none of them double-pronged*. The aroma of oak, cedar, ash, and pine drift through the air. A faint odor of wood smoke catches my nostrils. Someone is pressing too hard with a drill. But the scent is almost covered by the small oven where wood is being fire-etched and strengthened. There are stacking areas. Young boys carry the finished work to these roped-off places labeled "to upholster" and "ready for sale". All the work that used to be accomplished in a cottage until someone had the bright idea to move it to one poorly ventilated room where humans force other humans to work excessively long hours for farthings.

Speaking of which, I catch sight of the floor foreman coming out of the back office. An unimpressive middle-aged man with a chinstrap beard – though perhaps one who has recently come into some money. His trousers are blue with a matching waistcoat and pristine white shirt, and he has a fashionable dark-blue tricorne hat with gold braided trim in hand. *Fine clothes for a humble floor manager*. He waves off a worker as he shuts and locks the office door. As he steps away from the first, another man who isn't as easily put off comes up to him. I take the opportunity to move my way around the room. I come to a set of wide stairs leading down into a foyer with a few doors, including the large front doors. I arrange myself as if coming up the stairs, wait for the foreman to be near, and then drop my will. We nearly bump into each other.

"Oh, excuse me." My hand presses to my chest.

"Yes. My mistake," he nods, ready to pass me by, but stops upon a second look. He glances over my shoulder and behind himself, looking for my escort.

He looks back at me with curiosity.
"Are you lost, Miss?"

My presence has put him off, but
those worry lines I noticed on his
forehead as he came from his office are
still unmistakable. *Let's apply some
pressure*. "No. No, I don't think so." I
smile but glance back at the doors.
"Sorry, I'm a little out of sorts."

"Very well, Miss."

He addresses me with `miss,´ which
on the surface can come off as polite,
but in truth, it is a way to address a
woman the speaker feels lacks
respectability. He could have used
misses, or ma'am, or even madam. I try
to give him the benefit of the doubt
and assume he chose to use miss because
of my youthful appearance. "Misses,
actually, if you don't mind. I'm here
to speak with whoever is in charge
about some business." The worry lines
on his forehead vanish as his head
tilts and his eyes squint in curiosity.

"That would be me, Miss."

"Well, of course," I gesture to
his attire as I smile. "It's just - I
was making my way to this location when
I saw the most ghastly of things…" I
lean in as I continue, "A murder. And
just around the alley."

"Yes, well -"

"Did you know? I mean, it must have taken place in the basement of this building, certainly."

"I don't know anything about that, Miss," he says with irritation clearly taking over his curiosity.

"Misses, actually," I verbally poke him again. "Oh, I thought the city watch would have spoken with someone here. I mean, it was just around there," I say with some volume as I turn to point.

"Miss, please," he gently pushes my arm down.

"Yes, of course. I have no wish to upset you. You must have known the young man."

The worry lines are back. "Miss, I assure you, if one of my workers was missing, I'd know about it. And last I counted, all heads are here."

"But the alley door -"

"I don't expect you to know this, Miss, but if you know which doors to use, you can almost pass from one side of the city to the other without stepping outside." He's fidgeting with his hat, perhaps saying more than he had intended.

"Sorry, you're quite right. I'm being silly. It just - it was such a fright. I don't know how those watchmen

22

can stomach such a thing." I see him glancing at the door, eager to be done with this conversation or eager to be someplace else - or both. "That poor young man. He had been beaten so terribly. I can't help but think of his mother or friends." I watch his reaction - a wince and then the passing of his hand over his upper lip.

"Well, I can't speak to knowing anything about any watchmen or murder - "

"Oh, but that is such an unbecoming way to begin a conversation. Allow me to introduce myself properly. My name is Persephone Favreau." I put out my hand.

He begrudgingly takes up the tips of my fingers and gives a curt bow. "Wallace Graham. Miss Favreau -"

"Misses, actually. Or madam will do nicely. I'm here to do some business, perhaps. We're having a new house built,"

"Madam Favreau, we sell to businesses, not to individuals. There are many fine establishments that will gladly take your patronage. Now, if you'll excuse me,"

"Oh, but," I step in front of him, "Father always said, the best apples are plucked from the tree. And I do want the very best for the new house."

He passes his eyes over my red and green quilted skirt and bodice – though I'm still casting my will to obscure the leather back sheath snugly holding my morningstar. His frown would suggest my common clothing is not keeping up with my story. He's not sure why I'm here but, regardless, he's concluded that I'm not worth his time. "Be that as it may, Miss. We don't sell to individuals. However, if you would like to have your husband or father stop by, or if you like, leave me one of their cards, I will contact them at my earliest convenience. Now, if you please, *I* have important things to take care of. Thank you, and good day." With that, he crams his hat onto his head and walks away. He stops at the bottom of the stairs and turns sharply. "If you don't mind me saying, Miss, careful with that accent. France isn't too popular right now." He adjusts his hat and leaves through the front doors.

I'm not sure if that was a warning or a threat. Either way, I'm not bothered by it. I put on a slightly distressed expression and sidle over to the nearest workbench, where a burly man carefully applies wood stain to a freshly completed chair. "Is your foreman always so bristly?"

"Madam," he inclines his head but declines to say anything further.

"Well, perhaps it's the good Lord telling me to take my business elsewhere. Good day to you," I say politely and smile. It's followed by another "Madam," after I've taken a few steps. I turn back to the burly man, who had set down his brush and was wiping his brow with a sweat-stained rag. "Yes?"

He stares at me for a few seconds as if reevaluating his choice to speak up. With a sigh, he speaks. "He's a foreman, and they're paid to be loud and mean, but - Mister Graham... I'm trying to say, Madam - I've worked for far worse."

"Out of sorts today, then?"

"Yes, Madam, I'd say."

"Arrived in a bad mood?"

"No, Madam."

I smile and nod. "Thank you, mister..."

"Cunningham."

I bob a curtsy and turn to leave, but Mister Cunningham has more to say.

"Madam," he takes a step as he reaches out. He waits until I turn back. "What's bad for one is bad for all."

"I'm sorry?"

"I heard you say something about a murder, and there was a watchman up here earlier. I'm just saying I don't think Mister Graham is mixed up in any of that. He seemed very upset by the news."

Mister Cunningham's words more or less verify my thoughts. It would seem Mister Wallace Graham wasn't involved in the murder, but I'm very much certain that he knows more about it than he was willing to first say. "Very good, Mister Cunningham. I've reconsidered my reconsideration. I think Mister Graham will be seeing me again." I nod and turn away.

I step carefully through the main doors, glancing right and left. No Graham. I move up to the alley and peek around the corner. "There you are," I whisper, moving down the alley. I exert my will, but am extra careful to move slowly and stay close to the wall. An agitated mind is harder to convince not to notice me. And Graham is agitated. He appears to be using a calm tone, but his body language belies that.

"As I said, Sir, just a bit of unpleasantness. The Watch is handling it."

"And the killer?"

"Please, Sir. Move along. The cart will be arriving soon, so let's have some respect for the dead and give them some privacy during this disturbing moment."

Charles is likewise using a calm tone, but his body language also speaks volumes – his is saying that he's tired of being questioned. Wallace sets his jaw, gets a last peek over Charles' shoulder, and then moves away. Charles adjusts his stance and mutters, "Should have left it for the night watch."

I've seen all I need to - for now. No use in following Graham either. I'll find him when I need to. My next step is to see what the dead have to say. I try to avoid places where the dead accumulate, but I have a feeling that the victim will have much to say. Probably worth the risk. But first I need to message a friend.

CHAPTER THREE

The cart, the body laid out under a shroud, and the watchmen head north through the alley. Following them isn't difficult. Even without my will, they're well engrossed in a conversation about biscuits and beer. They almost miss it when they turn one way leaving the alley, and the cart is pushed along in the opposite direction. I leave Charles and James to their duty and keep my distance from the cart pusher. The pace is steady, but an ill-timed carriage breaks my line-of-sight, leaving me with nothing to follow. I guess at the eventual destination. Given the unknown identity of the individual, the body will probably be taken to the parish officials instead of the family. After some polite questions, I come to cross Poplar High Street and find I am correct.

Tucked back along a side street, I can see the spire of Saint Matthias Old Church. An unassuming brick and stone building that merged its classical and gothic features cohesively. "An architect with some talent," I mutter, staring up at the spire above me. But I'm unsure whether the church or the

almshouse next door should have my
attention. "Diligence," I say as I
skirt around to the back of the church
and gaze upon the graveyard. I sense no
disturbance – and this I find
frustrating. Annoyingly, it would seem,
more skulking will be necessary. I
follow a path that takes me to the back
of the almshouse. The large two-story
house could use some repair, but it's
the two doors at the back that I wonder
about. Both are attached to sections of
the building that appear to have been
added to the original structure. The
cart is here, left, hopefully, only
momentarily unattended in a somewhat
hidden shady spot. I could find a spot
to wait, or try the door, but it's a
busy area, and manipulating objects
makes it harder to hide myself. Rather
than risk the doors, and wanting to
finish my look around, I continue my
short walk around the side of the house
back to High Street. I spot a few boys
playing near the street.

    "Excuse me, young sirs." They
laugh at my greeting – *I think it's my
accent*. I guess their ages are between
ten and twelve.

    "What? Us?"

    "Why yes." They laugh again. "I
was wondering if you might do me a

small favor?" They exchange looks of uncertainty. "A pence if you say yes, and a shilling," I pause as I see their eyes widen, "each, when you return."

"What do you need us to do?" one of the boys asks quickly.

"Something very simple for such strong and smart boys. I need you to give someone a message for me. You see, I'm traveling with someone, and rather than doubling back to where we said we'd meet, I thought it would be easier for them to meet me here."

They nod. "What's the message?"

I fish around in my satchel and pull a small leather purse from it. "Here is the first half of what I promised." I hand each a shiny pence. "And this," I pull a small stone from the same pouch. I squeeze it once and then pass it to the oldest-looking of the boys. "Do you know the fish market —"

"What do you want us to do with this?" the boy interrupts.

"Now, now. Manners." The other boys playfully shove him. "As I was saying, do you know the fish market near here?" They nod their answer. "A little ways further along, there are some docks. And just at the end of that, there's a small shack. On the wall of that shack is a brass bell about that big," I ball my hand into a fist. "I would be very grateful if you would leave that stone on the ground under the bell."

"Just leave it there?"

"Yes. You're all undoubtedly very fast. I'm sure the task could be completed in just a few minutes, and then you can return here and continue with your game."

"And a shilling?"

"Yes. You have my word. I'll just be here." I look around and see an elderly man coming out of the building to rest on the stairs and smoke his pipe. "I'll just be here speaking with this fine gentleman." Seeing a grizzled man suddenly become sheepish at the prospect of speaking to a woman is always amusing.

With that, the boys give a final nod and run off. I turn my attention to the old sailor. Skin like leather, white hair, and missing an arm, he utilized his knees to help himself light his pipe. He gives me a polite nod as smoke drifts up between his lips. "Ma'am. French?" he asks.

I nod. "Is that a problem?"

He doesn't answer.

"I hope it's not too forward of me to ask for your company while I wait for those boys?"

He smirks and makes himself a little more comfortable on the stairs. "Ma'am, at this point in my life, what is or isn't socially acceptable doesn't really bother me. Not sure it ever did. You can call me Martin."

"Persephone," I move toward him. "You do strike me as someone who has lived his own life, and a very exciting one at that."

He looks down at his missing arm. "Not unscathed, I'm afraid."

"The heavens can try us," I say as I sit near him on the steps. For all his talk of going against the grain, it's longer than a moment before he relaxes again. "Have you lived at the almshouse for long?"

It is several puffs before he answers. "About five years now."

"Many of you in the house?"

"Near twenty. A couple of widows. Mostly addled old sailors like myself. And a few orphans. Those same boys you sent off are some."

"Oh? Good boys, are they?"

"Well," he grins. "We're all young at one point."

We both chuckle, and I wait as he takes a few more puffs from his pipe. I catch him out of the corner of my eye, watching me stare off in the direction the boys scampered.

"If you're worried about your money -"

"No," I cut in. "They appear trustworthy."

"Indeed. That older one is good with rope. A year or two more, he could find himself aboard a ship."

"You've been teaching them the skills of your trade?"

"No. Not me, Ma'am. The Company has a gentleman come in a few times a week. Teaches some mariner skills to any who wants to listen. It's mainly for the young and the widows. But I watch it sometimes. And the boys are there most days. I hear the Company had a schoolhouse and library in the building a while back."

"Oh?"

"Not now, though. Remodeled the place to make more room for us castaways."

I take the opportunity to see if I can find out where those back doors lead. "The place looks like it's been remodeled several times. And I'd say, could use a bit of looking after now."

33

"Well, it's an old building. When you get this old, you require constant care," he chuckles.

"Much in the way of additions, lately? Anything that makes you wonder, `Now why did they do that?´"

He squints at me with curiosity as he takes a few puffs. "I can't think of anything strange. The usual stuff. A new roof. A room here and there. Some stuff around back," he gestures, "near the chapel. Have you seen our Poplar Chapel?"

"I have. So, you say around back. Is there much around back? Probably a path between that very pretty church and the house." He smiles with pride as I say this.

"They say that every church dedicated to Saint Matthias has beams and planks from ships helping to hold it up."

"That's lovely. Do you attend services often?"

"Every day."

"And you have to walk all the way around?"

"No, Ma'am. As you say, there's a path at the back. Residents can use the door off the dining hall."

His eyes keep drifting away as if lost in thought. I feel like I'm losing his attention, so I press on quickly for answers. "The kitchen staff probably has access to the back?"

He looks at me strangely.

"For deliveries and such."

"Don't know. The only other door around back is the Dead House."

Yes! "Oh, my. Right here in the almshouse?"

"Oh, no Ma'am. It's just attached to the back. Only the Chaplin has access, and honestly, the undertakers are the only people I've noticed being allowed in there."

"Sounds like a place the children might get curious about and explore."

"Don't think so. As I said, they've got it locked up. Though, I suppose I'll get a good look at it sooner rather than later."

That long stare returns. Mournful and not, I think, for his long slumber. "You've got years in you yet, I dare say." He nods, though I can tell he disagrees. My mind searches for words of comfort. "The curfew tolls the knell of parting day, The lowing herd wind slowly o'er the lea, The plowman homeward plods his weary way, And leaves the world to darkness and to me."

He smirks and takes a long draft from his pipe. "Thomas Gray," he takes another long puff. "I've given my blood, sweat, and tears to the sea, Ma'am – and an arm – and honestly, there are days I wonder what do I have to show for it? But that church back there," he gestures over his shoulder. "The beams and planks. Good strong bones holding the roof up. Giving a safe place for those seeking shelter. It feels as if there's a little bit of me in that place, a little bit of me in those planks and beams, a little bit of me that will always be there to help watch over travelers and sailors." He shakes his head in sorrow, and I detect tears just on the cusp of falling. "Excuse me, Ma'am, legs gone a bit stiff." With that, he gets to his feet and wanders away.

I wonder about them sometimes. The mortals. So lost. So tiny. Yet, there are among them those who are insightful, intelligent, and kind. *Is it those that keep the gods attention and fuel The Game?* I watch Martin walk away, but my attention is almost immediately returned to the almshouse. Like the church, the almshouse was made of brick, and although both were historically intertwined with the East

India Company, only the almshouse had
the lion crest emblazoned in marble
high above the front door. My missions
are often about following breadcrumbs
of coincidence. I can't help but feel
that the fish market, the body of a
possible sailor, and a house operated
by the East India Company all add up to
something. A bigger picture, but one
I'm not seeing just yet. "Things far
afield brought together," I mutter. I
hear the scramble of tiny feet and turn
to find the boys running toward me.
"Mission accomplished?"

"As you said, Ma'am. Left on the
ground under the bell," the oldest boy
huffs out between breaths. "Can I ask,"
he stops for a breath, "a stone, Ma'am?
How is that a message to your friend?"

I smile. "You've all been friends
for a while, yes?"

They nod.

"If I had to guess, there are
times you know each other well enough
you don't even need to ask what the
other is thinking."

More nodding.

"My friend and I have been
traveling with each other for a long
time. We have ways to let the other
know what's going on."

"Oh, like a code?" the youngest boy asks. "My father wrote me once about rope code and flag code that he used on the ship."

"Yes. Like that. The stone was a code. She'll know what it means." And then it occurs to me that I might be getting myself into trouble. I have a French accent, and I'm talking about a secret friend and code. I quickly dig into my bag, retrieve three shillings, and flip one to each boy. "Now, off you go." They run off before I change my mind about the generous sum – each has a big smile.

Message given, but it will still be hours before Mym can get here. I glance up at the sky. "All for the best, I suppose." I say and then head back along the side path towards the church, "Speaking with the dead always goes better after the sun goes down." I don't know why this is, but experience has taught me it to be true. I pass by the door to the Dead House and notice the heavy iron lock dangling from the handles – and the cart is gone. Apparently, I missed the attendant while speaking with Martin. For most of my life, I have been reminded about the virtues of patience. In my experience, patience is another word for lost

opportunity. The words of my Patron are
in my mind as I stare at the lock. *The
Game is about subtlety. Do not draw
attention.* It is too bright, and the
area is too busy for me to break my way
in. I must choose caution, if not
patience, and turn away.

I don't like being this close to a
graveyard. The dead speak, but they
also watch and listen and can give your
position away. Rather than press my
luck, I avoid the graveyard. Thankfully
the church is open. It is a fine little
church. A rectangle with a vaulted
ceiling; oak columns upon ashlar
plinths divide the interior into a
nave, aisles, and five bays –
containing smaller alters and statues.
The pulpit lay ahead in front of rows
of pews, further enforcing this sect's
love of theatrics. I choose a back pew.
From this position, I have a good - if
obscured - view through a south-facing
window of the back of the almshouse.
Waiting is not a skill I've ever been
good at. Time spent not moving or doing
is time wasted. Yet, there are times
when there is nothing to do but wait.
It's not unlike my time spent skulking
around the docks waiting for my father
or news of him. Frustration abounds as

I find myself, like then, doing nothing but watching and waiting.

My gaze drifts back to the front of the church. I can't help feeling that I'm being watched – and not by those fiery eyes. I did not grow up in the Christian faith, though Marseille was in no short supply. Father never seemed to have favored any faith other than the sea, and Mother studied the ancient ways. Neither ever suggested what I should believe in – though the truth I know now is that it does not matter whom you pray to. All listen. "I wonder, new god, which champion you've chosen for the great game." Of course, there is no answer.

CHAPTER FOUR

Night approaches. A middle-aged woman holding a long taper moves methodically around the interior, lighting candles. After a day that has left me feeling like I've accomplished little in my mission, there is finally some movement. As she's nearly completing her task, I begin to see, in twos and threes, people leaving the almshouse through the back door. Their walk along the field path in the direction of the church is slow of pace – almost as if the process of getting to the church is part of the ceremony of mass. A few minutes later, the door to the church opens and begins filling with parishioners ready for the evening service. I catch sight of the Chaplin near the door. An austere statuesque figure in black and white vestments. A dour-looking fellow with a large nose, wrinkled features, but a full head of black hair. He nods slightly to those passing by and brave enough to make eye contact.

I have no interest in what I'm guessing will be a fire and brimstone lecture and make my way toward the door. It's no trouble to slip out

through the trickle of people entering
the church. The night air is crisp. The
daylight hours of the balmy early
spring weather have given way to the
nightly cling of more wintery
temperatures. Indeed, though there
won't be a frost, I can feel the chill
on my skin - but I'm not bothered by
it. I give the graveyard a wide berth,
even avoiding the path, and instead cut
my way across the rough field. I can
still hear traffic on High Street, but
it is much reduced. "Mym should be here
presently," I mutter. As my hand
reaches for the heavy lock around the
handles of the Dead House doors, I
fully recognize that it's my impatience
at work and not the knowledge that help
is on the way.

It is a sturdy lock. I can see why
Martin was unconcerned about
trespassers. I glance over my shoulder
at the sound of the stout church doors
being pushed shut. *This is too good a
chance to pass up*. It's all the
convincing I need to give myself. I
raise my hand over my shoulder, and in
a swift motion, my morningstar is
arcing down. A momentary clang of metal
on metal that I'm sure no one would
have paid any attention to and then the
lock is in pieces at my feet. I remain

motionless. My eyes move about the growing dark. My ears focus on any sound that might indicate an intruder coming up behind me. Nothing draws my attention. I return my morningstar to its sheath and turn the door handle.

There's no interior light. It is the pitchest of blacks. The faintest light from outside shows that I am standing at the top of brick stairs. I have no fear of the dark, so close the door and press myself against it. The smell of decay is paramount, yet not as pungent as I would have expected. My hands inspect the wall to either side of me in search of torches, and finding one, I apply some flint and steel to it. I light a second with the first, which bathes the room in enough illumination to make a proper assessment.

I can see why the cart was left outside earlier. The chamber is partially dug into the earth. Stairs lead down about ten feet to the main area of the Dead House. To my right is a mezzanine of wood that follows the walls around, allowing a good vantage point of the work being conducted below but also access to the back upper wall where several religious symbols are hung. On my left is a pulley lift upon which bodies are placed to bring them to the work area. With flickering light guiding my eyes, I make my way downstairs. Several shallow bowls are arranged around the small room, each with dried flowers, pine needles, and perfumed sachets. A large worktable is against the back wall. Clean linens are stacked there, as well as bottles of oils, rags, brushes, and a small firepit – currently cold – where a cauldron awaits wax to melt.

There are six niches in the walls. Three of them are filled with those who have already been cleaned, perfumed, oiled, wrapped in linen, and sealed with a thin layer of wax brushed onto the fabric. Preparations, duties, and tasks that undertakers are increasingly doing. Though I suppose not many of them have the same access to earthen chilled rooms to keep the bodies from decomposing too quickly. My quarry is upon the central table. His shirt has been removed, but otherwise, he remains clothed. His wounds have been cleaned though there is little that can be done with ragged flesh and a crumpled face.

I lay a solemn hand upon his chest. "Hold not onto your wrongs, regrets, and longings." I start to pull my hand back but quickly replace it.

"If this soul falls under your guidance, my Patron, be kind. I think he has been wronged in the name of The Game." I pull my hand away, and after a brief search of my satchel, I find the small leather pouch where I keep coins and stones. There is no need to pay the Boatman, and the pebbles are only to leave messages with Mym. However, there is a unique flat piece of blue-white marble that will be very useful in this situation. A gift from a friend – a brother – who said that if I continue to use rash actions, such a thing may come in handy. I run my thumb over the smooth stone and the rune carved into the surface. A symbol of life and death combined into what he called a *power rune*. It is of great annoyance that I have had to use this on occasion. I feel as if every time I use this, he somehow knows and smirks at being proved right.

Pressing the stone to the forehead of the corpse with my thumb, I take a deep breath and clear my mind. I reach out with hope, courage, and all the strength of will I can pull together. The Dead House drops away from my senses. The stone I press to his forehead shines brightly in my mind, expanding to become a doorway. There is a small window of opportunity to speak with the dead. Echoes in the ether can vibrate for decades, centuries, but there is only a moment, a chance, just after death when you may still actually speak with the dead. A spirit will find itself in a limbo created by its own regrets and longings as it tries to hang onto flesh that is no longer there. Or in one created by a psychopomp while judgment is conducted. In either case, a connection can be made while in that limbo, with questions asked and hopefully answered.

Without a name or a description to focus on, however, the sensation is not unlike shouting "Hey you!" into a crowded hall. My thoughts stretch out into infinity, shimmering motes of light to attract a specific fish. Minutes pass without so much as a nibble. I decide to change tactics. I begin to focus on the box. Old and intricate. Aged but strong wood. A unique item that would have been one of the deceased's last memories. A new thread of thought spirals through all that was and will be. Almost instantly, there's a tug. I feel myself physically leaning forward at the strength of the pull upon my psyche. My determination changes focus. Even though I have let go of the mental rope I had cast out, I can still feel the heavy hand of something using it to crawl toward me. *Wake up, Persephone!* I shout at myself, the thought echoing around the darkness of the space of eternity. *Move!* I shout. As I watch the rope of light I had created shrink with the approach of whomever I had contacted, I reach for a morningstar that doesn't exist in this place.

I gasp and stumble back - a *hand*. *There was a hand*. I scan the room, but nothing. The presence is already gone. Friend or foe? In my life, I have found them often to be the same thing. There is no time to ponder the event. I glance back at the body as it begins to twitch. It convulses with a tremendous spasm that arches his back. The table rattles as the body collapses. Like an ancient door opening, a groan emanates from the fractured maw. Gurgling sounds bubble up.

I rush forward and press my hands upon the table as I come face to face with the deceased. "You remember the box?" I speak into the dead man's ear. "What was in it?" I demand of the corpse. More gurgling - I hear H-sounds and K-sounds, perhaps something that sounded like an I. I try a different question. "Who did this to you?!" I command. An agonizing minute trickles by before I can ascertain another sound.

"...ham...."

The gurgle drifts away, and I'm left with nothing but an eerie whistle, like a frosty gust passing by the mouth of a cave. I open my mouth to demand more when the head slowly tilts to face me.

I see you.

The grotesque rumble of words is clearly spoken and instantly fills me with fear. "Thanatos -"

You dare to trespass. As the words come forth from the body, it sits up. The stone I had placed upon its forehead tumbles, clinks off the table, and vanishes into the dark.

I back away slowly. "It is not a transgression to question the dead that have not fully transitioned."

You presume to tell me the rules! The walls rattle with his words.

"My Patron has tasked me -"

My brother, as usual, oversteps. The dead are not his domain. He rejected his greatness, choosing

servitude, and has made it my problem ever since.
You will not pursue this conversation any further.

    I am, of course, familiar with the rivalry between these brothers. It remains a great shame of mine that, on one of my first tasks, I failed my Patron in a mission against Thanatos. I allowed myself to be intimidated and arrived too late to the final battle to change the course of events. The burden of the number of lives lost will never be taken from my shoulders. But — *I will not be intimidated again.* "My actions in no way infringe —" a wall of foul-smelling air erupts from the maw of the creature seated upon the table. I'm tossed back like a feather in the wind and crash against the wall where the dead await internment.

    My dominion is absolute! It is mine. I rule the dead. I choose —

    "But you don't choose. Do you?" I say, getting to my feet. His shove has knocked my fear out of me. "Those like my Patron ferry the dead. Care for them! Ease their passing. They have dominion over who goes beyond and who has gained special attention." I plant my feet in a defensive stance, my hand ready to grab my morningstar. "Charon chooses. Not you." *It was a mistake to mention my Patron by name.* I recognize this too late.

A ghastly howl echoes around the small room. **My power is absolute!**

I hear the tearing of fabric before I notice the bodies beginning to move. The creature on the central table leaps at me. I'm ready and easily sidestep the attack. But as I reach for my weapon, a hand from the niche above me reaches down to grab it first. The body is well off balance, and it takes little effort to pull it from its recess. It crashes to the floor as the Thanatos-creature lunges again for me. I avoid the swift flail of arms, but he catches the strap of my satchel and yanks me off balance. I feel the leather snap as my bag and its contents are cast to the floor. Before I can react, my feet are taken out from under me by the body I had tossed to the floor and the Thanatos-creature clubs me with its fists. From the ground, I see through the flickering light that two other bodies from across the room are walking towards me with all the speed granted to them during life.

I'm not unaccustomed to fighting the undead or the groups that worship

Thanatos in all his names, as the brothers are constantly at odds. The question to be answered is whether they are simply animated or controlled by Thanatos. I roll back over my shoulders as fists arc towards me, and as I get to my feet, I leap forward and push off the shoulders of the corpse as it tries to catch me. I land behind it and pull my fist back - but the corpse turns and grabs my fist from the air.

You cannot surprise me. The otherworldly hiss of words tumbles out of the wrapped face.

I'm held aloft by the throat and punched across the room, striking the central table and toppling it and me onto the floor. "Definitely in control," I mutter as I'm yanked to my feet and surrounded by the three other corpses.

I know everything. Generations of these small creatures have passed through my gates; all that they know I now possess.

I struggle against the hands. "That didn't stop me from besting your Champion when last we met. Fortuneteller assassins. You do love a show." Using the two to either side of me as support, I jump up and kick the corpse in front of me, which tumbles over the table. As I land, I pull the other two into each other and spin into a hook kick - the head of one of the creatures now held to the shoulders only by the remains of the linen shroud the body is wrapped in.

The creature I had kicked away - the poor lad from the chairmaker's basement - now stands. I watch as spidery thin lines of inky veins fan out across the poor lad's broken face, chest, and arms. *An angry god makes mistakes* - which I guess to be my best chance of getting out of here now. Angry gods also level whole mountains. "Let's see which way this goes." I take a defensive stance and taunt the Thanatos-creature to come forward.

As he takes a step, there is a sudden explosion of wood. Fragments and splinters fill the air as the doors to the Dead House are ripped from their hinges. A cannonball the size of a small boulder rockets down the stairs, smashing into the two corpses and the table at the center of the room. With the speed of a top, Mym spins rapidly in place, shredding the corpse she had landed on. She then launches herself at the Thanatos-creature with an eruption of steam. His arms spring up with amazing speed and catch Mym, and almost in the same motion, fling her away as if tossing away a child's toy. Mym is sent crashing into the back wall. The cobble and earthen wall collapse under the assault as Mym punches a hole through into whatever lay beyond.

The plume of dirt causes me to cough and cover my face. The distraction is enough that I don't react in time to stop the Thanatos-creature as it appears in front of me, picks me up, and tosses me through the hole created by Mym. I tuck into a roll and spring to my feet, morningstar in hand. I recognize an earthy basement when I smell one and assume we are now under the almshouse. I'm about to take the fight back to the creatures when I hear the cry of someone's voice.

"It came from over here!"

The Thanatos-creature hears it too, for it cocks its head toward the destroyed entrance. The gnarled face then looks back at its feet and bends to retrieve something from the floor. As it stands back up, it is holding the box I had removed from the site of the unfortunate sailor's murder. A haunting, growl-like laughter rumbles forth from the corpses as the Thanatos-creature slowly shakes its head.

Without warning, the stone wall
reassembles itself.

    Mym and I are left in the dark.

CHAPTER FIVE

In the dark of the basement, I hear Mym roll in front of me. I know her intent. "There is no winning this fight." I back away and begin searching the dark for the stairs. Mym remains ready to propel herself through the wall. "Others are coming." She remains stalwart. "Mym!"

She finally responds to the firm edge in my voice. I hear her roll away from the wall. I feel her rough texture brush against my leg and follow; we find the stairs a moment later. They're wooden, and I fear they will not take Mym's presence, but before I can say anything, I hear the spray of steam and the clunk of stone on wood. A moment later, there's another plume of steam followed by another clunk of rock against wood. "*Désolé*, but we do not have the time," I say as I lift Mym into my arms.

I dash up the stairs and shoulder the door open. I find myself standing in the middle of a kitchen. I am alone beside a few unattended, simmering pots of delicious-smelling soup. I don't wait. I'm through the door and into the central common area. I see the front door and quickly make my way to it and out onto the street. I linger in an alleyway and watch as torch-bearing nightwatchmen race toward the almshouse – one of those boys from earlier leading them.

I set Mym down. For all my strength, she is quite a task to haul around. Not that I would ever say that in those words to her. "We should not linger." I step away, and after a few moments, I hear Mym following behind. There is no way for me to explain how I can tell the difference between the sound of grit crackling under the weight of Mym as she moves along and the rumble and crackling of what she sounds like when she speaks to me. However, it helps when she adds an image to my mind. "Yes, it's been a while since I was hit that hard too." I rub my jaw, shoulder, and chest where the Thanatos-creature had pummeled me. *Pain is a reminder of failure*. I keep this thought to myself because I need it, but I don't want Mym to yell at me. "What was that?" I ask.

Rumble, Rumble. Crackle. Puff.

"No. It was a puppet. I've never known Thanatos to appear in person." I stop at the end of the alley and examine the road ahead. I'm not worried

for myself, but I've never been able to
completely obscure Mym from perception.
In an excitable environment, or if
people get too close, attention can be
difficult to shift. I assume it's
because she's too out of the ordinary.
How do you convince someone they didn't
just see a small boulder roll by – *no,
that was a cow, obviously*. Thankfully,
activity is low, and shadows are
plentiful.

    Rumble. Puff.

    "Yes, I'm heading back to the
docks. I need to think; there are
plenty of places to hide." I don't add
that I'm also unsettled by the fight.
The presence of my Patron inspires awe.
The presence of one such as Thanatos
inspires something else. The fish
market isn't much further, and hiding
from such eyes is difficult when my
mind is unsettled. It will be best to
take cover in more comfortable
surroundings. I doubt Thanatos will
search for me with his own eyes, but
his Champion is no doubt nearby –
fighting her can get very messy. Open
ground would be better, but I'll settle
for a less populated area. I'll find a
place to think or a battlefield at the
empty docks.

I test the door of the first
sturdy shack we come upon. Locked, but
the door is easily forced open. There
are no windows, but my eyes soon adjust
enough that I can find a pile of sacks
to make myself comfortable upon. A slow
sigh escapes me as I ease into the
burlap – a sigh cut short by a rather
curt puff of steam from Mym. "What did
I do?" There's some exasperation to my
tone – which isn't missed by Mym, who
gives an indignant low rumble in
return. "As I explained to Thanatos,
speaking with the dead is not against
the rules."

Rumble. Crackle. Rumble. Puff.

I choose not to respond. Although
– despite how it was worded – it is a
good question. Thanatos had reacted
quickly – and in person – to something
hardly more intrusive than a knock at
the door. And regardless of what Mym
might think, it _was_ just a knock. We're
always watched, my brothers and sisters
and I. Not all the time, but at any
time. Interested parties will turn
their gaze to us, some for fun, others
to interfere – though the rules govern
how much of this can happen. It can
become distracting to feel the presence
of so many exalted beings with their
attentions lingering on what you are

going to do. Most, however, have their own games or interests focused elsewhere. Thanatos' eyes must have been upon me for him to appear so quickly. And if that is the truth…

The nudge at my side breaks me free of my internal thoughts. I don't turn to her. There is no need. "I feel as if the brothers might be at each other once again." A long vent of steam follows my words. "It would follow the evidence at hand. It would not be the first time Thanatos has set his agent to commit wild acts of random murder."

Rumble. Puff.

"That is so. He hasn't appeared the last few times. But he did when instead of random murder, it was random mass death." Another long vent of steam. I reach out and pat the warm pebbly surface of Mym. "Let's not get ahead of what we know. So far, there has only been the one murder – and a coin box…?" My contemplation is again halted by a nudge against my leg. "The box? An old – ancient, really – box. Modestly adorned. Symbols on the outside I've never seen before. And the body, the murdered sailor – there was this human there. He lied about seeing others who had been killed the same

59

way. But why would he lie about such a thing?"

Rumble. Crackle. Puff. Puff.

"Perhaps. I don't know." I can sense the change in her demeanor. Perhaps it was her own, or perhaps she was picking up on my worry, but she seems nervous now. Confident Mym can be brash. Nervous Mym can be unpredictable. We sit in silence for several minutes, each in her own mind. *What was that journalist's name? William, wasn't it? Apparently, he has a knack for finding trouble. Or trouble finding him. Coincidence, I name you clue.* A long vent of steam grabs me away from my thoughts. I pat her stone surface again. "We will not know until we come to it. We must follow this path and see where it might lead." I shrug. "The mission is what matters." She rolls away to rest nearer to the door. *Brash is better than unpredictable.* "By the way," I say smugly, making myself more comfortable on the sacks. "Nothing can be done with it now, but you should know I had unlocked the Dead House door for you. A simple push would have opened them."

Rumble.

"No, I'm not ungrateful."

Rumble. Rumble. Puff. Rumble.

"No, I'm not saying that either. But you mentioned drawing attention -"

Puff. Puff. Puff.

"Maybe. Best we sleep on it." With that, I roll to my side and close my eyes. Sleep isn't something I generally need, but I do enjoy dreaming. Drifting off, I can hear Mym pacing. It strikes me as less nervous and more irritated. I smile and allow sleep to take me.

A nudge against my leg awakens me. Instinct has my hand reaching for my morningstar. "What's wrong."

Crackle. Rumble. Puff.

I move over to the door and press my ear to it. Mym says the fish market is waking up. I ease the door open. It's still dark, though the slight tint of orange to the sky suggests dawn is approaching. I catch the faint echo of voices. "Time we moved on."

The morning air is chilly and damp but also refreshing. I take a deep breath as we walk. Dreaming usually pulls at threads allowing me to focus on my path. But this sleep was unhelpful, filled with dreams of my family before I had been chosen and reenactments of the fight with the Thanatos-creature. I woke several times. The morning air, however, is

doing what dreaming had not. As we move
from alley to alley, my mind begins to
peel back all of yesterday's
interactions. The young man at the fish
market. The body. The guards. The
journalist. The almshouse. The church.
The Dead House. *None of them appear to
be connected in any meaningful way
other than to draw me in a direction*.
"Stepping stones across the river," I
mutter as we once again come to Poplar
High Street. Standing at the base of
the stairs leading up into the
almshouse is a member of the city watch
- polearm at the ready.

    Rumble. Puff.

    "I was hoping to find my bag and
maybe, though unlikely, retrieve that
box. But now I'm thinking we need to be
somewhere else."

    Rumble. Crackle.

    "Of course I can get over there."

    Crackle.

    "Fine. Wait here," I snap at her
and exert my will. I walk across the
road and along the almshouse to the
field behind. Another guard is here,
standing at the broken doors of the
Dead House. Using the flick of a stone
and being fleet of foot, he notices
nothing as I move into the crypt. The
light of day streaming into the room

makes it easy to see the damage, though attempts have been made to clean up the mess. The broken table is now in a neat pile at the center of the room. The scattered tools and broken bowls are laid out in a heap. The dead, torn and mangled, are back in the recesses. Fresh wrappings have yet to be applied. More importantly, however, my bag and the box are not here. There's no reason to linger, and I am headed up the stairs when I hear voices from outside. I quickly press myself against the wall.

"Can we continue our work this morning?"

"The Lord's work must be seen to. It is shameful to allow those poor souls to remain in their current state."

The two men do nothing to hide their irritation, but the guard sounds unmoved by their words or presence.

"No souls in there, just the dead."

"And until they've received their proper burial, their immortal souls could be in jeopardy."

"Don't know nothing about that, vicar. I was told to keep people out."

"Surely that doesn't include us. We have a duty -"

"I have my orders."

"Are there more questions to be asked? Hmm?" The clergyman speaks with a curt high-pitched tone. "We spoke with your watch commander. We even answered that other young man's irritating questions," he continues, but then pauses before spouting, "We have a duty -"

"Watchman Thorne, isn't it?" The second clergyman cuts in over his partner. "You must be a man of God. What if that was your body in there waiting for your final resting place?"

"Can't say I'd be in a position to complain much, vicar."

"What about your family? Wouldn't your family want your remains to be treated with care and honor?"

There's a long pause before the guard clears his throat. "I have a sister."

"Ah, there you see. I'm sure she would want you looked after properly."

Another pause before the guard clears his throat again. "Alright - but you make sure you're available for more questions if they come up. Even from irritating young men, if that be the case."

"Thank you. God be with you."

Those I thought were two priests
are actually a layman and a priest.
They stop at the top of the stairs.
"It's even more devastating in the
light of day." The priest lays a hand
on his friend, and they both begin the
work of redressing the bodies.

Slipping away is easy enough, and
I'm standing with Mym within minutes.
"Before you ask, no I didn't. But I'm
sure of it now. The breadcrumbs I've
been following lead me further into the
city." I peek out around the building
and look west down the road. "It seems
there was an irritating young man here
at some point last night. And I think I
know who that may be."

Rumble.

"What? No," I say sharply. "Now
come along. This is going to be
tricky."

There was hardly anything in this
area the last time I was here. Now,
heading west into the city proper will
take us over a couple of busy streets
with tall buildings - some with three
levels - pressed against each other and
few alleys to weave between. A less
direct route would be better for
concealment but would take much longer.
I glance down at Mym, and we both know
I'm not going to take the circuitous

path. "Let's hope my will is up to the task."

Convincing people that she's not there can be difficult, so I decide to project the impression that I'm taking a morning walk with my loyal sheepdog. Adding is always harder than subtracting, and I can already feel the strain after a block. Thankfully, other than a few nods and comments on the "beautiful animal," there aren't many paying attention to the two of us. Until -

"Good day to you. That is a fine beast."

"What a lovely animal."

An older couple, her arm around his, stops beside us.

"Samuel, look, it's so much like our Daisy." The woman dabs at her eyes.

"Daisy was a working animal, my dear," he clears his throat, "but yes, coloration very much like Daisy."

Despite his gruff dismissal, I can see the emotion in his eyes. I also notice a folded bit of paper just sticking out of his waistcoat. It's a newspaper, and I'm staring at a rough sketch which resembles me. "Mym," I say absently.

"Your name is Mym, dear?" the woman asks.

"No," I laugh and point.

"Oh, yes, of course. Why hello there, Mym."

As she leans in, I'm suddenly very nervous.

"Oh," the woman blinks and stands straight. She rubs her eyes.

"That's a lovely accent you have. French?" he asks.

"Sorry to press on, but," and then I can't think of how to end that sentence, so I just start walking again. After putting some distance between us and them, I lean forward a little and whisper to Mym, "We may be in a little trouble."

Rumble.

"If I'm in trouble, you're in trouble." She doesn't respond to that.

The closely packed buildings soon give way to open land. I drop the perception aura around Mym. Projecting that deception is not unlike carrying her. I feel a great weight lifted. It's still cool, the sun is still hours from noon, but I wipe sweat from my brow. "The road is more open from here out until the city. I'll hide us if we see anyone coming our way." Along this section of the road are a number of fresh houses, some of them no more than a few decades old, each with a bit of

67

land attached. *Won't be long before all of this is part of the city*, I muse to myself. Occasionally a carriage or wagon rolls by, and I quickly project the image of Mym as a dog or simply have us stop and pretend I'm resting against this rock by the side of the road. After several lengths of the road, we finally come upon our first pedestrian. A young man ahead of us quickly marches towards Poplar Ward. I opt for resting along the side of the road and waving.

"Morning," he says in passing.

"Morning," I return and notice he's holding several newspapers. "What's that you have there?"

"What? These? Delivering the day's editions. Finished, but I grabbed too many on my way out and was hoping to sell some of them –" the young man cuts himself off.

I smirk. "*Accidentally* grabbed too many?"

"Well," he returns my smirk and rubs at the back of his head, "I don't think the *Gazette* will miss a few farthings."

"I don't say they will." I laugh and quietly pull a button from my sleeve. "Well, here you go. One farthing."

"Careful, the ink's still wet on some of these." He hands me a sheet and waves goodbye.

Hopefully, my sleight of hand and trickery won't get him into too much trouble. "The *Gazetteer and London Daily Advertiser*," I read aloud for Mym's sake. I glance over the page. It's a standard newspaper - articles on the front and advertisements on the back. However, two stories immediately grab my attention. "Crusher Strikes Again," I read, and then, "French Spy Targets Dead House."

Rumble.

"As I said. If I'm in trouble, you're in trouble." I quickly read the articles. The first describes two brutal murders. The author refers to a previous article but does describe victim one as a professor. The second victim is the lad from the chairmaker's basement. It's the accompanying sketch that causes me to bite my lip. The second article is much smaller and describes a break-in at a Dead House in Poplar by a suspected French spy. It's not typical for stories to indicate the author, but I am not surprised to see that both articles are authored… and by the same person. "William Monkton.

These are going to get him into trouble."

Rumble. Rumble.

"Indeed."

CHAPTER SIX

I always feel guilty for passing pebbles and buttons off as currency – though it hasn't stopped me from doing it. Normally, I keep several currency types in my bag, but that has inconveniently gone missing. I hand the carriage driver a few pebbles and keep him distracted with a question as Mym gets herself down and rolls under the shadow of a platformed wooden staircase. "You're sure this is where the *Gazetteer and London Daily Advertiser* are printed?" The carriage rocks, but I pretend not to notice.

The driver pauses for a moment before answering. He looks at his horses and tightens his grip on the reigns. "Yes, Ma'am. Down this lane right here." He points. "Ink, paper, and such, barrels of'em, always clogging up the street."

"Thank you," I smile and step away from the carriage. Glancing about, I marvel at modern London. At the center of the world for sure. It is a layered amalgam of staggering poverty and extreme wealth, all on top of each other. Smokestacks belching black plumes high above. Shacks precariously stacked, teetering atop each other. Grand stone and marble edifices cluster together like trees in an inhospitable environment. And all of it separated only by the length of a city street. Pater-Noster Row, this fairly narrow road paved with cobblestones where I find myself standing, is one of the nicer spots in the city. A few upscale homes, but mainly sellers of books and clothing – though I am enjoying the sweet scent from the pastries a few storefronts away. All in the shadow of Saint Paul's Cathedral. It is a busy place, but also lovely.

I join Mym in her shady spot. "The morning has given way to a busy afternoon. I fear moving around might be more difficult."

Rumble.

"I wasn't going to point that out, but yes. Perhaps it would be best if I looked around. If I can't get back here, I will get you a message."

Crackle.

"What do you mean, no?"

Rumble. Rumble. Rumble.

There's no use arguing. "As you wish," I say reluctantly. "We'll try *walk the dog* again." Mym rolls up beside me, and we step out of the shade of the stairs. The most attention we draw as we move along is a smile and a few tipped hats. I sometimes wonder about my abilities. There are basic skills all my brothers and sisters have access to, but on the whole, we each have talents the others do not. Walking at a slow pace next to Mym, altering how others see her, I can't help but wonder about the extent of my powers. Hiding myself or something I'm holding requires little effort. Mym can take a bit more concentration. But, will there be a day when I'll be able to hide something like a cart or a building – or shift a whole city out of perception? And then an unsavory thought occurs to me.

Could my opposition be using the same perception filters? We share talents, and I'm sure someone else can also bend perception. "But certainly not as good as I," I mumble. I must admit, however, there is a possibility. I continue thinking about shifting a whole city – there are those far older than I…. I feel my mind wander and shift away from Mym; I catch myself. Thankfully, no one seems to have noticed. With attentions diverged by the commerce along this street, it is not too difficult to conduct ourselves unnoticed. *Stay focused on the task at hand – there's a door that needs kicking in.* I know our destination. According to the pamphlets I glanced at previously, I'm looking for The Globe. Following my memory to that location led to an irritating, *I told you so,* when we discovered this did not mean the theater. It took some questions, but I'm confident we are on the right path now. However I can already feel myself becoming impatient. Glancing at stalls and shopfronts is a tedious affair. Every face and action is a story to be read, and it's never too difficult to figure out the ending.

A vendor of scarves. There are far too many scarves of varying colors and patterns for her to have knitted with only her two hands. She employs at least one other. That, the well-maintained cart, and the smattering of exotic textiles all suggest a woman doing well for herself. She is probably making enough for her own shop. Though I doubt it will ever come to that. There is genuine joy on her face as she entices potential buyers to come and peruse her wares. This and her clothing tell me a few last things in passing. This is someone who likes to hunt for a sale. Enjoys the interactions. Who will never grow tired of working. Someone who could afford more but accepts less fashionable clothing and the comfort of an established shop for the increased revenue it means for her. The flesh is weak, however, and age will make the lure of indulging in the comforts of her means harder to ignore. I'd guess, in ten years, she'll have at least one other cart – probably somewhere near Drury Lane – both operated by employees while she enjoys late morning rises and comfortable carriage rides between indulging in on-the-spot check-ins of her vendors.

I see a young man making his way leisurely along a bookstand. Even before the boy's hand is in motion, I can see the pocket he'll try to pick. The thief hasn't learned to mind his surroundings. Certainly not new to the life of a street urchin, but probably his first solo grab-and-run. I've seen the bushy-mustached bookseller glance at the boy once already. A bookseller who sells alone, otherwise he would not be out here trying to ensure this well-dressed man doesn't walk away while customers mill about inside. A bookseller with a shop placard worn by the many years of its presence. A bookseller comfortable enough with his surroundings to have a number of his books in the open for those passing by to touch and consider. This bookseller knows this street and probably that boy. The young man will try and fail to pick the pocket of that customer because the bookseller will stop him. There'll be raised voices, and then the bookseller will assure the well-dressed man that the boy will be dealt with. The bookseller will drag the boy inside, set him in a corner, deal quickly with his customers, and then deal with the young man. And then this bookseller will offer this urchin some food and a place to stay.

I'm several paces past the bookshop when I hear a cry of anger followed shortly after by the shouts of a young voice and the chime of an entrance bell. In moments, the well-dressed man from the bookshop passes us. I take in his story as he makes his way down the lane ahead of us. I noticed the callused middle finger of his right hand and ink stains while he was standing at the bookshop. Now I see his new clothing and his occasional stopping to adjust his shoes - also new. A writer, no doubt, and one who has recently come into some money. I denote a swagger to his walk. There's a

confidence there that doesn't come from
gaining wealth by means of attrition.
I'd say he's finally sold his work.

For the simple reason we are
headed in the same direction, Mym and I
follow him to nearly the end of the
street where he stops and enters a
public house. The face of the pub is
dark green and brown — it blends with
the earthy tones of the rest of the
street. *Odd*, I think. Despite being in
line with the other storefronts, it's
almost hidden by its understated
appearance. A large, multi-paned, front
window shows the busy interior. The
sign over the door reads: The Globe.
"Stay," I say and don't wait for an
argument.

The interior is lively, with five
of the eight tables occupied. Like the
nameless well-dressed man I followed,
several people here dabble or make a
living painting pages with words. It
would seem I've stumbled upon a haven
for satirists and journalists to meet,
show off, and exchange news and ideas.
Perhaps this is the reason for the
understated exterior. There are more
pressing mysteries, though. It is my
experience that storytellers have eyes
for the world, so remaining unseen
could prove difficult. As I prefer to

be the one asking questions, I allow myself to be seen rather than be discovered and make my way to the bar. Behind the bar stands a beardless man with large arms and a bruised cheek, wearing a simple gray linen shirt with threadbare shoulders. He nods and smiles at me.

"Can I do something for you?"

I remind myself to avoid my usual accent. "Yes, thank you. I'm looking for William Monkton?" I catch the sudden suspicion in his eyes. The only thing better than a lie is the truth seasoned with a lie. "I know this might seem strange, but I'm a journalist, too. I work for the *Oxford Gazette*. You see, I've been tracking whispers of a killer -"

"Dangerous work for a lady," he grunts and says - though his relaxed posture and lean forward suggest he finds this alluring. I lean in and whisper, "My mother enjoyed reading Mary Astell." I lean back and say in a normal volume with an air of faux confidence. "I like to challenge conceptions and push against complacency."

The barman's lips press into a wry smile. He thumps the bartop and shouts,

"Eh, you lot. Have you seen Will today?"

"He's in the back," resonates from several throats.

The barman cocks his head to the right toward a door along the far wall and says, "He's in the back."

I smile and step away. I feel as if permission has been given, so I don't stop to knock. I open the door into a small square room. A beast of a device takes up half the space. The wood and iron machine is splashed in ink and operated by means of a large lever. There's also a low table with stacks of paper, a desk with ink wells and parchment, a couple of crates, a barrel, and a cabinet with drawers and nooks filled with small letters. A couple of lamps and a backdoor which stands open, allowing in the daylight. A man in breeches, tan stockings, and a blue waistcoat sits at the desk with his back to me.

"William Monkton?" I ask as I close the door behind me.

There's a moment where the only sound is the scratching of quill on parchment. "Yes and no."

"I'm sorry -" I begin, but am cut off.

"I am William, but not Monkton."
He sets his quill down and stands to
face me. "Oh, my. You are pretty,
miss?"

"Misses, actually,"

He steps over to me, takes my
hand, and kisses it. "Misses.
Wonderful. Pretty and caught. My name
is William Arnall, and I am at your
service."

He smells of grease and sweat. His
sleeves and the front of his shirt are
splashed in dirt and ink. None of that
is what makes my lips cringe. I slide
my hand from his. "Do you know when
William - the other William - will be
by? Or where I may find him?"

"I honestly don't know. William
loves his daily stroll. He's usually
gone for hours. Always returns with a
good story, though. I'm sure, however,
whatever you are looking for, I can
help."

Information is information, and if
this irritating little man can help, it
will save me from having to come back,
so I allow a small smile to creep over
my lips and say, "I wanted to ask him
about one of his stories. In the last
edition, he wrote about The Crusher. It
was wonderfully written and so
informative,"

"I wrote that." His arrogant leer is off-putting.

"Did you?"

He inches closer. "Well, you see, William can be a bit flowery. You've got to excite the reader." He grabs and squeezes my hands tightly as he says this.

"So, you could say you made the story better?" He nods. "Well, that's what I'm hoping to do. I've been investigating a similar story for the *Oxford Gazette* -"

"Impossible." He frowns and takes a step back - thankfully, dropping my hand.

"Why?"

"Well, to begin with - you're a woman. I'm all for women pushing boundaries, but wouldn't you be better suited writing about fairs and such?"

I'm about to respond but stop as he snaps his fingers.

"Oh, the Society - the, um, The Society of Artists of Great Britain. Their exhibition is coming up -"

This time, I cut him off. "The Crusher," I clear my throat and add pleasantly, "please."

He frowns again. "You see, that's the other part." He taps me on the shoulder and draws his mouth into a condescending smile – though I'm sure he thinks it charming. "William brought me that story, and I'm sure he made it up. I mean, I looked at his notes, and I couldn't see what he was going on about. But it will sell papers… and if he is right, then at least we own the story." He retakes my hands. "Now, where were we?" He strokes my hand and then pauses to examine them. "A bit rough. A farmer's daughter?"

His smile is unpleasant, but I step closer and whisper. "No, no, no. Not rough from the farm. It's from years of crushing skulls." I give him a peck on the cheek and feel a slight tremble in his hands as I squeeze them. He pulls, but I hold for just a second before allowing him to withdraw his hands. I turn slowly but keep eye contact as I leave.

I storm through the pub but stop at the door. *He knew what a pummeling looked like.* I click my tongue against the roof of my mouth as I step over to the barman. "I never got your name."

"Arnold."

"Well, Arnold, I'm rather cross, so I will only ask this once. That bruise on your face and your knuckles are swollen. I doubt you got those from this lot, and I'm certain you didn't lose the fight, not with just those injuries, or it wasn't a serious altercation. But your clothes…"

He steps back and awkwardly fidgets with his shirt. "What's wrong with my clothes?"

"Nothing. But they're not the clothes of someone winning paid fights, though something tells me you do know about such things. So, Arnold - where would someone go to make some money on fighting?"

"There's a fight club just north of the city. Mary Le Bone Fields -"

I cut him off with a raised finger. I allow the tension to hang for just a moment. "Arnold, I didn't ask about a fight club."

He licks his lips and peaks over my shoulder. He leans in a little and whispers. "You didn't hear it from me. Tottenham Court Road, tonight. But Miss -"

"Misses, please, or ma'am."

"Ma'am, it's a dangerous place."

"Thank you, Arnold." I smile and turn away.

Once outside, I stop and lean against Mym.

Rumble. Crackle.

"No. But I know where he'll be."

CHAPTER SEVEN

Standing outside The Globe, I'm once again drawn to the towering brick stack belching black smoke just over the tops of the buildings. A giant chimney of some enormous furnace. I can't help but imagine a day when the city is blanketed in such things. It occurs to me that it has been a while since I visited London and a lot has changed, leaving me with an irritating sense of lack of direction.

"Tottenham." I tap my lips as I think. The Crown had, or still has, a manor house north of the city called Tottenham Court. "We head north," I say as I pat Mym. "Ready, my pet?" I smirk because I know she hates it when I refer to her as such.

Crackle.

"What do you mean no? Are you staying here?"

Crackle.

"Alright, then what?"

Crackle. Rumble.

I sigh and lean back against her. She's right. I'm drawing attention to myself, and she doesn't mean the occasional eyes cast in the direction of a woman seemingly chatting with her dog. Using our powers draws attention. It's a bell that rings in the ether where the gods exist and to which my brothers and sisters are connected. Certain talents use more power and thus draw more attention. There are ways to hide, both from the gods and others. But no distractions or cover offer complete protection, and determined opposition will eventually be able to trace the ripples of energy. "Walk the dog has been working. Being more serpentine will take time, and I'd rather be direct. I promise to be careful."

Crackle.

"What do you mean, no?" I hear how sharp my tone is as my anger gets the better of me. "If you want, you can find a hiding spot, and I'll -"

Crackle.

"Stop saying no!" I snap. More eyes drift in our direction, and I laugh it off. "You stubborn beast. Come along." I begin to walk. She'll follow, or she won't. She does. By the time we reach the main road, I admit to myself that she's probably correct. What truly troubles me is that my opposition has undoubtedly gotten a sense of my presence but, as of yet, I've picked up nothing - *a further clue as to my*

certainty of whom I'm playing against.
Less direct may be the better way
forward for the time being. I don't say
anything, but I take us back to the
alleys and backroads.

We skirt Fleet Street and make our
way over back plots, side roads, and
alleys to arrive at Lincoln's Inn
Fields. The area is a mesh of upscale
buildings, homes, and open public
lands. I remember cows walking in the
pastures the last time I was here. It
is now much more of a park surrounded
by an iron railing. Still, plenty of
places remain to hide and cover our
passage through the area without
tapping my power.

More side streets and alleys lead
us to a broad and busy street. We stand
across from a garden plaza and an
impressive stone building. The British
Museum. New for me and new for the
city. I would often marvel at the
oddities my father brought home from
his adventures. We had a sizeable
collection of books, scrolls, and
objects by the end. I sometimes wonder
what became of them. I wonder now if
any reside in that building. If not
here, then probably lost among
artifacts of some other museum. Or
simply lost.

I must have been standing transfixed on the museum for too long because I'm pulled back to the present by a nudge at my leg. "Just getting my bearings."

Puff.

"No. I'm not lost." I glance right and then left. "I'm fairly certain we need to move east and north a bit more."

Puff. Rumble. Puff. Crackle.

"I am aware." I glance up. We are well into the afternoon hours. "Step back." Mym rolls back along the alley wall. When she settles, I grab the first person passing by the alley. It's an older gentleman dressed in a red coat and vest trimmed in gold. I press him against the wall of the alley. "Tottenham Court Road?"

"What is the meaning of this? Unhand me…" his voice trails off as he notices I am a woman. "Really, this is unbecoming,"

I press my thumbs into his shoulders.

His face winces in pain. "That way _"

I step back, and he races away.

Puff. Crackle.

"Like I said, getting my bearings." We continue in silence as we travel more or less parallel to the main road through the alleys. At the intersection of several roads and lanes, we spot a playhouse and a plaque naming the street in front of it as Tottenham Court Road. We are certainly near the limits of the city. Large houses, farms, and fields with clusters of poorly maintained housing stacked tightly together dot the area. Further out along this street is the Crown's manor house from which this road gets its name. But I don't believe we'll travel that far along this path.

I don't see a clear path to get us through this intersection unseen, so I decide it's worth the risk. I lay a hand atop Mym and begin to draw on my power. Everything in the universe vibrates with invisible energy. The air around us is a weave of ribbons, auras, and ripples of this energy. It all goes unnoticed by the average eye, but to some - certainly my brothers and sisters - this weave can be seen and felt. A trick to going unnoticed by those who can see and feel the weave is to sink into it. It's much like hiding footsteps in the snow by stepping into someone else's footprint. It takes far more concentration, and one must move slowly to not cause undue ripples - but

it can be done. Instead of exerting my
will, I draw from the weave around me,
pulling from horses, people, and even
buildings as I push Mym out of
perception.

"Slowly," I say. My hand still
atop her, I lead Mym across the street
toward a narrow brick building opposite
the theater. Cause and effect are still
part of my world, and I can already see
some signs of my interference. A man
pausing to rub at his forehead. A
sudden confusion in that horse. They'll
find a few buildings in this area
needing some fresh paint sooner rather
than later. Nonetheless, we make it to
the building without an incident.
Unfortunately, I can't release my will
just yet. Hand still upon Mym, I take a
quick look around. The theater. A few
homes. The building we stand in the
shadow of – I notice a sign indicating
this place rents rooms.

Not what I'm looking for, I'm
afraid. I lower myself and kneel.
"Unsanctioned prize fighting is not
unlike dueling. Not illegal, but
certainly frowned upon. It's not
something that will be done in the
open. However, it is something that
will draw a crowd - even if it is just
a select crowd. We need a large, out-

of-the-way building. Something people are going to see but not think about." I tap Mym, and she begins to roll with me as I proceed along the road. It's not long before the cluster of buildings amassed near the intersection gives way to open, untamed land. Here and there, further along the road, I notice a few more clusters of buildings, but I see now what I am looking for.

We slowly approach a timberyard. There are a few smaller buildings within the fenced-off area, but I'm drawn to the large warehouse towards the plot's back. Far fewer pedestrians and carts are here, so I drop my will. "I think this is it. Would you mind having a look around?" Mym rolls away while I find an out-of-the-way spot to sit. Resting in the shade of a tree is relaxing. For a moment I allow myself to forget my mission and enjoy the spring breeze. But just for a moment. In the calm of my mind, I recall something. When I made contact with the sailor before Thanatos arrived… he mentioned something. "Ham?" I glance up and down the road. "Tottenham Road. Tottenham – ham. Why would he send me here?" I contemplate this but nothing with a satisfying answer manifests. "I need more information."

Mym returns a short time later, splattered in fresh mud. *Rumble. Rumble. Crackle*.

"Several paths leading back into the city and some men carrying crates into the warehouse. Any carriage tracks?"

Rumble.

I glance up at the sky - late afternoon. "We wait. Such things will not happen in the light of day," I say. I wish I could say I always arrive where I need to be exactly when I need to be there. But I don't. Far too often, I find myself having to pause and wait for what I'm tracking to catch up or time to pass. Having Mym close by always helps with the waiting, though the time isn't usually spent in conversation. Her presence is enough, and I feel she is of the same opinion. I sometimes read from a book… something I typically keep in my bag. There's nothing to do this time but wait as the darkness creeps around us.

I watch as the buildings around me become highlighted in the flickering light of torches and candles. The working hours have passed, yet I observe a line of rough-looking men enter the timberyard and make their way to the warehouse. A few minutes tick by, and I hear the approach of the first carriage along the back paths. A few minutes more pass, and pockets of three and four begin arriving. I even catch a pair of night watchmen entering the building. *A much larger crowd than what I was expecting.* "Taking full advantage of the it's-okay-if-it's-unseen-and-unspoken mentality. That's something I'll never understand about humans – I'm not sure I understood it even when I was human. These arbitrary social walls that they insist on putting up. This is acceptable if you're this, but not if you're that. You can do this, but only in the dark. This person is different from this person because of a simple quirk of fate. You know?" I look at Mym and get the impression she is asleep. There's no outward change to her appearance, but I can usually tell where her focus is and right now there is no focus. "Wake up, you great lump." I shove her – which amounts to rolling her about an inch. "It's starting."

I maintain that it will be better to enter through the back of the building, and so we make our way through the pasture and trees to the rough paths behind the timberyard. It is instantly apparent I am correct. There is no hiding the small collection of personal carriages dotting the area behind the warehouse. I watch the most recent arrivals, a pair of gentlemen – one very large and wearing a heavy cloak, the other dressed in expensive clothing – enter a propped open door. As no one else appears to be arriving imminently, we both pass from carriage to carriage and arrive at the door.

The interior of the timberyard warehouse is what I expected – though the dark makes any purposeful assessment difficult. However, sneaking around is unnecessary; cheering and shouting can easily be heard coming up some stairs set into the floor. A large and sturdy door normally covers the subterranean passageway though currently it is likewise propped open. "There is plenty of darkness. I'm not expecting a fight,"

Crackle. Puff.

I smirk. Her wit is sharp for something so round. "All the same. I will call if I need you."

Mym rolls away without further comment, and I begin my descent. I enter a chamber I was not expecting. Great care and ingenuity have been

undertaken to carve out and illuminate
a relatively large space. A series of
lamps and torches with mirrors to
augment the reflection gives the room
more than enough light to see by.
There's even a makeshift pub present.
Nearby to the beer and liquor is a
waiting area for contestants and space
around the ring to stand and watch.
Slightly elevated over all of this is a
platform with chairs for those who wish
to watch the proceedings but would
rather pay for the comfort of sitting
while they do so. The ring itself is
actually a square made up of a wooden
fence and a sandy floor. Individuals
move around the room taking bets for
the house, but I also see the winks and
nods of personal bets between watchers.
The chamber could do with some
ventilation as the aroma of beer and
sweat fills the room. The smell
notwithstanding, the air is charged
with excitement, and it is hard to stay
focused and not be drawn in by the
bare-knuckle fighting.

As I step away from the stairs, I
instantly take notice of a few shocked
and disapproving glares. A couple of
men press their way through the crowd
in my direction. I pretend not to
notice and make a quick effort to get

behind a noisy group near the pub. It takes but a breath to shift perception away from me, and despite Mym's warnings, I even alter my appearance to one more befitting such a gathering. The men attempting to catch the woman suddenly look lost and bewildered. In such a place, I won't be able to keep myself hidden for long, so I leave them to their confusion and continue to pass through the crowd, searching for William Monkton.

There's a sudden swell of cheering, and I can't help but stop and watch. The pugilists are exchanging blows furiously. Both men are broad in the shoulder and thick in the neck with hairy chests and hairy faces. By design or accident, the only way I can tell them apart at a glance is by the tan trousers of the one and the burgundy-colored trousers of the other. An excited hush silences much of the crowd as Burgundy strikes with a devastating cross, followed by a hook and an uppercut. Tan stumbles back from this onslaught then charges forward with a roar, attempting a clinch, but Burgundy sidesteps as he brings his fists down on the back of Tan's head. Tan trips forward into the sand. Burgundy rushes forward, flips Tan over, and assails the prone man with a series of blows. The crowd's energy shifts to anger as there are a number of "He's down" and "Corner" calls in an attempt to end the fight.

I glance past the fighters to the stairs on the other side of the room as I take note of a trickle of new faces entering the arena. One of those faces is William. I feel zero shame for the sense of smug satisfaction at the end of a successful hunt. He makes his way to the beer vendors, and I move to join him.

Something shatters behind me. Close enough that I feel shards pelt my leg. Before I can turn, there's a roar of a thunderous gale, and I am thrown forward through the fence of the square and tumble over the sandy pit. Sand and debris kick up into a choking cloud that quickly causes chaos.

Not unlike the depictions of the Amazons of old, a figure steps through the gap in the fence I had created. As the wind dies, flowing dark hair settles onto the shoulders of the lean, powerful woman standing before me. A familiar person from my past - real in every way, yet still a mask. The cloud begins to dissipate, and with no clear egress and far too many people to leave

unprotected, I exert my will and shift
our appearances. There is no need to be
careful about not drawing attention as
she is standing right there, so I put
the full weight of my concentration
behind a believable disguise. To
onlookers, as visions begin to clear,
they will see two massive wild dogs
snarling and barking at each other in
the middle of the ring. I can now hear
calls from the crowd as the men hurl
themselves over each other and up the
stairs.

"How did they get in here?"

"Untamed beats! Where are the
Night watchmen?"

"Someone's idea of a joke."

As I get to my feet, I catch sight
of William, who seems he would rather
stay but is pushed along with the
exodus. At this distance, I have no
problem locking minds with Mym and
sending her an image of William.
Follow, I think at her and then quickly
add, *Do no harm*.

My opponent and I circle each
other – as we do, I watch as she drops
her mask. The features of the lean
woman shift. Black hair becomes gray
and coarse. Youthful flesh becomes
wrinkled. The lean physique becomes
stout and stocky. Despite how her

clothing now fits, her overall appearance is matronly. "I know you like an entrance, but you should know I'm not surprised. Your Patron's appearance was a big hint, but really, not sensing you and knowing you must be around, gave you away. Though, I must ask, those puncture marks – a new way of drawing blood for your potions?"

She doesn't respond at first, but then a demure smile appears. "Protecting the Humans? You care too much for them," she says.

"I see no reason for any of them to get involved, Elizabeth. Or are you still going by Catherine?"

She shrugs. "I go by Mary these days. Mary Kelly." She gives a quick bob.

"Elizabeth, Catherine, Mary – whatever you are calling yourself – I defeated you in Nyirbator, in Paris, and I will do it again here in London. Flee or fight." I reach up and pull my morningstar from my back.

"A task has been given. A mission is in motion. I will not back down. But, if I am to fail, at least I can do as much harm as possible on the way out." Her words switch between Greek, Hungarian, and French accents like a poorly prepared performer. "Do you remember the screams? I do. Shall we see how many I can make scream now?"

She turns to the crowd, hand reaching for a small vial secured to the strap across her chest by a leather loop. I pounce, star raised high, but come down on nothing but sand. Mary comes at me with a cross, but I parry the blow with my morningstar. We both take a few steps back from each other. I twirl my star and take a ready stance. She laughs off my attempt at intimidating her – our kind is not easily menaced – and pulls from her bag a thin dagger of black and green. "What is your business here?"

"Oh, I think we are on the same business."

"What do you want with William?" I shout at her.

Mary's head lifts in a cackle. "Just beginning and yet so far behind already. I knew you'd lead me to him." Her face becomes one of scorn. "Your Patron will always be in the shadow of his brother." Mary lunges. As I spin away from the attack, I feel the edge of the blade slice fabric but not flesh. I pivot with a back twirl of my star to gain momentum and come at her with a strike at her left. She raises her bare forearm to block, taking the full weight of my strike. There's a grunt of pain, and I see a smear of blood, but this doesn't slow the viper-like thrust of her dagger toward me. However, I'm already spinning out of the way - getting behind her. I come down on her shoulder with my morningstar. Mary crumples to the sand, blood dripping from forearm and now shoulder. I raise my star for a head strike, but she twists and entangles her legs in mine, sending me sprawling. I scramble to my feet but Mary is still seated on the sand. Her face is a testament to pain. She draws a small bottle of green solution from her bag and quickly drinks it. There is an instant change to her demeanor as an ugliness that defies description overtakes her appearance. It isn't so much a physical change as a change in presence. As if anger could manifest as a shadow. There is none to bear witness to this but I, as the room had finally emptied.

Mary leaps at me with speed I've never seen her use before. Her fist uppercuts me and then slams relentlessly down onto my face. In my daze, I don't realize at first that I've dropped my morningstar. With a grunt of effort, Mary tosses me to the other side of the square. My eye begins to swell, and I can feel the blood pouring from my nose, but nonetheless, I spring to my feet. "Why did you kill that sailor?"

Her answer is an unintelligible shout.

"What was in the box?"

She charges, fist coming for my head, but I react fast enough to catch it. We stand, arms quivering with the exertion. Her eyes yell *that's impossible*, and her mouth is nothing but a howl of frustration. I lean in with a head-butt, a push-kick, and a hook-kick. Mary stumbles away, falling against the wooden fence – using it to help keep on her feet. She looks at me over her shoulder with rage in her eyes. "He's. Not. The. Only. One. I've. Killed," she grunts out with each breath. She returns to the center of the ring, unfortunately standing between me and my morningstar. Propelled by another howl of anger, she charges. I meet her halfway, roll low under her strike, dash forward, grab my star - hear her behind me - and swing as I pivot, driving my weapon into the side of her head.

Mary stumbles sideways with the strike's momentum and stands, legs shaking, back to me, shoulders hunched, a few feet away. I watch as the aura of anger she had wrapped herself in dissolves, the haze I was viewing her through vanishes, and although she never actually grew in size, the air of strength is gone. "Many more will die. That is the will of Thanatos." She slowly turns to face me. "I admit it. Brawn to brawn, you are the better warrior." Her black and white frock now torn and covered in blood, she lifts her hands in defeat. "Brain to brain, however, there is no contest." She reaches into her bag and pulls out two small vials, one muddy brown and the other a light blue. She holds one in each hand, but she is distracted from her next comment by the sound of two people thumping down the stairs — one with heavy boots.

Mary quickly drinks the muddy potion, and I watch as there is a physical change this time. A shimmer of dancing light sparkles around her, and when it fades, standing before me is that meek, elderly, woman I saw standing in the alley outside where that sailor had been murdered. A tingle of terror and curiosity ripples through me as I stare at her. I can see her; she stands there, but I no longer sense her as one of my kind. She winks and tosses the second bottle at me, which I knock away with my morningstar. A crack of lightning knocks me back. My eyesight is nothing but a red blur for several seconds. Through the haze I see Mary racing toward the stairs, crying out, "I'm here. Please help."

"By the stars, Ma'am. What are you doing down here?" It's William – *of course he didn't leave.*

Mary doesn't reply but allows William to take her hand and help her up the stairs.

I rub at my eyes trying to force away the red blur. I take an uncertain step as my eyesight clears. I see the melted sand and a patch of burning ceiling that is quickly spreading. I honestly don't know what the guard that came down with William sees. Is it me? A wild dog? Animal or woman, the guard flinches as I race by him and up the stairs. There are several people still about. Some are glancing curiously at me, but most are staring and gesturing with distress across the warehouse to the broken door and the Mym-sized hole.

CHAPTER EIGHT

The light is dim, and attentions are distracted enough that I don't wait to hide myself. I take a step; any still watching, will be asking themselves if they really saw a woman or if it was a trick of shadow and light. I follow the line of gouges and scratches on the stone floor to the warehouse door. I could already tell by the time I reached the wall that she was moving fast. The hole isn't actually in the warehouse door but in the wall beside it. There was no stealth here. For all her brashness, Mym wouldn't have exposed herself without reason – not with this many witnesses. I push open the door and slip outside, taking a last glance behind me as I do – hoping to see Mary but not expecting to.

Every carriage is gone. Those with means and reputations seemed to have taken no time to retreat from this scene. The lingering presence will fade quickly, but my first breath in the open air tingles my nostrils with the scent of oil, leather, horses, and – blood. Fresh blood. My head twitches. No one is about. No one running away.

No one hiding in the shadows. My eyes quickly scan the ground around the door. I follow my nose. A few paces away from the door is a small splash of blood. It's not Mary's blood. Our blood doesn't pool. It doesn't remain. We leave only memories - not even memories, if a mission is performed properly. *William*?

Mym's tracks stretch out into the night and, despite the dark, are easy enough to follow. At the edge of the timberyard, not far from where I had waited while Mym initially scouted, her tracks become scrambled. Patterns of her circling about, overlapping, and here - rapidly back and forth as if pushing against something. There's a scent here, too. Acidic. I find soot and can smell the sulfur - an explosion. I gently tiptoe around the crisscrossing pattern of Mym's movement and notice there are a lot of other footprints here, most obliterated by Mym, but enough. Small feet with a light step. Mym wouldn't have tackled a human; it must have been Mary.

My heart is suddenly pounding in my chest.

I find the break in the back and forth. Her tracks lead off into the night again. However, perhaps thirty feet along, I slow to a stop as my senses tingle. There's more blood here and shoe scuffs in the dirt. Another back and forth but between those with two legs. *Interrupted as Mym catches up.* Footsteps lead off the road, as do Mym's tracks, while a second set continues quickly toward the city. *Mary chasing William, and Mym chasing Mary.* I should follow William, but I don't. I follow Mym and Mary. I race into the pitch-black countryside, losing the tracks, doubling back, and following them once more. Well off the road, I find the ground ripped up. An earthen wall, crumbling now, blocks my way forward. I pass my hands along the rough surface, feeling places where Mym had thrown herself against it. I find the edge of the wall and work my way around the other side, stopping when I sense the use of magic I'm more familiar with. The ripple of energy spirals out from a central location - *Portal magic.*

My mind is a storm of anger. "Both!?" I shout, not caring if anyone can hear. "Where?!" I spin and face the city. "William." I race back toward the road. Maintaining the perception filter while running is very difficult, so I don't even bother. As I approach the end of the lane.where it joins the city, I gain the attention in the form of glances. I slow to a walk when I come to the first cluster of hovels – all anchored on a gin shanty. The night had brought out a completely different array than what I had passed through during the day. Already there were children huddled in doorways, and men of all sorts passed out from drink. I reach out with my senses, searching the ether for my connection to Mym. Within several steps, I catch a familiar echo – *here*. The vision of a brick building drifts like mist at the edge of my senses. I follow the ribbon of energy, the image gaining clarity with each step. Then I recognize what I'm looking at – the boarding house across from the theater.

"Mym," I sigh in relief as I arrive. She remains nestled against the front stairs, but I sense her attention focused on me. I lean with both hands pressed against the top of her. "I thought," I clear my throat. "Doesn't matter. Are you injured?"

Crackle. Crackle.

"I'd say I'm sorry, but you like scorch marks." I glance up at the building. "William?"

Rumble. Rumble. Crackle. Puff.

"I know. I saw the blood and the tracks. I also see you forced Mary to retreat." I smirk, but it's because I sense the flash of pride wafting off of Mym. I adjust my garments from the tussle caused by my run, and once more presentable, I start up the stairs.

The door opens into a short hallway with stairs at the back and an archway to either side. To the right is a parlor with a door at the back. To the left is a dining room with a door at the back. I'm drawn back to the hallway by the sound of someone coming down the stairs. A portly middle-aged woman with silver hair approaches me with a broad smile.

"Looking for a room, Dear? I have to tell you, I don't rent to, ah – single ladies." She smiles sweetly – though that fades as she decides she doesn't like what she's looking at.

"I'm not looking for a room. At least not one to rent. I'm here to see a gentleman."

Her expression changes instantly. "No. No, Miss. Not here." She begins to usher me to the door.

"I just –"

"Not my business, Miss. But not here. I rent to families, honest men, and actors. And I'm already too busy keeping my eyes on those actors. I'm sure you'll be able to find another place to sleep for the night."

I expect the door to slam, but it's actually pushed gently shut. I pick up confusion from Mym but hold out an irritated finger before she can ask anything. I wait a second and then quietly open the door. I can hear the woman in the parlor. I exert my will and wrap myself in the aura that keeps humans from noticing me. Following Mym's instructions, I climb the stairs to the second floor and make my way down the hallway to the corner room facing the street. I stop at the door as I contemplate knocking or barging in.

I compromise by knocking but not waiting for permission. I step into a large single room furnished in luxury and good taste. A fine chest of drawers and an armoire are under and next to the window, respectively. A small table for eating is close to the fireplace. A large, comfy chair is at the end of a thickly padded bed. The floor is wood, except for a rug by the bed and one at the center of the room, both with an agreeable pattern. All of this is in stark contrast to the mess. Piles of clothing lay on the floor between the armoire and the chest of drawers. Pages, half written on, are scattered about. An uncapped inkwell and several quills are a jumbled mess on the table. Near the bedside are several empty and half-empty bottles of wine.

William rests in the chair at the end of the bed with a bottle of wine in hand. He is shirtless and barefoot in his breeches – and not as unfit as I assumed, given his breathless state when I saw him in that alley. He's sacrificed a shirt to fashion makeshift bandages to wrap the upper portion of his left arm as well as his abdomen – which must be the deeper cut as blood is already staining the fabric. His surprise resolves to calm. He sets the bottle he's holding down and then, without warning, leaps from his chair in a race to beat me to his chest of drawers.

He opens the drawer, but my hand is firmly on his wrist, preventing him from reaching in. I take a peek. Set in the empty drawer are two pistols. We stare at each other for several breaths before his eyes squint slightly, and his head cocks to the side. "You seem familiar." A moment passes before his eyes drift to the top of the chest of drawers and the sheet of parchment there. It's a rough drawing of the official image released by the paper. "Oh," his voice quivers a little. "Well, I assumed you'd come looking for your bag eventually. Though another night would have been preferable."

"I'm not looking for my bag. I'm looking for you."

He swallows. "Yes. I see that as being slightly different and yet far more frightening."

"Sit," I order.

He nods but passes the chair and moves toward the door. I brace, ready to chase after him, but he doesn't run. He shuts the door and then takes his seat. "You're in danger," I say.

He glances down at his bandages and then laughs. "I'd say."

"I need to know everything you know."

His thoughtful expression shifts into a smirk, "Twenty-eight years will take some time to explain."

I suppress the urge to drive my thumb into one of his wounds. "The Crusher. Tell me everything you know about The Crusher."

"Ah."

"Ah?"

"Well," he stops as he adjusts uncomfortably in his chair, "I'm trying to understand our relationship,"

"We don't have a relationship."

"Of course. But being interrogated by a spy who is also The Crusher is worse than just dealing with a spy."

"I'm not The Crusher," I huff as I step over to the window. He has a good view of the playhouse across the street.

"I can't help but notice you didn't deny the spy part."

His words are strained as he shifts in his seat to pick up the wine bottle. I stared down at the rough drawing of me that had been left on the chest of drawers. *He's good. Talent or education, maybe both*. I doubt a journalist makes much money... yet the luxury around the room would suggest family money, which means parents who could afford to indulge a young William with artistic tutors. The boy with imagination has turned into a man with a mind for stories. I decide to let him keep thinking of me as a spy. I answer by not answering.

"Are you going to kill me? I don't think I can stop you; I'd just like to know." He finishes the last dribbles of wine, looks at the bottle momentarily as if contemplating it as a potential weapon, and then winces as he sets it back down beside the chair.

I'm intrigued by how bravely he faces potential death. There's a flicker there, something behind the eyes. An expression of hope if I'm not mistaken. *Odd*. I slowly step back over to him. "My bag?"

"Second drawer."

I reclaim my bag from the chest of drawers in order to end something that is a great distraction for him. His wincing about is bothersome. I fear he may succumb to his wounds - either through drink or distraction from the pain - before I can get any worthwhile information out of him. "Lay on the bed." I'm surprised by the apparent flush on his cheeks. "Lay on the bed," I insist. As he arranges himself on the bed, I examine the contents of my bag and find the silver and glass bottle I want. "This will sting."

"Apothecarist as well?" William grunts as he shifts his body away from the edge of the bed, allowing me a few inches to sit by his side.

I unwrap the scraps of shirt from his upper arm and abdomen. Thin red spiderweb lines are snaking away from the wounds - a slow-acting poison. The plan may have been to subdue, question, and then let die. It is odd behavior for Mary to apply a cut that kills her victim out of sight. Acids, explosions, and yes, poison, but she enjoys watching suffering. She's picked up a new toy and is still learning to use it. Otherwise, I think William would be dead by now.

I lift the silver lid of the canister. "These are not bad. Stop wincing." I apply some ointment to the upper arm – jerking my hand away as he recoils in pain, "I said stop it." The abdomen wound is to the side and much deeper. I'm surprised he was able to walk away, let alone run. I apply two coats of the ointment. There's an old wound on his shoulder and upper left arm that I take a moment to inspect. The telltale scarring from a fire. He catches me looking. I awkwardly clear my throat and wipe my fingers on my skirt. I place the bottle back in my bag as I get up. "In a moment, those will heat up. In about an hour, a clear crust will form. The crust will be slightly flexible but don't expect to be doing much, or you'll rip them open again. In about a day, you should be able to peel them off like any scab." I place my back against the chest of drawers and fold my arms. "Now. Tell me what you know."

He stretches ever so slightly, testing the extent of the medicine I had applied. With an approving nod he begins. "I was at this sparring match, as I usually am when I know about a fight. And, and, these dogs, these enormous dogs broke in. I don't know how. They began ripping at each other, and everyone scattered. I managed to work my way back, to see what was going on, but then there was this woman, this elderly woman." He ran his hand through his hair and pinched the bridge of his nose. "What was she doing there? Not a place for a -" he glances at me. "Anyway, I escort her out, and as I do, I'm asking some polite questions - and then she stabs me." He places a hand on his side. "And, then," an exasperated chuckle escapes his lips while he rubs at his eyes. It's as if he's trying to scrub the memory in order to make sense of it. "And then one of the dogs leaps through the wall of the warehouse and begins chasing me, and then the lady begins chasing me… or maybe they were chasing each other. There was no time to ask any questions. A short time later, she catches up to me and tries to stab me again, but just slashes my arm this time, mainly because that dog rams into her. They began to fight, and I didn't try to stick around this time. I'm not ashamed to say, I ran for my life."

I could see it on his face and in his breathing. Even in this safe place, the excitement and fear of that moment are very real for him. "And The Crusher?"

"Why do you want to know about The Crusher?" His head tilts to face me. "Odd for a spy to care about something so domestic. Or is this a spy-on-spy affair?" The tone of his voice goes up with excitement. "Do you have a rogue spy on your hands?"

"I'm perfectly capable of making you bleed again." The threat is serious, yet he smirks and looks away.

"I'd show you my notes, but most are at The Globe."

"I'll take whatever you can remember."

He sighs. "William said this would cause trouble." He looks back at me. "He said – no, laughed really, and told me I was all over the place with this one, trying to make a bigger story out of it than it is. I insisted they were all linked, but he runs the paper, so there was only so much pushing to be done."

"What was linked?"

"I've cobbled together several murders that I think are all related." Despite my warning to remain still, William gets himself up into a seated position. "I got wind of a story of a wealthy family in Kent. House broken into. Some staff were killed, burned with acid, and beaten. I sent a letter and received a reply informing me that a small family heirloom, a stone knife, had been stolen. Then there's the Nivens, working class from the Soho area. Never did any harm to no one. Whole family murdered, beaten to death. I spoke with a guard friend, and he says the father's last words were, `Cup, she kept demanding a cup.´ Maybe it's nothing, but I tracked down their things. All were donated to Saint Anne's. I spoke with a priest there, and he rattled off the list of things donated. This was a family of three, but only two cups were included in what was donated."

I was beginning to see why the other William had scoffed at this. "And the professor mentioned in your article?"

He paused briefly before adjusting his head to stare at the ceiling. "Why did you ruin the Dead House? Looking for something? Were you caught in the act? Smashed tables, scattered bodies, I'm certain there was a fight. Why leave your bag? I knew it was important. Knew whoever did this would come looking for it. So, I didn't want the Watch to have it. I told the guard, `This can't be important; otherwise, why would the attacker have left it?'" He laughs and turns to look at me. "You weren't there to make a mess. Unless you carry that weapon just to make a mess?" He flicks his head in my direction, indicating the morningstar strapped to my back.

"You can see this?" My hand lifts and touches the points of the star.

"Yes. Why wouldn't I? How many ladies around town have a weapon strapped to their back?"

I found his perception irritating. Also, his questions. It reminds me of one of my brothers. I'm fairly certain it's a technique to throw a person off their guard. It's annoying how often it works. "The professor?"

He tries to reach for one of the half-empty bottles of wine but stops at the pain in his side.

I sigh, stomp over, and hand him the bottle.

He smiles. "Thank you." And takes a sip. "Professor Robert Wren. Chemistry and math, taught at Oxford. Wife Jane. Son Arthur. Rumors travel fast through the upper class. It took a few days, but when I heard about it, I knew it fit with everything else I had found. I took a trip out there hoping for… I don't know. Maybe a clearer picture as to why this keeps happening. I spoke with the son and the widow. Robert was found in the doorway to the study, beaten, nearly crushed. Arthur said he was upstairs. He remembers hearing the front door open, and then, about ten minutes later, a bit of shouting followed by thumps. The Widow Wren said, insisted in fact, that she wasn't at home during the attack. When I pressed her on that, Arthur made me change the subject. Something never sat right with me about that. Moreso, though, why was Robert killed there? Why not run for the door or up the stairs? Or call out for Arthur. No weapon was found near or on him. In fact, the guard said it was like he hadn't defended himself at all. Yet, he was struck down in the doorway to the study - as if, I don't know… as if trying to block someone's path. And then I get this." It takes him a moment to get to his feet. He inspects the pages on the table before holding one out to me. "A letter from Arthur. It arrived too late to add any of it to the article. Essentially, he says that his mom has been missing for a few days, and if I'm still investigating his father's death and I happen to uncover any information about his missing mother, to please contact him."

I read the letter and then passed it back to him. I pace back and forth from the window to the door and back again before sitting in the chair at the end of the bed. "It doesn't fit."

"What doesn't fit?" William asks, making his way back over to the bed.

"I keep coming back to something that…" I trail off. *How can I tell him?* "Something that was told to me. I feel it's important somehow, but it doesn't seem to fit with any of my information." I fall into silence, and thankfully, William refrains from asking any questions. Round and round `Ham´ spins in my mind. I sigh. "I was informed that this sailor – he was dressed as one, I'm not at all sure that was his profession – that his final word was `ham.´" I lean around the chair to catch his reaction.

William's face scrunches in confused thought.

I sigh again and turn away. *His reaction is an honest one. He has no more idea than I do.* "I know. I thought for a moment that `ham´ was him trying to say Tottenham Court Road. That somehow, the two of you were linked. Now I doubt that."

"Perhaps he was just hungry."

The dead don't reach out to mention their favorite meal. "I feel it is more important than that." My mind drifts back to that moment. "There was a sadness to it. Pain. Perhaps betrayal. Or maybe concern. As if he was trying to speak to someone familiar," I say more to myself, forgetting for a moment that William is in the room.

"You were told that his last word was said as if in betrayal?"

I can feel his quizzical eyes on the back of my head. I thump the arms of the chair and stand. "Thank you, Mister Monkton. This hasn't been a complete waste of my time." I move to the door.

"What? That's it?"

"Keep your head down." I don't mention that I hope the use of my powers doesn't lead Mary to his front door.

"There's a story here. I can't just sit here." He stands.

"That crazy old woman may come back to finish the job. You are of interest to her. Stay put for a few days."

"Because of The Crusher?"

"Because," I sigh. My shoulders droop. I can't think of a lie. "Because her interest in you is complicated. She doesn't like that you're writing about her antics. She's worried your research will help me. Now she's failed her assassination attempt - and she doesn't take failure lightly."

"All the more reason for us to stay together. I'd rather not be her or this Crusher's - mayhaps they are the same - either way, I don't want to be the next victim."

My hand hesitates on the door handle.

He takes a step closer. "Maybe we should both rest. We can come at this fresh in the morning. The bed is yours. I've fallen asleep many a night in that chair." He waits. "I don't claim to know what's going on here - though I am beside myself with anticipation in trying to unravel this — but I see you've obviously been in a fight and could use a moment yourself."

"Obviously?" I touch my face. Definitely tender.

"If you open the armoire door, there's a mirror there."

I do. A silver-handled mirror rests on a small shelf. It's very pretty. Something that you would find among a woman's things. Something that was probably given to her as a gift. Curious that William would have such a thing. I observe my reflection. Nothing that won't fade in a few hours, but perhaps a few hours of sleep would not be an outrageous indulgence.

CHAPTER NINE

I smile as I become aware once
more. I play my dream over in my mind
one last time before it fades away. A
serene day of sailing. The sea air
whipping at my hair. The splash of
water against the hull of the ship. The
fresh, briny air fills my lungs. That
feeling of moving faster than you've
ever moved before, yet at the same
time, the world around you appears not
to move at all. Oddly, though, all the
while feasting on a pork loin. I
stretch and feel the bed under me and
the blanket above me - both are
exquisite. I have to imagine that
sleeping upon a cloud must feel the
same. The sound of the door opening
throws me off the bed. I leap onto my
feet, morningstar in hand.

William stands at the door. The
objects upon the tray he holds rattle
as he's startled by my sudden action.
He gently pushes the door closed with
his foot and takes a tentative step
into his room. "I brought you a few
things if you wanted to refresh
yourself."

I allow a second to pass and then nod at the table as I slide my morningstar into its proper place.

"There's a washing basin. A few clean rags. A water jug. Some brandy. A sponge. And a collection of my favorite herbs and spices," he lists off as he sets the tray down. He looks up with a satisfied smile.

I roll my eyes and glance out the window. It's still dark. *How long was I asleep?* He notices my stare.

William crosses to the window and pulls the curtains a little wider. "It is the hour of the bread makers." He peers out.

I join him at the window. "I've rested. I feel much better. Thank you."

"You look all the better for it. Quite remarkable." He smiles warmly as he reaches up to touch my face. I don't have to stop him; he stops himself. The smile vanishes under a weight of — *What is that? Shame? Guilt?* He quickly returns his gaze to the window.

"Time for me to be on my way," I say.

He clears his throat and gently thumps the top of the dresser. "Right. Let me get my coat."

"You are staying here."

"There's a story here. A huge one. I'm not staying here."

I step up to him. "You will stay here," I say and then add. "For your own safety."

William swallows and takes half a step back. I can tell he's intimidated. "There's a story here," he says nervously but with conviction. "Innocent lives are certainly at risk. Now, I can come with you and offer a modicum of assistance, or you can be on your way and have to put up with us constantly running into each other as we pursue this separately."

A moment passes as we stare at each other. "You will wait in the salon."

He nods, but as he steps away, he pauses and glances wordlessly at the window.

I can see his mind and step away from the chest of drawers to examine the tray. "The salon, William. I will join you in a moment."

"Of course." He grabs his coat from the back of the chair and a satchel from the floor by the door and leaves the room.

I decide to partake of the supplies he had gone to the trouble of setting out. "It's bad manners otherwise, right?" I say to myself… or maybe my Patron if he's listening. I freshen up quickly, grab my bag, and leave the room. As I descended the stairs, I know full well I could walk on by without him ever taking notice and that by the time he realized I'm gone, I would be well on my way. "He's going to get himself killed," I sigh and step into the parlor. He seems genuinely surprised by my appearance.

He clears his throat. "Shall we?" He gestures to the door.

The night is cool and dark. These are not streets bestowed with lamps and burnt out are the torches that offered a semblance of flickering illumination. The faint shuffle of footfalls tells me we aren't the only ones to transgress the tranquility of the dark. In a moment, our eyes will adjust and shadows will take form, allowing us to move about without too much trouble. Mym is alert and ready for trouble – I doubt she slept. She is a stalwart friend, scout, and warrior. No doubt she feared what I feared, which was Mary showing herself. I feel her focus shift to me and then to William as we make our way down the stairs. Reaching the street, I'm hit with the possibility that upon meeting Mym,

William may decide my world is a little too strange to dip a toe into and return to his room.

William comes to my side, "Where do we begin?"

"Introductions."

"Pardon?"

"Mym, this is William Monkton. He will be joining us, at least for a short time. He has talents that may prove to be useful."

"Mym?" William looks around, peering through the dark as if trying to see through the glare of the sun or a smoke-filled room. He jumps and grabs my arm in fear as Mym rolls forward. "That's the beast that chased me," he leans forward. "Wait. No beast, but, ah, but – what is that thing?"

His hand tightens around my forearm. "Careful, you'll make her blush. This is Mym." I turn to walk away.

William sputters but collects himself quickly and asks, "Hold a moment. Did you say She? Her?"

"She. Yes."

"She?"

"She."

There's a pause. Even without looking, and now a good thirty feet ahead, I can tell they are scrutinizing each other.

"How can you tell?" he mutters curiously.

"Why does it matter? Come along if you're going to." To his credit, William does begin to follow – though there is a small yelp as Mym rolls by him.

I lead the way south and east back into the heart of the city. I'm once more confident on my path. I'm also confident that Mary is along the same path – though I do not know her endgame. I fear that regardless of her goal, she will now direct her attention to me. She will revel in tripping me up, delaying me, frustrating me, and hurting me. But there is an advantage to this if I can keep at least one step ahead. My pace quickens.

I don't bother with alleys and side streets but stick to the main thoroughfares. We passed a handful of people, each focused on their destination and not on us. I don't even bother to hide Mym – which I take as a blessing. It means there's less for Mary to track; at the very least, it will make it harder for her to follow us. About an hour into our march, I see the first light of day begin to paint

the sky. It's also when I start to see
more people appear on the street as the
workday begins. When I pause to wait
for the first carriage of the day to
pass by, I hear the puff of William
catching his breath. I press on before
he's ready. I hear him shuffle to keep
up, but he's beginning to fall behind.

"I say," William says, "where are
we going?"

"The dead only speak with
importance."

"Yes, yes, very enigmatic, but
where are we going?"

"I have a sense that a man has
lied to me. I will have words with
him."

"Just as illuminating." He pauses
as he quickens his pace to catch up.
"It's only that we seem to be in a
hurry,"

"If you can't keep up -"

"No. No. Nothing like that…"

He doesn't finish his thought. I
glance back over my shoulder. He's in
his own head, his finger making small
gestures as if pointing at an invisible
map. He stops, and his face lights up.

"Just a moment," he says and races
down the alleyway he'd just stopped in
front of.

Mym doesn't stop. *Rumble. Puff,* she says, rolling by me.

"Maybe. He'll catch up or he won't," I say and fall in alongside Mym. "Although, it will only get brighter now. At this point, maybe we should get off the main roads. I want to avoid walk the dog for now."

Crackle.

"Back to where we started. Near enough, anyway." I am worried by the number of people I'm seeing and the light of day now fully creeping across the sky. As it happens, Mym and I have stepped into a length of this road where several side streets and alleys branch away. The race is on. However, zigzagging through the city will take time. Before I come to a decision, a carriage speeds towards us. It rumbles to a stop, nearly in front of me. The side door opens, and William's head appears.

"So there I was, worried I'd hold you back, when suddenly I recalled a one, Mister McAllister, a carriage driver who favors Chancery Lane and the corresponding roads. I wrote an article on carriage drivers a few months back and recalled his usual route. I took a chance, and here we are. He's happily

agreed to take us anywhere in the city
as fast as his horse will travel."

He's very proud of himself, and I
can't help but smile in return. "Move
over," I whisper to William and then
take a step to the side and address
Mister McAllister. "Do you know the
fish market of the Isle of Dogs?"

"Yes, Ma'am."

The carriage is jostled as Mym's
puff of steam lifts her up and into our
transportation. I hear a surprised
"Oh!" from William, which is mostly
covered up by the horse pawing at the
ground in agitation, but McAllister has
a firm grip on the reins. "There,
please. I'll tell you when to stop."

"Yes, Ma'am."

The driver waits until he hears
the door close before calling his horse
to motion. William was not wrong about
the speed of travel – though the rattle
of the carriage is obnoxiously loud.

"Be there in no time," William
says just above the din of noise.

I don't notice at first because
I'm enjoying the speed at which we are
traveling, but when I glance toward
Mym, I see that she and William are
staring at each other – although he is
probably unaware of this.

Puff.

William's eyebrows go up, and he flinches back at the sudden eruption of steam.

"She would like you to stop staring at her."

William nervously clears his throat and says to me, "Sorry."

I shake my head and nod to Mym.

"Sorry," he says to Mym before adjusting his position to stare out the window.

Mym is still staring at him, but as William doesn't know this, I don't scold her. I watch him, however, out of the corner of my eye. His attention keeps wandering, drawn to our rocky companion taking up most of the interior foot space. Hardly a few minutes later, he is staring once more at Mym. "I feel compelled to ask, how did you meet, ah - how did you meet Mym?"

"We found each other in Norway," I say, pretending to be interested in the passing scenery. "While exploring a waterfall."

"You were both exploring the waterfall, together?"

"No. We were both there, but not together. I was -" I pause and turn my full attention to him. *How much should I tell you? How much am I allowed to say? I feel as if a line has already been crossed.* "I was chasing someone."

"Another rogue spy? Is this a common problem in France?" He smirks.

"Yes, something like that. Unfortunately, they surprised me. I was knocked into a river and then over a waterfall. I hit my head and took in too much water – I nearly lost consciousness. I remember just as everything was going black, the force of the falls pushed me right down to the bottom of the lake. Right to the bottom. I felt myself hit the rocks below, and then I was being pushed. This rush of water pushed me away from the turbulent water enough that I was able to float to the surface."

"A second waterfall? Like a current of some sort?"

"No. By chance, I had been pushed onto Mym. Seeing my plight, she pushed me to safety using her vents."

William nods and then shakes his head. "Wait. Why was Mym at the bottom of a lake?"

"When my senses returned to me. I dove back into the water to investigate this strange occurrence. I found and rescued her in return."

Crackle. Crackle. Puff.

"Yes. Thank you for reminding me."

134

"What did she say?"

"She was pointing out that she rescued herself. She reminded me that it took several tries, and ultimately, it took both of us to rescue her from the bottom of the lake. You see, she had-"

Rumble. Puff.

"Oh, I think I do. I mean, since we're relating all the details to William after all. We need to tell him how you got there in the first place." I wait for her to respond. She doesn't, so with a malicious little smirk, I continue. "She was playing by the river, rolling around in the mud very close to the waterfall, when she slipped. She was forced down the falls and landed in the water with such force that she lost consciousness. When she awoke, she was wedged between several rocks. Try as she might, she was trapped."

"How long was she -" William shifts his focus from me to her, "How long were you down there?"

Crackle.

"She doesn't know."

William leans back in his seat, his face contemplative. He suddenly turns to me, and then to Mym, and then back to me. "Sorry, I'm not sure who to ask this?"

"Then just ask."

"You said she lost consciousness," he says, and I nod. "Does that mean she, you, can feel pain?"

I feel this is now certainly headed in the direction of bad taste. She would not enjoy us discussing her frailties any more than I would enjoy discussing mine. "She feels a great many things," I say carefully. I glance out the window and recognize the area we are in. I thumped the roof of the carriage to get the driver's attention. "This will do!" I call out, and the carriage begins to slow.

I exit quickly and get my bearings.

William steps down from the carriage and over to the driver. "My good sir, if it is no trouble, I would like to procure your services for the rest of the day."

I see William hand McAllister several coins.

Eyes wide and a smile to match, the driver nods. "My pleasure, Sir. Shall I wait here?"

William looks at me. Thankfully, the driver is too well engrossed in his windfall to notice Mym getting down from the carriage. She rolls straight away into an alley. "There's an almshouse just up the road here. Could you wait there?"

"I can, Ma'am." He pockets the money and pulls away from the curb.

From where we had disembarked, it is but a short walk to the familiar alley where this all started. Mym slips just inside the alley and settles against a wall. I lead William around to the front of the building.

"Care to illuminate me?" he asks.

"I told you someone lied to me, and I'd like to know why."

We are not the only ones entering the building. A steady stream of men flow through the doors and up the broad stairs to the work area. The large windows offer some light at this hour, but much of the interior is still cast in large shadows. The smell of fresh wood and oils permeates the air. The workers, for the most part, are uninterested in the two of us as they engage in their daily preparations before the tasks begin in earnest. The office door at the far end of the factory floor has light peering around it.

I don't knock.

Wallace Graham is seated behind a desk. His coat and tricorne hang on a few hooks. His attention appears to be focused on orders laid out in front of him on the desk. His head jerks up in anger. Eyes fuming, words on his lips, but he stops as he's taken aback by the appearance of someone other than whom he was expecting. "What is the meaning of this?!"

William takes a step to the side, lingering at the back of the small office. I hear him close the door as I approach the desk. I allow my presence to become recognized.

"Miss, um, miss – I've forgotten your name," Wallace glances behind me, "but I see you've brought your husband this time. Well done." Wallace slicks back his greasy hair and comes around the desk, his hand out for William.

I step in front of Wallace. "Mister Wallace Graham, you lied to me."

"Ah – ham," William mutters.

"Nonsense. I told you to bring your husband around. And you have. Sir," he tries to press around me.

I take his shoulder and throw him against his desk, scattering pages. I press my knee against his back and bend his arm into an awkward and painful angle.

"What -" he begins to shout, but I clamp my hand over his mouth.

I hear William nervously shuffle and then take up a position in front of the door.

"What do you know about the sailor?"

"What sailor?" Wallace mumbles from behind my hand.

"The young man who was killed here the other day."

"Nothing. I don't know him."

"You do. I saw you."

There's a knock at the door.

"Our time is running out…" William stresses.

"Tell me." I sneer. I pull his arm a little more.

"Alright. Alright," Wallace cries.

"Anything above a whisper, and your arm is mine," I say and pull my hand away from his mouth.

"I was curious. Yes. I went to look because I knew the owner was going to be asking me questions."

There's another knock at the door - more insistent this time.

"Continue," I say.

"His face was gone," Wallace's voice trembles. "It was the most horrible thing I've ever seen."

He becomes lost in the memory. I nudge him.

"I admit, I did recognize him. His missing earlobe -"

"Missing earlobe?" I ask. I had notice this, but his whole face was splashed in blood; I had assumed it had been damaged in the fight.

"I've seen him before. He's been here before."

Another series of knocks on the door. Harsh and forceful, the whole door shakes.

Wallace continues without prompt. "He's friends with one of my workers."

"Who?" Both William and I speak at once.

"Henry Cunningham. I have questions for him, but he hasn't shown up to work. He won't have a job if he doesn't show up today."

"Where does he live?" I pull his arm.

Wallace speaks through gritted teeth, "I don't know."

William steps forward. "Have you seen him walking in a particular direction? Is he married?"

"He's not married as far as I know, but he has a woman. I've heard Nancy mentioned."

"Think very carefully. Anything, anything at all that might suggest who this Nancy is?"

"She's a whore for all I know."

I slap a hand over his mouth and yank his arm out of its socket.

William approaches and leans in. "Anything? When he would mention Nancy, did he come in eating a pastry? Did he comb his hair differently?"

I can see Wallace thinking. "Low tide. He smells of low tide — and he was talking one day of getting her a new knife."

The door rattles again.

I push his arm back into place and help him up. "Send whoever that is away. I have more questions."

Rubbing his shoulder, Wallace pulls the door open.

A small, frail, elderly woman stands on the other side.

William recognizes her as the lady who stabbed him.

I recognize her as the form Mary used in the alleyway and to escape from the fight arena.

She smiles, uncorks a small bottle, and pushes it and Wallace backward into the office. He tumbles into William and falls to the floor. A sickly green smoke begins to pour forth from the bottle – the plume envelops Wallace's face.

In seconds, the office is filled with this smoke. It begins to filter into the main work area. I grab William and pull him from the office. "Out!" I yell. "Everyone out!" I race toward the main doors and crash into the open air. I drop William's hand and spin around, searching for Mary.

"Cunningham," William coughs, "she'll be after him next."

I rush over to the alley. "Make your way to the carriage," I say to Mym, "Mary may double back and attack the driver." I glance back over my shoulder, "William!" I call as I dash away.

CHAPTER TEN

William and I sprint along the road, cutting our way around - and sometimes over - other pedestrians. As we come to the market, I draw close to a shack and peer around. There are stalls and huts and people and carts pushed to and fro, streets and alleys branching away like the tunnels of an ant colony. "Which way?"

"Let's ask?" William steps away from the shack and approaches a group of women under the awning of a small stall. Each is at a task, either mending a basket, looping a net, or filleting some of the fish. All work with a knife. "Graham said he overheard Cunningham mention getting his lady a new knife. She may be a fishmonger or someone who repairs or crafts tools for the sea," he says to me as we approach. "Ladies, a fine morning to you all."

They nod. "What can we do for you, good sir?" the lady prepping the fillets asks.

"I'm sorry to say nothing you are providing here. But, I am willing to pay you for your time." He reaches into his satchel and pulls out a small leather bag, which he shakes, causing the coins within to jingle. "We are looking for a craftsman, a sculptor of chairs and other furniture. We have a specialty job for him, but unfortunately, he was not at work today. I am told he is seeing a young woman who is engaged in your type of work. Do you know of such a couple?"

The women share glances. "Can't say we do. But," the basket woman shrugs, "Madeline, maybe?" A round of nods meets this.

"Madeline?" I ask.

The basket woman sets her work down and comes to my side. "That way," she points, "nearer to the docks. There's a shack with a well-rusted anchor leaning against a bit of stone. That'll be Maddy's hut. She bakes muffins and such, but if there's gossip to be had, she'd be the one to know it."

I begin walking, leaving William to thank the women.

"Greatly appreciated," he says. I hear a few coins drop into someone's hand.

He catches up a moment later. "We haven't time for this," I say to him.

"I gladly submit to your expertise if there is another path you wish to try or something else you would like."

144

I find it interesting that he used the word *path*. We are playthings to the gods. Toys that are argued over and sometimes broken in a game I don't bother to understand. I enjoy what I do because it allows me to save lives. As long as I am allowed to keep doing that and bashing things, I'm willing to ignore the unsavory aspects of those beyond this realm. We all have our place and missions to be done. What I do, what my brothers and sisters with other Patrons do, is essential. The weave of the ether is such that chaos is at odds with balance. I maintain the balance against my kindred with missions to do otherwise. The path I am set upon matters. I save lives – *I try to save lives*. My eyes blur a moment, but I fight away the tears. "I would have liked Mister Graham to have been honest with me in the first place. I would have liked Mister Cunningham to have said something more when I spoke to him the first time. What I would like is for men not to lie. What I would like is a straightforward fight. As I don't have any of that, let's see where this leads us." I don't mean to grouse, but I do wish I had a better idea, and I truly am tired of being lied to.

"You spoke with Mister Cunningham before?"

"Briefly. He told me that he didn't think Mister Graham was caught up in the murder. Which was both the truth and a lie."

"An omission, if it turns out Mister Cunningham knew anything about this matter."

"An omission. Yes, I suppose that is how your kind would see it." I hear William about to speak but interrupt him. "I think we're here. There," and dart over to a shack with an anchor as described. The door is open, and the air around the hut does smell of baked goods. I don't knock as I enter. "Madeline?"

The inside is basically just a kitchen. Countertops with bowls. A shelf with several jars. A pile of sacks in the corner. A large oven. A woman in a floured apron and her hair pulled up with sticks turns as we enter. "If you're here for some of my goods, you'll have to wait a bit. I've sold out of my morning muffins."

"Are you Madeline?" I ask again.

Her eyebrows go up; there's a hint of concern as she looks from me to William. "Yes?"

"We are told you are a woman who knows things."

She flashes a prideful smile. "I listen, you know," she brushes some of the flour from her apron and pulls back a strand of hair that had fallen out of place. "And who ye be?"

"I am Persephone," I watch her eyes flick to William. "I am looking for a craftsman by the name of Henry Cunningham. He makes chairs. He is with a woman, Nancy, who works the docks making nets or such."

"Oh, aye." Madeline nods.

"Are you sure?" I take a step; she responds with a step back.

"Yes. A nice couple. Be a better couple if he married her. I hear," she leans in a little, "I hear there's carnality there." She raises her hands and lowers her head. "Not that it be my place to judge, but I ask you, if he's already getting what he wants, what she got to get him to make her an honest woman?"

"Indeed. You know where I might find them?" I brush away her comments and take a firm grip on the strap of my satchel. *I don't have time for this.*

"I'm unsure where he lives, but her house is on Foxglove Lane. It's just north of here. A short walk just across the way. Third in from the corner on the right. I live on the lane myself, and this one day, Mister Cunningham wasn't available. You see, sometimes he helps her with her sales. Anyway, I see her struggling a little with her cart - she has this push cart she sells from. Oh - nets, scoops, hooks, some fine baskets - anyway, she's struggling a bit, and I ask her if she needs help. Anyway, turns out we're on the same lane. Oh my, her house. So many flowers. Dried, fresh - just a bushel of them. Not sure if her man spoils her or if she spoils herself, but just this wonderful smell. Though, been thinking of using that myself. Working down and along the docks here can leave a fishy smell on your clothes. Then again, I come home smelling of baked bread more often than not -"

"Thank you." I cut her off and leave the hut, William following right behind. I follow her vague directions and stop at a street labeled Foxglove Lane. A line of small homes - mostly with single levels, though a few with double and one or two with three - are built along the lane and follow it as it curves out of sight. According to Madeline, Nancy's house is the third on the right, but I don't need that information to find her place because Mary is here. The small, frail woman approaches the house, a bottle of green swirling gas in her hand. "Mary!" I call out, but she has already stopped. I'm pretty sure she sensed my arrival. "Mary, your fight is with me."

"My fight," she responds as she turns to me, "is with whomever Thanatos tells me my fight is with." As she says this, she spins, and with a strength that belies her frame, she back-kicks the door open and lobs the bottle over her shoulder into the house.

Before I can stop him, William takes off, running towards the house. "What are you doing?!"

"I don't know!" he calls over his shoulder.

Mary doesn't stop William as he charges by her and through the front door – from which green smoke is now billowing. "Two with one stone." She takes several steps towards me.

I match her, and we meet outside the second house in the middle of the lane. I draw my morningstar, and she a green-tipped dagger – and, oddly, a chisel. She holds the woodworking tool out to me.

"Location spells are so easy. You just need something personal to the subject. Shame you don't use more of your talents." She drops the tool. "You must enjoy arriving late only to find death and destruction?"

With a burst of rage, I swing for her head.

She dodges. "If it eases your spirit, we've both lost something here. The stray you've picked up, and the information you were hoping to gain – both dead, and you at a dead end. And me, this form. I have enjoyed it, so unassuming, but alas, it has drawn too much attention."

I lunge again, but she's able to leap back in time and deflect with her dagger. "Fight me!"

"When I'm finished torturing you." She pulls a small vial from behind the scarf around her waist and tosses it at the nearest house. It clinks against the stone and comes to rest right outside the door.

As I reach the piece of glassware, the stoppered end begins to spark and the red powder within glows. I wrap my hands around the vial as it explodes. I'm knocked back into the street. It wasn't enough to do much harm, but my clothes are scorched, and my hands will need to heal. I roll onto my hands and knees, but the portal Mary had created was already spiraling shut. "Merde." I reclaim my morningstar. I should run. I should at least move, but I can't. I stare at the tiny house and the green smoke pouring out of the open door.

I catch a faint cough – and then another closer and louder. I race to the door, and reach it just as William, supporting most of the weight of the husky Mister Cunningham, falls through the opening, collapsing onto the street. Both men are coughing and sputtering but alive.

"It was like a miracle," William is interrupted by a coughing fit. "A miracle. The gas filled the house, but the flowers – some of the flowers would," he rubs his stinging eyes, "they would poof as the gas came in contact with them. It created these clear pockets –"

"Not a miracle, just magic." I plant the pointy end of my star near his head and lean in over him, supported by the butt of the shaft. I am planning on scolding him again, but I find myself staring at the bump on his nose. Broken at some point in his life, recently, and didn't heal quite right. Another puzzle piece falls into

place. I decided not to berate him.
Instead, I yank both William and
Cunningham to their feet. I glance over
their shoulders. This is a working-
class neighborhood in the middle of the
day. Most of these houses are empty
right now, but the noise still drew a
few people. I stick a finger in
Cunningham's face. "You will follow.
You will stay silent. You will not fall
behind." I look to William, who nods. I
dash away with the two of them
following.

A few streets later, I slip into
the first alley I find. I gesture for
them to rest. Mister Cunningham leans
against the wall and vomits. William,
appearing a little green, sits and
hangs his head. I stand behind
Cunningham as he spits to clear his
mouth. "Mister Cunningham, you failed
to mention you knew the deceased."

He turns and leans his back
against the wall. He squints at my face
and then recognizes me. "I didn't think
it proper."

"How 'bout now?"

"Didn't you have an accent?" he
asks.

"Mister Cunningham, you said you
didn't think Mister Graham had anything

to do with the murder of that sailor. It seems, however, that you did."

"I didn't," Cunningham snaps.

I judge his face to be a mix of fear and anger. "But you knew him?"

The anger slips into sorrow. "He was my friend."

"Omit nothing, Mister Cunningham. Your life and the lives of others remain in danger, and I don't have time for what is proper."

He sighs and nods. "His name was Jacob Alexander, and he was my friend since we were children. He was a royal courier, but…"

"But?"

"He took other courier jobs as well. Jobs that weren't always safe." Saying this, he looks away and slides down the wall.

"You helped?"

He nods.

"Did you get him killed?" Out of the corner of my eye I see William's head snap up as I say this, but I hold out a finger to keep him silent.

"The storage room. Almost no one knows about it. We used it to store some of the stuff we were moving and as a meeting place to hand things over."

There's a long pause. His mind is elsewhere. I squat to be eye level with him, and with honest care, I ask, "Henry, what happened?"

"I have this cousin. He's done very well for himself. Smart. Teaches at that school -"

"Oxford?" William cuts in.

"There, yes. I wouldn't say we're close, but we're family, and word gets around. Anyway, I received this letter asking me for help transporting something. I knew Jacob would be up for it; he loves to travel and being a courier takes him to all sorts of places. So, I told him about the job and that he needs to see my cousin. He tells his boss he must visit his sick mother, and off he goes."

"Where did he go?" I ask.

"Don't know. Far," Henry shrugs. "He was gone for a couple of months. I don't have the details. I'm just the middleman. It was far. It needed to be done fast and quietly. And the handoff was supposed to take place in the storage room." He shakes his head, perhaps anticipating my next question. "I don't know why my cousin wanted to come here to pick up the item." His head slowly lifts. He stares into my eyes. "I thought, as you must be thinking right now, why did my cousin so brutally murder my friend? But he didn't. I've since learned that my cousin is also dead. Both dead. I feared for my safety; rightly so, it would seem."

"And Nancy?" I ask.

"Alive, as far as I know." Henry scrambles to his feet. "I, I should find her. She may be in danger, too."

I don't stop him as he moves away.

"Hold a moment," William calls out. He uses the wall to help get himself to his feet. He pulls a small leather pouch from his bag as he approaches Henry. William examines the coins within and then cinches the small bag shut. "Take your love someplace new. Start over together. This won't last you long, but it will get you there. You both have talents I'm sure will benefit you." William places the leather bag in Henry's hand.

"May God bless you both," Cunningham says as he leaves.

"See, we're not all bad," William says after Henry has left our sight.

"He lied," I hold up a hand before William can speak. "Omitted. Graham lied. If truth had come naturally, we might be ahead of this."

"You were a stranger to them."

"Does a stranger deserve less than the truth?" I begin to walk at a quick pace because Nancy isn't the only one that needs to be checked on. "And I think it had less to do with our level of acquaintance and more to do with the clothes I wear." After a few steps, I add. "I doubt you'd understand." Several minutes of silence pass before I realize I have annoyed William. It takes him several minutes to work up the courage to speak, or maybe he needed those minutes to calm himself.

"You assume wrong to think I do not understand hardship. It's also folly to assume just because we share the same sex that all of us are in any way the same."

"I didn't mean… have you never cast stones?"

The words are hardly out of my mouth before William responds. "Never have I, nor never will I assume that a person's ability to accomplish anything in this life is measured by their sex or appearance."

"Well then, you are in the minority."

"I tell you, I am not. That flocks of geese cluster together and can prove to be a bluster of noise does not mean that the quieter pigeons are not equal to or outnumber them."

He begins to outpace me. I allow him to pout and follow at my natural stride. We reach the almshouse a few minutes later. William approaches the carriage without care, but I linger in the alley across the street and find Mym.

Rumble. Puff.

"Don't worry about it. We should go."

Rumble.

"I'll explain once we're on our way." I project my will, walk my dog across the street, and help her into the carriage.

Before I can give the driver our destination, William speaks. "Oxford, my good sir."

"That'll take a day, Sir."

"Then we better be off." William closes the door, and the carriage rolls away from the almshouse. "Hopefully, I have not assumed incorrectly."

I don't answer. He still looks grumpy, so, I address Mym. "Mary beat us to Mister Cunningham. We managed to get him away, but I am disturbed by the encounter."

Puff.

"I can't sense Mary. I can't track her type of magic either. The way she hides herself…"

Crackle.

"No, this isn't shapeshifting. I know a shapeshifter, and this isn't that. She… she changes. I don't know." I sigh and lean back into the seat as I close my eyes. The ride is silent for some time. I open my eyes and find Mym asleep and William staring out the window. He's slumped, suggesting more fatigue or maybe embarrassment rather than anger – or Mary's smoke taking its toll on him. I don't feel I was incorrect in anything I said, yet his mood, irritatingly, is affecting my mood. "I apologize," I say.

He answers without pause. "Please do not apologize." He turns to face me. "Your opinion is warranted. I am well aware of the privilege that the luck of my birth has given me. I am well aware that men of like minds congregate and sway society to belittle and rule women. I am aware that otherwise good men are silenced by fear or complacency. I am aware of the terrible oppression and subjugation your sex endures." He takes a breath. "I apologize. You have a right to your anger, and I should accept that in support."

"I do not have a right to slap an ally."

"I feel that actions that are good and right for you to take supersede anything I am bound by."

There is something telling in his words, but I balk at a response. I nod and shift my gaze to my window. My mind sifting through the Rules; *What can I tell him? What is he allowed to know?*

CHAPTER ELEVEN

The carriage ride was bumpy and slow. I'm certain Mister McAllister handled his horse with expertise, but the distance was not easily overcome. Not counting a brief detour before leaving London for William to acquire more funds, Mister McAllister had driven the carriage through the rest of the day and the night without pause or rest. As we neared the periphery of London, both Mym and William were asleep. I watched him occasionally, wondering about this man who had insisted on taking such a dangerous journey. A man of questions who has asked few. There are assumptions I have made about him and questions I would like to ask, but I feel letting him sleep to be best right now. As he rested, I noticed the green tint to the skin around his neck and cheeks - lingering effects from Mary's attack, slowly fading as the hours drifted along.

With a fresh day rising, I hope William will awake in better temperament and I will be a few steps nearer to discovering Thanatos' machinations. Trees and farmland give way to homes and the usual trappings of society. The carriage crosses a stone bridge as we enter the outskirts of the city. I nudge Mym and William, "I believe we have come to Oxford." There's a grumble from both.

William wipes sleep from his eyes and glances out the window. He thumps the ceiling of the cab. "Driver," he calls out, "a right on the next road."

If McAllister verbally responds, it's hidden by the clop of horse hooves. As commanded, he directs the carriage to the right as we come to the next major intersection. The road curves along the edge of the city. Small homes pass along our left, and to the right, there is a park and gardens. As the serenity drops away, we are again riding in a valley of brick and mortar. These homes are far larger, some surrounded by fenced property.

"This next house, my good man," William shouts to McAllister.

The carriage comes to a halt in front of a gated home. Beyond the stone wall and the iron gate is a brown-stone house with several street-facing windows, including a lower bay window and a columned doorway. As I move to exit the carriage, I hear William clear his throat. I look back at him.

"Arthur is not a chatty person and can become quite defensive if the wrong word is spoken. I wonder if perhaps I should address him?"

I momentarily contemplate if I should tell him my plan just involves me sneaking in. I decide to adjust to what William is suggesting. "If Arthur has any further information, I have confidence you will get him to speak of it." I climb out of the carriage and lean in through the window. "Whether he does or doesn't, keep him distracted." I signal to Mym to stay and walk around to the gate. William joins me.

William opens the gate and allows me to pass through. A broad but short garden path between a few hedges leads us to a stout oak door with thick iron hinges. William uses the knocker to alert the household to our presence. A moment later, the door inches open. Standing behind a gap hardly half as wide as a person is an older man with thin white hair dressed in a tan and blue-tailed dress coat with a white waistcoat. His eyes drift down and up William before addressing him.

"Yes, Sir," he says.

"It's Poole, isn't it?" William smiles as he removes his tri-hat and holds it behind his back.

"Yes, Sir."

"I don't know if you remember me. I was here a few weeks ago when Professor Wren was murdered."

"Ah, Mister Monkton. I have to say, the Master is currently out. Though we do expect him back soon."

"Excellent. I wonder if I may indulge in your hospitality. We have been on the road all night -"

"`We´, Sir?"

"Yes," William stammers at Poole's raised eyebrows. He glances over his shoulder to ensure I'm still there, but he quickly turns to face the butler when he sees my head slowly shaking no. "Um, yes. My driver and I, of course."

"Yes, of course, Sir. Please, come in. I shall set you up in the receiving room." Poole steps back from the door, allowing us to enter.

The entry chamber is comprised of a white tiled floor and darkly stained wood. Narrow benches are built into the walls, and at the center is a small round table with a large glass vase displaying several early spring flowers. I move quickly around William, keeping myself well to the side. Poole shuts the door. "This way," he says.

He leads us through to the hallway. Four doors are here, and there

163

is another small chamber at the back of the hallway where the stairs are located. I can make out two archways there, though I can't see where they lead. Poole stops in front of the first door and escorts us into the room. The sitting room is small, decorated in soft green and white, with floral carvings around the fireplace and a large portrait of a sunflower hanging on the wall. A couch matching the decor sits under the street-facing window.

"I will see that refreshments are brought to you." Poole nods, but as he's leaving, he stops. "If you like, I will also see to your driver. There's a service gate. I can have him move your carriage to the stables where he and the horse can rest. And I'll have one of the maids bring him some food."

"Wonderful," William smiles and makes himself comfortable on the couch. "Oh, Poole," he calls out just as the door is about to shut.

"Yes, Sir?"

"A small basin, if you don't mind. I'd like to splash off some of the grime of travel before I see your Master."

"Yes, Sir." Poole departs.

I note how comfortable William seems in these surroundings. He sits with his back in the corner of the couch, an arm draped over the back, eyes glancing out the window at the street beyond. I can tell he's lost focus and I'm sure he's fallen into my perception ward. I'm about to get his attention when I see the faint smile, driven possibly by memory, fade into a frown. I sit on the cushion next to him and watch his eyes blink as he notices me again.

"Oh, Persephony. My apologies. I was lost in thought there for a moment." He clears his throat. "What's our next move?" A boyish grin comes to his lips.

"Where was the professor killed?"

"The doorway on the left. The one closest to the stairs. That's the study."

"Wait here. Keep Arthur busy while I have a look around." I move to the door. I ease it open and check the hallway. Before I leave, I hear William speak up softly.

"Poole, he – ah, he didn't see you."

I say as I slip out, "He didn't *notice* me." From further down the hallway, I hear the clink of dishes. The door to the study is only a few steps away, and I cross to it. I inspect the area around the door, though I'm not expecting much. We leave traces - especially when we use our abilities, but much like water on a hot day, those traces tend to evaporate. Besides, I know who I'm looking for. Mary was here. The question is, why? *Probably in your guise of that meek, old woman. Why would you come here, though? You managed to surprise Professor Wren. Did you insist on something that he wouldn't give you?* I step back from the door, trying to take in the larger picture. *He wasn't up against the door. He was in the doorway. The door was open. Why were you trying to get into this room? Why was he stopping you?* I hear footsteps hastily coming in this direction, so I quickly open the study door and dash inside. I hear the front door open, and Poole says, "Welcome home, Master Arthur."

"They want me to take up my Father's old seat."

"Congratulations, Sir," Poole says as he shuts the door.

"Not yet. They want me to write a paper and present it to them."

"Ah -"

"Yes, you see as well. I have Father's love of mathematics and science, but the written word…"

"Speaking of the written word, Sir, Mister Monkton has called on you. He's in the sitting room."

"Perhaps he has news on Mother."

The door to the sitting room opens, and I lose track of the conversation. I'm not sure how long William will be able to distract Arthur, so I return to my investigation. A large bay window bathes the room in sunlight. To either side of the window heavy blue curtains are tied back with a braided golden rope. A small table with a thin rectangular black box and two comfortable chairs are at the window. Books and bookshelves surround the room, and there is an ornate desk to the far left and a fireplace to the right.

After glancing around the room, I start with the desk. The desk is old and well-maintained. Right off, I notice a stack of handwritten pages. A polished stone acting as a paperweight. I pass my eyes over the pages. *An unfinished book by Robert Wren.* My attention passes to a small desk key seemingly haphazardly tossed into the position where it now lay. All the desk drawers have locks, but, as I test each one, none are locked. I open each drawer. Nothing grabs my attention until the last. The bottom drawer has several books, a journal, and a crumpled piece of paper. As with the other drawers, the state of the items suggests that the drawer had been rummaged through and then shut – perhaps forcefully. There's no way to tell if anything is missing, but these items in the deepest drawer interest me. I recognize some of the authors – Greaves, Kircher, al-Maqrizi. Other books I have no knowledge of, though all in some way seem to deal with Greek and Egyptian history. Distant history. The loose, crumpled page, has a list of names and places, some of which are crossed out. *The handwriting does not match that of Robert Wren's unfinished manuscript*. As I contemplate the page in my hand, I hear the sitting room door open.

"Please, Arthur, hear me out," William pleads.

"I assumed you came calling because you had information. Instead, I see you are here pursuing lies."

"Arthur, your mother is missing because she was a witness to something...

or is at least thought to have witnessed something - or maybe knows something. I cannot help if I don't have all the information."

"It's indecent -"

I hear the fluster in Arthur's voice even through the study's door. And he's not flustered because he believes that's what this is - *he's hiding something*.

"Arthur," William says in a conciliatory tone, "in the weeks or even months leading up to your father's murder and your mother's disappearance, did either of them - especially your mother - have any new interests or hobbies? Anyone new in their lives?"

Some words are spoken that I can't discern, and then the handle on the study door begins to turn. I return the crumpled page to where I had found it and slide the drawer shut. I step back and silently make my way over to the fireplace as the door opens. Arthur stutter-steps as he comes into the room. He was reluctant to place his feet on the doorway floor, so he took a slightly larger step as he entered. He doesn't notice me, and William, focusing on Arthur, doesn't either.

"This is the study." Arthur nervously clears his throat. "As I'm sure you recall, my father was murdered just there." He points to the threshold. "And my mother was – ah – just there." He glances at William but doesn't make eye contact.

"But you said… and your mother –"

"Yes, you were told otherwise," Arthur's tone is mournful. His presence is sheepish, like a child caught in a lie. He comes to stand next to the desk. "Have you ever had to fight for your mother's love?"

The odd question takes William a little aback, but he answers honestly. "No."

"I thought that to be the only answer myself, but then my mother died." Arthur sighs. "The woman you met did not give birth to me. She was my father's second wife. Though I did call her mother for nearly ten years, she never referred to me as son."

"At the risk of sounding indelicate, how did your birth Mother die?"

"She got sick," Arthur shrugs.

"And Jane?"

"The maid, or was. I was a boy at the time. I didn't interact with her all that much."

"And they married right away?"

"No. More than a year later. You see, my mother, my actual Mother, was kind, insightful, and a lover of books. I don't think my father loved Jane. I think my father missed my mother, and when he found out that Jane had a mind for history and science, he married her because she fit the memory. I missed my mother's love, and when I found out my father was to remarry, I did everything I could to regain that attention. So, I hope you can understand that when she asked me to lie for her, William, I - I -"

"Of course, Arthur, there are no ill feelings from where I stand."

Arthur nods. "She was here on that day. In this room. She would not say what she saw, only that she was here and that I was to tell no one this. I was to say she had been out when Father was attacked. She was scared. Of what, I know not. But she was very insistent that if anyone were to ask, I was to say that she had not been home." His eyes focused on a spot in the middle of the room as if he was seeing and hearing her now. "I didn't know what to say. She had never asked anything of me before. It's terrible to say, let alone think with my father dead on the floor not feet from us, but I admit to a

flash of happiness, a feeling of
longing fulfilled. Of course I agreed."
He takes a breath and sighs. "It was
all for nothing, it would seem. But
even before her disappearance, she was
always distant with me. My efforts to
gain attention and affection only
seemed to make her more apathetic to my
existence. I would listen sometimes
when they would work in here. She'd
write letters for him and collect books
for him. She would even do research for
him."

"What were they researching?"

Arthur lays a hand on the pile of
pages near the corner of the desk. "*A
History of Egypt: A Culture of
Mathematical Precision*. Father was
convinced that the ancient cultures
were far more advanced than is
currently known. Maybe even more
advanced than we are now. He had
friends, other academics, in places
like Egypt and Greece, and she would
routinely contact them in his name
regarding information pertaining to my
father's book." Arthur turned and ran
his finger down a line of books on a
shelf behind him. "Books on Egyptian
history and the meaning of their
glyphs. Borrowed, bought, and gifted
thanks to my moth – Jane." He chuckles

to himself. "My father described a lot of it as mystery and sorcery, but he very much enjoyed the rather detailed descriptions of some of their architectural achievements."

Lost in his memories, Arthur absently crosses the room to the small table and sits under the bay window in one of the cushioned chairs. "She would sit here and open her correspondence." He smiles wistfully, but the smile is short-lived as his face furrows into thought. "You asked me about recent interests. There was one. Or at least one that I'm aware of. Jane had become fixated on objects from that region." He points to several items on shelves around the room. Statues, metallic boxes, and silver scrollcases glistened in the light shining through the window. "I assume her readings had given her fanciful notions. They're trinkets. Replicas that did not keep the promise of their description. However, I do remember them arguing several months back. It was odd because they rarely argued – seldom spoke unless it was about research. He was at his wit's end regarding her trinket obsession. You see, Father was a serious man who took his research seriously, and this shift away from

written, measurable accounts had gotten
him some looks from his fellow
academics. Nonetheless, she convinced
my father this item was proof of what
he was saying in his book. A physical
artifact that she promised would show
the mathematical and mechanical
advancement of those bygone
civilizations. He agreed but insisted
that it be kept secret. I don't even
think he planned to have it shipped
here."

"Do you know what this item was?"

He laughs. "Something, I'm sure,
which would have looked nice on one of
these shelves."

"So, you doubt that it was the
promised proof?"

Arthur taps idly at the thin black
box on the table. "I've come to realize
that Mother Jane could be distracted by
shiny things," he absently flips the
lid up and closes it again – the tiny
hinges squeak a little. "I said I don't
think my father ever truly loved her,
but in the same breath, I'm sure she
never truly loved us either." He flips
the lid open again, only this time it
stays open. "Oh, I say, it's gone."

"What's gone?" William comes to
the small table.

"There was a knife here - a dagger. My mother would use it to open her letters. After she went missing, I came here looking for a clue, a hint, anything. Why was Father killed? Why let my mother live only to abduct her later? I can't believe I missed this."

I approach slowly, staying against the wall, keeping to what little shadow there is in the room. This close to them, with this much emotion, keeping myself unnoticed is difficult. If either looked this way, I'm not sure I could maintain the perception filter. But I want a closer look at this box. On the underside of the lid, I can see a symbol hidden in the wood's dark stain but visible as the light catches it. A symbol made up of four other symbols. From top to bottom, it reads Tau Theta, and from right to left, it reads Theta Tau. *From life to death and death to life - the Cult of Eleusis.*

"Would it have been left someplace else?"

"No. It should be here. I don't understand. Excuse me, I need to speak with Poole."

After Arthur had whisked himself down the hallway, William slinked to the desk, thinking I had hidden myself there. "Are you here?" he whispers.

175

"Yes," I say from behind him.

He jumps up, startled. "Have you been here the whole time?"

"Yes," I say, returning to the desk and the drawer with the crumpled page. I lay it on the desk, and William leans in to look.

"The handwriting doesn't match." He nods to the unfinished book.

"Jane wrote this. I think this drawer, in fact, is full of things that were hers and kept secret from Robert."

He begins to read from the list. "Bone? Saint Magnus the Martyr? Saint Magnus is under construction. All part of the bridge reconstruction. Jar and The Society of Artists of Great Britain? The Society of Artists is having an exhibition at Spring Gardens in… oh, I think tomorrow. Key and The Natural History Museum. Nothing of note I can think of regarding that. And what is this? Some of these are crossed out. That one there has been crossed out a few times. What's this last notation?" William squints as he tries to read between the scribbles. "Bill – Billings – Billingsgate. Oh, that's where –"

"Yes. Shhh. Let me think. She was here. Left alive. Left alive because she had something."

"Or knew something."

"Yes. Needed to be kept alive for answers. Probably threatened."

"Watching Robert being beaten to death - an excellent threat."

"Indeed. Mary got what she wanted. Got what she wanted and left."

"Why leave Jane alive if she was no longer of any use? Or did Mary come back to finish the job?"

"I think Jane may have disappeared for other reasons."

"Oh?"

But I don't elaborate. I stare at the list. "Who do I chase? Mary or the Cult?"

"A cult now? How exciting."

I give him a side glance. "Mary has whatever was to be handed over at Billingsgate."

"Which do you think she'll try for next?"

I don't answer. *I think Mary and the Cult have been nipping at each other over these artifacts for a while now. Slowing each other down. But who do I chase after? Crossed out must mean the Cult has it. If they fear this information has been discovered, they'll be moving to collect in a hurry. All at once? That could draw too much attention. One item at a time. They'll move down the list. And Mary... I*

might get ahead if… My finger comes
down on the words Natural History
Museum. I say to William, "I get the
feeling that Mary finding this
information has accelerated events.
She's had a few days, but she thinks
I've hit a dead end. She's not a
sprinter. She likes to take her time,
so if she thinks she's in the lead,
she'll be in no rush."

"And why not Saint Magnus or the
Society?"

"I'm tired of trying to catch her.
Time to let her come to me." I drop the
page back into the drawer. I move to
walk away, but William grabs my arm.

"People are in danger."

"All the more reason for me to get
ahead of her."

"And wait?"

"You usually do when you're going
to ambush someone."

"But people are in danger,"
William stresses. He pauses and glances
at the open door. He begins again in a
whisper. "You wait for her; meanwhile,
she could hurt more people. The Society
has put together this event at the
Spring Gardens, and lots of people will
be there. She'll be there looking for,"
gesturing toward the paper, "a jar." He
throws his hands up and steps back.

"What happens if she can't just take it? And what of this `cult´?"

I don't answer.

He opens his mouth to say more but stops as Arthur returns. Arthur's eyes fall on me for just a moment, and then he shakes his head. "Sorry, I thought - " he clears his throat. "Poole has set up some refreshments in the dining room. If you like, we can eat and you can ask more questions."

"Yes, thank you, Arthur."

I watch as they walk away. I tell myself to leave. *Leave right now. Leave right now and he can still live to be an old man.*

CHAPTER TWELVE

As day had turned to night, clear skies also turned dark and pendulous. Rain, heavy at times, falls upon us as McAllister drives his beast of burden back towards London. The rumble of the carriage wheels along the road has become reminiscent of pigs wallowing in mud. Our progress is slowed, but the storm has not forced us to seek shelter. Mym, always one to sleep given a choice, dozes snuggly between the two of us, and the carriage bench takes up most of the interior space. Unlike our first passing along this avenue, William is wide awake. He slumbered briefly after we had set out from the Wren house but fitfully.

Glancing at him now across the carriage, I can tell his eyes are peering out into the rainy night, but his mind is elsewhere. I stare for several minutes, wondering – *what did I ponder when I was human?* I return to my book. My satchel had become laden as we departed Arthur Wren's home. The hours ahead of me in this carriage prove an opportune time to examine my loot. Three books, a notebook, and that

crumpled page from the desk's bottom
drawer in Arthur's study. Books and
notes belonging to the missing Jane
Wren. Jane Wren, who I'm sure belonged
to the Cult of Eleusis.

I note the past tense in my mind.
The Cult trains their operatives well.
If anyone were to look into Jane Wren,
they would find that no such person
exists other than perhaps a marriage
certificate to Robert Wren. Equally,
much like myself and my kind, they move
around a lot and know not to leave
anything that could be traceable.
Nothing noting their intentions or
interests. Nothing to suggest where
they are or where they will be. Jane,
however, had gotten sloppy. These books
and notes certainly have been
overlooked as nothing more than
Robert's research – but I'm seeing
something more.

The writing is a puzzle. Sentences
with missing words. Pages that make no
sense to me. I find myself staring,
trying to read, only to catch myself
turning the page. But I get the
impression that she was tracking
several objects. And not just her.
Different quills, different inks,
different handwriting, lists, and
descriptions fill the notebook. Entries

have been updated and added to. Jane seemed particularly focused on these older passages, the ones mentioning and describing things and events in Egypt. Scribbles in her hand dot the edges of these pages.

I pinch the bridge of my nose and look up from the journal. I feel I am missing something. I feel as if the answers are in my lap, but the story isn't revealing itself. And I'm bothered by this information even being associated with the Cult. It's a shift from what I've known about the Cult. These are assassins who aim to create chaos and then rise from that chaos to reshape the world in their image. They murder kings and queens. They insert themselves into positions, whispering to those they have sway over, advising tactics with only one aim – death and destruction. My most recent encounter with the Cult involved them masquerading as governesses and au pairs to raise children into monsters. *Socially speaking. But this –*

"I've never been able to read while traveling," William says.

I welcome the interruption as an invitation to rest my eyes. Mym can heat sections of her body into a molten glow, but reading by this dim red light is hard on the eyes. I rub my eyes and stretch my neck, which William takes as an opening to speak more.

"I used to travel quite a bit, but reading to pass the time always made me dizzy and my stomach angry."

"Instead, you ponder the passing scenery to pass the time. You must be terribly bored." I nod at the night and the rain out the window.

"I enjoy the rain. But yes, there's not much to look at just now. And actually, watching the scenery also leads to dizziness and an unsettled stomach. I usually try to sleep."

"Aren't you a fun traveling companion?" William's smile as I say this is radiant. He chuckles to himself and looks away.

"That's what she used to say."

"The woman who belongs to that silver mirror in your room?"

William nods, the smile slowly drifting away. He sighs and looks down at the books on my lap. He's contemplative for a few moments. "Forgive me. I was just thinking about the moral ambiguity of thievery. Is need greater than ownership?"

"My need is always greater."

"So it would seem," he smirks. Bathed in the dim red illumination of

Mym's glowing patches, there is a sinisterness in the innocent expression. "What need drove you to take Arthur's things?" He leans in closer, taking a moment to read the titles of the works. "Or is there something you have seen - worth taking - that neither Jane nor Mary noticed?"

"You ask a lot of questions?"

"I do."

Our eyes meet. "And are polite enough not to ask others."

"Smart enough, at the very least. I ask the questions I feel have the best chance of being answered."

"You're very good at reading a situation."

"Perhaps. I dare say your literacy extends beyond that of words on pages."

I find myself once again stepping up to that imaginary red line. *How much do I tell him? What has he figured out?* I have, on occasion, been forced to work with humans. A general rule I use to guide myself when explaining things to them is to stop when I come to information that would have befuddled my mind when I was human. I think he senses my reluctance, for he leans back with a nod and a brief expression of disappointment as he returns his gaze to the storm beyond the window. I wish

I could mock him, call him a pouty human, and get back to reading, but I can't. He's not pouting. He's accepted it. He's accepted that there are things I can't, or don't want, to tell him.

We're jolted then as the carriage skids briefly to the right before being corrected.

William puts a hand out in an unnecessary protective gesture.

I nod.

He nods and returns his attention to the window.

I return my attention to my books. After a moment, I sigh as I decide to put a toe on the red line. I pull the crumpled page from where I was using it to mark a page in the journal, but William speaks up before I can say anything.

"Jane isn't missing, is she? She's dead. You think Jane died because of what is on that piece of paper." He doesn't turn around. "Or rather, because she allowed Mary to see what was on that piece of paper. A secret society?" He turns to look at me and raises an eyebrow. "Secret societies?"

I nod.

"Then why leave the notes? Why not take them or have them collected?"

"Because the absence of a thing, or attempting to collect said thing, would draw attention. It is better to let them hide in plain sight among other tools of research. Besides, they know where to find them. They can always come back for them later."

"Them? They?" William smirks.

"As you say, secret societies."

"Of course."

I look down to hide my smile. "But, I feel the reason for leaving them behind is simple. They don't need them anymore. Mary finding out probably means they'll act now rather than take their time."

"Ah, leading us back around to something you had said before. I don't suppose you've thought about what I said in response?"

He's seeing faces, while I'm seeing numbers. I need to be focused on the bigger picture – *some will have to die so that a great many others can live*. Somehow, I don't think he'll respond well to that if I say it out loud. *Maybe if I can get him to understand*. "They're building something. They've been searching for the pieces for a long time and appear to finally have what they need or know where to get them." I put the pile of books to the side, all except the journal. "I think they targeted Robert because of his interest in Egypt. It appears as if several of the pieces were to be found in that region."

"But there are others who do the same research."

"Robert fit their criteria. Respected and rich enough to get things done but a small enough fish in a big enough pond that his life would go unnoticed. Plus, an opportunity to insert themselves."

"I'm amazed by how much of this *secret* society you understand."

The carriage jolts violently just then, and we are both caught off guard enough that we have to brace ourselves. I hear McAllister call out to his horse, and a second later, the carriage is traveling along safely again. However, our speed is further reduced.

"I'm troubled by these symbols. I've seen these glyphs before. Recently. Jane was particularly focused on them. This scarab and… what would you call this, a mushroom? This kingly figure. A loaf of bread and a horizontal line. Jane has written several translations, crossing them out as she refined her knowledge. Mind. To change. To alter. Be cautious. A

warning – she circled this one." I sigh
in frustration and close the book. "I'm
usually very good with languages, but
this journal…"

"And where did you see these
glyphs?"

"On a box."

"On the box Mary killed for?"

I nod.

"Tell me about the box."

"Small. Ancient but well-kept.
Plain, though it did have these
symbols. I think it was a coin box."

Mym's light goes out. She shudders
a little, her coarse surface scratching
against the wood of the interior. She
settles again, though the dim red light
doesn't return.

William and I sit in silence and
darkness. The drumming of the rain atop
the carriage. The slosh of wheels over
the wet and muddy surface of the road.
The eerie slam of a gust of wind
against the side causes the window
shade to flap. I try not to feel it,
but I sense I'm being told something.

"You know," William's voice
interrupts my thinking, "a society of
artists might know something about such
a decorative box."

"And getting ahead of this will
make such a decorative box

unnecessary." I hear him adjust in his seat, but he says nothing. "Though, perhaps the museum is too far ahead. A museum is a big place, after all, lots of places to hide something. Saint Magnus – as you say, it is under construction and might be easier to search."

"I submit to the greater wisdom. Compared to the many, what is one life – or a few?"

There is silence between us for the rest of the storm.

The long hours give me time to think. I could be rid of William instantly. The irritating smirk. The questions. *He's right. And I hate that he's right. I would have come to the conclusion myself. I was already aware of it. There will be bloodshed at the Gardens if Mary is confronted. But, there's a chance here to get ahead of her. To set a trap. Why do I allow him to make me doubt myself? Why did I allow him to stay? Was it convenience? Selfishness? Advantage? Does it matter?* My mind spins around this subject. I find myself staring at him in the darkness. *The mission is what matters. But so does he. So does everyone. Protecting everyone, isn't that the mission?* And then something occurs to

189

me. *Despite the danger, his safest place may be in his element. But if Mary sees him - Oh, but if Mary sees him and not me…* I'm not proud of that second thought. *There's a choice here.* Contemplating that choice carries me through the night.

The bustle of the early city awakens my traveling companions this time, not me. With a yawn and a stretch, William first and then Mym become aware that we've returned to London. "We should be arriving shortly."

William nods. However, his glance out the window sparks confusion. "We're nowhere near Saint Magnus. What time is it?"

"Must be nearly noon," I say as I place the books into William's bag. "Our pace was significantly slowed last night. Besides, poor McAllister and his horse are exhausted."

"What are you doing?"

I look at him for a moment as I confirm with myself that the choice I made last night is the best idea. I'm honestly not expecting much at the Gardens. I feel the opposition has been on the move long enough that the Jar is probably in someone's hands. *He'll probably be safer here, observing.* "I'm

going to find some new transportation.
You, since you insist, will go to the
art society."

"But -"

"If Mary sees you, you're dead.
She won't appear the same. She could be
any woman." And it's not just Mary he
needs to worry about. "In fact, if you
see - a group of women, don't engage."

"There's likely to be a lot of
women there."

"Don't engage," I snap at him.
"And you're going with him."

Rumble. Puff.

"You are. I'll meet up with you
later - and you, if you're still
alive." That said, I open the door and
step from the moving carriage.

I don't look back as McAllister's
carriage trundles away. The timing
couldn't have been better. After a few
quick steps, I'm out of the street and
waiting at the curb as another carriage
pulls up. Two men exit and, even with
my will untapped, they never notice me.
I slip a coin into the driver's hand.
"Saint Magnus."

"Ma'am," he nods.

This driver does not have the
skills of McAllister, and I regret not
pushing Mym and William out of the
carriage and taking it the rest of the

way. The better part of an hour passes before we roll along Thames Street. The ongoing construction can be seen. Scaffolding, that unsteady weave of metal and wood that always appears to be seconds from collapsing, trusses bridge and buildings. The sounds of hammers on stone and nails ring out over the babble of city life. "This will be fine, Driver," I call out. I wait for the carriage to come to a stop before exiting.

As part of the bridge reconstruction, the road is being widened along this area. Stone workers are busy cutting away the old and laying gravel for the new cobbles and blocks. Several buildings have been knocked down in the name of progress, though a damaged warehouse bearing the scars of a fire still stands beside the church. A lot of the debris waits to be carted away. The Church of Saint Magnus the Martyr is not immune to the march of time and change. For hundreds of years, the building has stood as the guardian - a welcome sight for travelers crossing the northern side of the Thames. But now, somehow, with all the construction going on around it, I get the impression of a grandfather asleep in his chair while the family makes merry in the next room.

The grand tower of the church seems to have been refaced, the archways widened to make ready for the new road and pedestrian footpath. Some supports hold up the new archways, and nearby is a pile of stone which a mason peruses for his next choice. I slip by him unnoticed. I'm in the vestibule, stairs to either side of me leading up. Along the nave are rows of pews and pillars coated in a matte finish of dark stain. There's no sound other than what drifts in from outside.

"Am I too early, too late, or have services been moved elsewhere during the construction?" I whisper as I make my way cautiously toward the pulpit. My eyes dart around the interior. *Places to hide, but if someone were going to sneak up on me, it would be from behind.* I glance back; the church doors are open, but only the sound of the street is there. "It could be anywhere. Has it been hidden to be never found? Maybe hidden and only for the chosen to see." I allow my fingers to glide over the outside of the pulpit, hoping to trip a hidden latch or spot a panel that isn't quite like the others.

"I assure you, only for the chosen to see."

I step back to get a clear view of the person who just popped up from behind the pulpit. Glancing up, I see a figure dressed in a wrap-shirt with cap sleeves and a light, flowing skirt – an ombre of blue to black from bottom to top. A cloak and cowl hide her face, but strands of blonde hair can be seen. This could be Mary, but I think more likely, "Eleusis."

"We are the many," the cloaked woman says.

I hear the shuffling of soft shoes and then the closing of the church doors. I take in the room without losing sight of the woman atop the pulpit. These new figures, hair short or tied back tightly, with shirt-wraps and skirts of white draped in tabards of burgundy edged in gray. *I spot six, but I know there are probably nine*. "Acolytes and a Priestess. A standard cohort," I say to the woman atop the pulpit.

"There is nothing standard about us, Avatar. We are the Sisters of Hera, here to end your meddling."

My head tilts to the side, and I allow myself a cocky smile. The Sisters of Hera are elites among the Cult of

Eleusis. Specially trained to take out my kind. "I've always enjoyed fighting the best." My feet are moving before my morningstar is in my hands. I charge right, dashing into the south aisle and the nearest cluster of three Sisters. I hear the *thunk*, *thunk*, *thunk* of throwing daggers behind me stabbing into pews as I run. I glance to the side and see the three acolytes absent from my initial count up in the gallery. They let loose another barrage of daggers. I slow, skid along the stone floor, and lean back. Three daggers pass ahead of me. As they do, I reach up and snatch the nearest one out of the air, whirl around for some added momentum, and send it sailing back at its owner. I don't look but hear the cry of pain and the tumble of a body from the gallery.

As I race by, I grab the second dagger jutting out from the pew. There's almost no weight in my hand. It is a light and elegant weapon – an elongated, slender arrowhead weighted slightly at the tip which is coated in a green crystal or resin. I waste no time in tossing the dagger ahead of me. The attack is easily deflected but renders my target off balance. I bring my morningstar down on her head as I sidekick the next nearest cultist. The third, however, slips in under my arm and slices me along the bicep as she tumbles out of the way of my swing.

Dark hair, light hair, no hair, similar height, all fit, dressed the same – when they're in a group, it's hard to tell one from another. The best my mind can do is – this one is unhurt. An unhurt Sister charges up to me. Punches are thrown and blocked. My morningstar clangs off her armguards. Her hands are quick, and I'm forced to step back, but nothing she sends my way lands. She plants a foot on my chest and vaults backward as two others come forward, fall to their knees, and slide under my swing, slicing me at thigh and side as they roll into a tumble and out of reach.

The deadly circus act is going to kill me by a thousand cuts. I clutch my side. "What's this? Too afraid to come at me all at once? Ten to one isn't the best odds for you, but at least try."

"Don't insult us, Avatar. You understand our tactics. There is honor in understanding you have lost to the greater effort," says the dark-robed woman from the pulpit.

The circle tightens. Seven burgundy tabards stand around me. I can see a few of them tense in preparation for their next pass. "I'll say this,"

"Yes?" As the woman from the pulpit speaks, the acolytes reset to ready stances.

"I applaud your ambush. How did you know I'd be here?"

"You forced your way into our home. You took our man. You threatened our Sister. You forced us to take action against our own. You got our attention. We weren't sure where you would turn up, but we knew you would. This is on you."

The smirk was irritating, but the tone was angry. *Good. Never fight angry.* "I would love to take credit for all of that. But that wasn't me."

Her eyes dart to a particular set of three, "But you were seen."

"Not me. Another, yes. But not me. Though, I do appreciate you acknowledging that I'm on the right path." I charge forward, dodging knife edges, ducking fists and kicks, diving into a roll, and coming up running as I fling myself at a pillar. I crack through it, land on the other side, and rise to one knee – morningstar ready.

There's a creak and a groan as the ceiling cracks and crashes down on top of three of them. I hook a pew with my morningstar and fling it at the others charging at me. One takes it full in the face and two others are knocked aside. Not dead, but not moving either. There are only a few left standing - plus the Priestess at the pulpit. But I think I need to be someplace else now. I thought I could get ahead of this – ahead of Mary, at least. Turns out I'm right in the middle. *They didn't know where I'd turn up – or rather, where Mary would turn up*. I flash them a smile and dash for the door. Once outside, with the focus off of me, I flex my will. No one notices me as I grab onto the back of a passing carriage and let it carry me west along the Thames.

CHAPTER THIRTEEN

I can feel my sliced flesh
burning. My arm. My thigh. My side. I
inspect each with quick glances while
dashing between alleys and grabbing
hold of the backs of carriages. The
wounds are cracked and swollen.
Tendrils of green and black reach out
from each of the raw lacerations. I
have to keep blinking hard and forcing
deep breaths to stay awake. "The
Sisters of Hera," I slur. I hadn't
faced them the last time I battled with
the Cult of Eleusis. I hop down from
the back of the carriage I'm currently
clinging to. "Provoked into being by my
actions? I'm honored," I cough and
startle a young couple as they suddenly
become aware of me. I want to run, but
I'm already winded. It's painful even
to clench a fist. Thankfully, the
Spring Gardens area is at the end of
this row of houses. I can already hear
music in the air and the sound of
muddled conversations.

*Nearly there. You must move
faster.* I encourage myself, but not
with a gentle tone. They probably

already had the Finger Bone but stayed behind to lay a trap. *They stayed behind to lay a trap. Now move!* As I enter the Gardens it is easy to see that the event has been well received. The area is festooned with banners, garlands, and ribbons. There are food vendors, tables and booths displaying art, and tents with open flaps allowing patrons entrance to enjoy whatever delights are within, as well as temporary pavilions – grander tents where I'm sure the rich and famous have set up their own displays and rest areas. I can see that some of the bordering mansions have opened their homes to the festivities. There are dozens of people out on the fields enjoying the open air and minstrels.

For my purposes, it is very crowded and busy, something I don't generally mind - except for the fact that I am not at my best right now. Thankfully, the bleeding has stopped. I stroll around the perimeter, my mind reaching out for Mym. I should be watching for suspicious activity. You can read a room – or an open field full of tents and tables. Someone trained to blend can sometimes lack the natural spontaneity of interaction. The Cult is a group of trained assassins and spies, but they don't play well with others in more everyday settings. *And then there's Mary. She could be any face.* But I'm not focused on that because I can't be. Like a kite caught in a strong breeze, I allow myself to be pulled along as my mind searches for Mym's familiar thoughts.

After about a hundred yards of wandering behind tents at the edges of the exhibition, I get a sense of her. I find myself walking towards a large red and gold pavilion. Out in front of it is a cluster of smaller dark blue tents, and the grouping all have royal insignia. "What is she doing over there?" I stumble between tents and find her. Someone had set a tray of empty glasses atop her. I swipe the tray away – thankfully, the thump of the wooden tray and glasses is muffled by the grass into which they fall.

Crackle. Rumble.

"I'm sorry, I didn't realize that was part of your disguise." I slump and put a hand onto her coarse exterior to steady myself.

Crackle. Puff.

I try to put my thoughts into order, but I find myself sitting beside Mym and resting my head on my knees instead. "There is too much." I dig around in my satchel for a small stone. I squeeze the stone and then drop it in front of Mym. I feel her roll slightly forward and then back. I wait, happy to be resting. And as I do, I hear William's voice. I glance around. His voice is coming from the other side of the large tent of red and gold. "What is he doing in there?!" I feel Mym nudge me.

Crackle. Rumble. Puff. Rumble. Puff. Crackle. Puff. Rumble. Rumble. Crackle.

I'm momentarily stunned as it's the most she's ever said at any one time... *and she's yelling at me.* "I handled it."

Rumble. Rumble.

"It got handled. I'm here and I'm speaking with you. Can we focus on the fact that the Cult probably has whatever was hidden there? I don't think they'll be here distracted as they search for the Jar. They may already have it and are just waiting for me. They've probably set up similar ambushes at every place on that list. We need to be careful... and now I'm thinking, I've played into their plan, if they are here." I lift my head, scanning for anyone, but I'm well hidden here. "If they're waiting for me to show myself..." I hear William's voice

202

again. "And what is he doing in there? I told him to avoid any contact." I want to rage to my feet, but I need a few more minutes.

Rumble. Puff. Rumble.

"He's speaking with the Queen?!" I do stand this time, but I need a moment to settle the spinning in my head. I can feel the last of the poison working its way out, though I'm not at peak just yet.

Rumble. Puff.

I manage to take a whole step away before stopping. "You're right. I can't just barge in there." I take a deep breath and feel perceptions drifting away from me. "Now I can." But, to be safe, I search for a back way in. The tent is well staked down, but I find a loose peg and get in under the pavilion. There are two rows of tables, each with displays of odd and grotesque art. Twisted figures. Impressionist objects. Many styles reflecting an odd similarity of technique from across many lands. By far, most of the art to be seen are statuettes, nude, sculpted in great detail, and some in risqué positions. Ten guards protect the displays, though the six people idly walking among the tables take very little notice of the stern faces and halberds. As I watch, another two patrons enter the tent and begin their visual tour.

Besides the art displays, there is a large unlit crystal chandelier above and a comfortable seating area, though it is currently unoccupied. Three small tents of dark blue have been set up at the back of the pavilion – one of those has its entry flap pulled shut. The dark blue tents are closer to where I had been sitting outside, and I trust I'll find William there. As I approach, I hear him laugh. I gather at least three people are inside and are focused toward the front of the tent. I slip in as I did before and stand quietly at the back.

It's as if someone had plucked a salon from one of the mansions nearby and dropped it here. Around the central tent pole are couches and chairs. To one side is an open firepit. Art, displayed on tripods, is along the walls. William is here, stretched out on a chaise lounge – drink in hand. A second man is also here. He is thin with a round face, his hair neat on top but bushy with natural curls at his ears. He's smartly dressed in a burgundy coat and high-collared shirt. Seated in a high-backed chair between the two men is a young woman with a long neck in a white and light blue ruffled dress. A silver circlet with a purple stone rests atop her head. She's currently chuckling into a hanky – a chuckle that turns to a cough. She waves off both men and the guard at the tent entrance as they all lean forward.

As she opens her mouth to speak, she becomes distracted. She cocks her head to one side and then the other as if listening for something. Then, somewhat unsettled, she addresses her guests. "Please, you must stop doing that." She wipes her lips. "You've all acted most honorably in your concern for me. But, I am perpetually laden with this blasted illness. You will tire yourselves before I stop coughing."

I misunderstood Mym. Not queen, but a young princess. I edge myself around the room in William's direction.

The Princess sputters into her cup as she tries to take a sip – she begins to cough again.

"I will never stop being concerned for you, Your Highness. Your father would kill me." The thin man stands and fetches a pitcher of water to refresh the Princess' goblet.

"You are my most favorite shadow, Mister Walpole." The Princess smiles. "And you, Mister Monkton, I gladly count as a new friend."

"You honor me, Your Highness."

"Please," the Princess takes a sip of water. "Please, tell me more about this Crusher. Do you really believe it is a woman?"

"I do more than believe it, Your Highness. I have seen her in action."

"Have you notified the constables?" Walpole asks.

"They would believe me no more than you," William and the Princess laugh. "I can see it in your eyes. But what I say is true. A woman. A murderess. When I feel I can predict her next actions, I will do my best to have the guards ready with an ambush."

"How very exciting." The Princess coughs again. "I dare say she should be examined inside and out once caught and put down."

"Your Highness," a shocked Walpole says.

"I mean it. She is an oddity. A dangerous one." The venom in her words is hardly covered by her playful tone. There's a brief awkwardness before both men clear their throats and shift in their seats.

"You're not wrong, Princess. We could learn much from her. Maybe enough to stop someone else like her from doing the harm she has done."

"Well said, Mister Monkton. What say you, Mister Walpole? Knowing is always better than not knowing, yes?"

Walpole contemplates this before responding. "I think, Your Highness, that you are very young yet and that your very dangerous thinkings will get me hung one day."

As the Princess and Walpole begin a friendly bickering match about dangerous thinking, I slink up behind William and crouch behind his chaise. I reach up and pinch his neck.

"Ow!" William says as he sits up. He rubs his neck and glances around the room before becoming aware that the other two are watching him. "Sorry. It's an old injury. It sometimes grabs me when I've been in the same position for too long. Your Highness, may I beg my leave? It is probably time for me to meet that friend I was telling you about."

"Of course, Mister Monkton. But I insist we meet again. I extend to you an invitation to that little club I mentioned," she looks at Walpole as she says this – who fidgets a little ill at ease. "I won't take no for an answer."

"I am yours to command, Your Highness." William bows and leaves.

I sneak out with him, and within two steps of the pavilion entrance, I pull him to the side where Mym waits. "What are you doing? I said don't engage," I say in a stern whisper.

"You look a fright –"

He takes my arms, but I brush him off. "What part of `your life is in danger´, don't you understand?"

For a moment, his face is a mixture of shame and concern, and then a broad smile creeps over his face. "I have so much to tell you."

I walk away. I hear them follow. I lead them away from the exhibition and find some storage shacks at the edge of the Gardens. I wave them in. The fit borders on uncomfortable with all three of us, but we all find a place to settle. "Talk," I order.

"I want to assure you that I have kept my eyes open, but also my ears. I felt the less foot traffic, the better, so I asked Mym to follow me to the royal pavilion. I made sure she was well hidden and then went about exploring. There was a theft late last night. It seems that many of the art displays were being stored in nearby homes. A Mister Wainwright of Hay Market Street was safeguarding a great many pieces. His home was broken into, yet only one thing was stolen. Now, he praises his guard dogs for this…"

"But you think otherwise." His smile is infectious, and that's annoying.

"The thing stolen was a jar. According to the Art Society people I spoke with, a decorative crystal jar with a human eye floating in it."

"You have my attention."

"I thought I might," he says and leans forward, lowering his voice. "The only record on the object is that it came from the Far East. The jar has been examined on multiple occasions. Experts on the craft have found no seam, and by all accounts, the eye is just – floating. The jar doesn't seem to hold any liquid or gas to allow for such a state." He slaps his knee and leans back.

"A jar. It can't be a coincidence."

"I thought not."

"Mary," I growl and stand, slamming my fist into my hand.

"Perhaps, but I think more likely this Cult. The word is that there were three hooded figures seen. But, there's more. I asked a few more questions. It turns out the Art Society people were in a bit of a buzz about this theft. I mean, there's the issue of the item being stolen, but more importantly, according to their sources, it turns out Princess Louisa is interested in the Occult. They - the Art Society - had it on good authority that the Princess was making a special trip to the exhibition to see that very piece."

"And you offered your services to help smooth any disappointment."

"I did."

"You lied that you knew the Princess."

"I did."

"Go on." I don't sit. I turn and lean on the sill and look through the window to the Gardens.

"It turns out that the Princess is an art lover. Did you happen to see any of the pieces she had on display in the pavilion?"

I nod.

"Her taste is, ah, eclectic. It also seems our Princess has a penchant for adventure and has been caught more than once in places where she ought not to be."

"What does this have to do with the jar?"

"Tangential, but please, I feel the information is important. Since the death of her sister, now a few years passed, she has been more mindful of her family station, and she has limited her outings. Though, to hear them talk, I believe it has been Mister Walpole who has been the limiting factor. Anyway, it turns out her sister, the Princess Elizabeth became ill after an official meal with a few French dignitaries."

"I'm sure that did not help relations."

"It did not. But, the war aside, as poor Elizabeth continued to succumb to her illness, a woman was mentioned. Highly recommended… Mary Batteman."

"Mary?"

"So it would seem. Elizabeth did not recover and what's more, Princess Louisa soon became ill as well. I don't believe Mary was there just for the sake of chaos. As you've explained, such unrest seems more like the calling card of the Cult of Eleusis. I think Mary was there for a reason, possibly looking for something, and the sick Princess was the door she used to get in. Sadly, Elizabeth passed quickly from whatever had befallen her, and in desperation to remain on the grounds, Mary poisoned Louisa."

"Overplayed her hand. She does that."

"Indeed. The guards went after the nursemaid, but she escaped."

"And she blamed me for having to get rid of that disguise," I muse – then I feel the air in the room shift, and a presence emerges. I turn to the sound of William gasping.

"By all the heavens!" William scrambles to put some distance between himself and the figure now taking up what little floor space is at the center of this shack.

Charon stands there. The slightly tattered wool coat, linen trousers, and shirt flicker as if a breeze surrounds him, though I feel no air moving. His hunched frame, always reminiscent of a Shepard's crook, stands over me. The flames of his eyes are particularly intense and pass a sickly red-orange glow to the ancient flesh of his face.

I bow. "I –" My apology for my poor performance at Saint Magnus is cut off as Charon grows to fill even more of the limited space of the shack. I dare to glance up. His eyes fill my mind – and then a river of images.

Full of face and with sad yet intense eyes, a man sits upon a rickety boat being punted along a wide river. Somehow, I know him to be Sir Hans Sloane. He's speaking and saying many things, but his words become more apparent as he mentions a key.

"I donated the bulk of my belongings to the Natural History Museum for their collections, but for a few small items I gave to others, and... this key. I can hardly put it into words. It brought fear to my blood, yet there was this compulsion to keep it. I had the presence of mind to recognize it as evil and that no one should hold it. So, I left instructions that it should be hidden. The weight of this secret to be held by only one person – have I damned them by doing this?"

He receives no response.

"Perhaps it was foolish. Perhaps I should have had the devil melted from it? You see, I enjoyed the botanical gardens of Chelsea. There is peace there. I particularly loved the walks among the many different trees. I hoped that the purity of those grounds would hide the key. Tell me, Boatman, was I wrong? Have I cost myself passage to the other side? Will you not speak to me?"

The image fades. I blink and find myself once more looking into his burning eyes. He lifts his hand, and Jane's journal and the crumpled page are there, floating in the narrow space between us.

NO LONGER HIDDEN.

The baritone rumble of his voice shakes my soul. "I understand."

Charon shifts, and his finger moves to point at William. No words are spoken.

I take a deep breath, my lungs filling with sorrow. I fight the urge to protest and simply nod as I say, "I understand."

CHAPTER FOURTEEN

The journal and crumpled page drop to the floor as the shadows of the shack creep in around Charon and swallow him. The heavy thud of both book and page far exceeds their weight and, to my ears, rings of heavy bells. He often warns me with all manner of chimes and gongs. The tinkle of a sleigh bells. The warm mellow of wedding bells. The turbulent cries of alarm bells. The mournful tolling of a steeple's iron bells. Some of my kind look for messages in omens. Others in the wind. I prefer the acoustical melody of forged materials.

I go to my knees and pick up the book and page. I gently run my thumbs over the worn leather and the rough texture of the parchment. My mind is flooded with new knowledge. "How did I miss this?"

William takes a long, deep breath – as if finally remembering to breathe. "Did he point at me?" He moistens his lips. "He did, you know. Point at me."

"We need to go. Now. The Chelsae Gardens –"

"Why did he point at me?" He forces a chuckle. "I don't want to assume the obvious. I'm sure there -"

"William, settle your mind."

"It's not my mind that is unsettled."

I stand, most of my attention still on the book and page. I'm vaguely aware of William clumsily getting to his feet as well as his voice, but my mind is elsewhere.

"Persephone?"

I look at him. "Yes?"

"Perhaps it is improper, but I have questions."

"And I have a lot to process." I step to the door. "We can talk while we move. But we need to move now." My tone does the trick. I see the worry drop away from his face.

"Right. I'll get us a carriage. Chelsea, was it? Not much on that side of the city. A few hamlets. Farms. Estates. Never mind," he clears his throat. "Give me a moment, and I'll have us on our way."

There is silence for hardly a moment after William leaves the shack. **Rumble. Puff.**

I don't answer. Guilt prevents me. I don't think I'll ever get over that early failure. The guilt of so many -

countless - lives. *If I'd been better. If I'd been faster*. Guilt has been a companion for far longer than Mym. *I strive to be better. To do better. To be faster. Fear of that failure - fear of adding to that guilt - drives me. But, they all can't be saved.* My eyes drift to the door. "The mission is what matters."

Rumble. Puff.

"Yes!" I snap. I pause to steady my mind. "Yes, I'll tell him. Once we're on the way, I'll explain everything to him."

The door opens and William sticks his head in. "Your carriage awaits, Ma'am."

We rush away from the shack. I make the conscious choice not to guard us against notice. The waters of the ether are rippling; for the mission's purposes, we can better hide in those ripples and avoid making any additional wake.

The carriage is not far. I move to speak with the driver, but William puts his hand on me.

"If I may? I have an idea that may get us there faster."

I step back and help Mym get settled. I overhear William telling the driver to get us to the nearest dock as quickly as possible. "The river?" I ask as William steps in, and we pull away from the curb.

"The way west is a narrow and rough country road. A pleasant bit of travel for those not in a rush. At a dock, we have a good chance of getting the attention of a waterman. Travel along the river will get us to the gardens faster than taking the road."

I am not going to argue about water travel and set my head back. I know my silence is not what he would have preferred, but I need time to sort out what had been said and unsaid. "I know you have questions," I say with my eyes closed. "But my communications with my Patron are a lot like communicating with Mym. Our conversations are subtle and nuanced." I hear him shift, but he remains silent.

The carriage ride to the Thames is not a long one. Almost before the driver has pulled his horse to a halt, William is already leaping from the carriage. He races down to the docks at a determined pace. I assume William had settled accounts but use speaking with the driver as a distraction for Mym to extricate herself. "Has my partner…" I pretend to fumble when speaking to him.

I see some worry in his eyes as he glances at my torn, rumpled, and singed attire. I'm not sure what he assumes, but he simply nods.

"Yes, Miss. Never you mind. You best keep up with your man."

I give the driver a demure nod and approach the docks. I spot William waving at a gray and grizzled fellow lounging on the foredeck of a small boat.

"My good man. Hello! Is your wherry ready for departure?" William calls out, still several paces from the ship.

"No punts, just a sail. But yes, Sir, I'm a waterman. I'll get you where you need."

"Well, then," William leaps the narrow gap onto the ship. He slips around the sailor, pulling his attention away from the docks. "Set your sail. The best speed you can manage. The Gardens at Chelsea."

Both men turn sharply to a loud splash. They find me standing at the dock edge. I wave. I see William pass a fist of currency into the sailor's hand – regaining the man's full attention. "Chelsea," William reiterates.

The man nods and begins the business of unmooring his boat. "You and your miss can make yourselves comfortable in the cabin, Sir."

William comes and opens the hatch for me. I step in. The cabin is hardly larger than the interior of the carriage but, to a degree, more comfortable. I choose a seat. William sits opposite me. I watch through the small window as the sailor sets sail and tacks into the wind.

"Mym?"

"She enjoys mud," my eyes still out the window, I shrug. "And with no one watching, she'll probably get there before we do."

"She knows where to, to, come up for air?"

"I gave her an image. It's wildly outdated, but it should get her there." I look back at William, and before I can stop myself, I feel the shift in my face.

"What's that face?" He smiles and leans back into his cushioned seat. "You have an infinite ocean of emotions. I've seen the gentle laps upon the shores of your face, though you keep the great waves well out to sea. But that face," he points at me. "A face of genuine sadness. What do you see now when you look upon me?"

"I see what I have always seen. A man who seeks out danger and pain to punish himself." His jaw falls slack as he hears this, and he looks away. "I also see that your tricorn has gone missing." He turns back around, his hands going to his head.

"Oh, ah – I think I may have left it in that shack. Oh well. I remember the important things." He pats his bag.

Something in his tone suggests he's not speaking of whatever money he may have stashed away. I do worry, however – such resources are not infinite. And, as my attempts to keep him hidden were for nothing, he may have need of his wealth now more than ever. "I suppose hats are easy to come by. On the other hand, you have been shoving money at people for several days now."

"Don't worry about me." His eyes close slightly. He takes in a breath and sighs as if free of some weight. "I've been selfish with my money for a long time. Sure, I allow myself to live comfortably, but other than drinking too much and eating when I have to, I spend very little. It just sits there, making more of itself, like a bunch of rabbits."

"And this upsets you?"

"Always has," he muses as his mind drifts out beyond the wherry. "I don't," he stops and begins again. "There was a time," again, his words fail him. "There's so much suffering, too much," this was not to his liking either. He smirks and runs his hands through his hair. "My family tried to have me committed to an asylum once. Apparently, giving away money was not to their liking."

"I get it. You're a selfish man who can't find a reason to spend his money."

He laughs at himself as he stretches out on his side on the cushioned seating. "Yes, that's it exactly."

"Until you found someone who didn't mind you giving away your money," I say softly.

He nods. "Yes, also true." He rolls onto his back.

We both know he doesn't mean me. Despite the sadness in his last words, his mood has lightened enough that I feel I can relax. I allow myself to enjoy the sway of the ship. It's as if the vessel had become the cradling arms of a gentle parent. A sensation I miss. I slap my knee – *focus on current matters!* I look back over at William.

He's staring at the sky through the window. He senses my attention and returns my gaze. "I will spare you the compliments of being a tolerable representation of your sex -"

"Thank you?" he says.

"Don't interrupt. As you have said, you are aware that there is more going on here than mere intrigue and beguilement. I have sought to limit your knowledge to keep you safe. That, it seems, was in vain." I stop somewhat abruptly. I have no idea how to continue. *How do I summarize the vastness of ethereal existence?*

"You started well," William says after more than a minute of my silence.

His face is turned away from me, but I don't need to see his face to hear his smirk. I feel the urge to smack him. "Charon did point at you." This gets his attention. He sits up slowly, a bit paler than a moment ago. "He doesn't cut the skein or weave it. He doesn't know when or how you will die. And, although stories of him have spawned fanciful images of a hooded figure with a scythe, he doesn't carry one, nor will he collect you when it happens."

"You've ruined my childhood. Tell me he has a boat, at least."

I can't tell if he's being silly or serious. "The boat is true. He's a psychopomp – a gatekeeper. There are several; they each do it a little differently, but all have the same job. They sit vigil over the ways into and out of the Beyond. They are escorts for the recently deceased. They will ask you about your life and guide you through the transition, but ultimately, they are there to judge you."

"They decide if I go to heaven or hell?"

"They decide who gets you and how pleasant your experience will be. There are those who would find being placed in Thanatos' shadow a heavenly experience and those who would find it very unpleasant."

"And Charon pointed at me because…?"

Transitioning is rather cut and dry compared to what I need to explain next. I take a deep breath. "You have to understand that there are things that I don't know. But I will try to the best of my knowledge. There are great and powerful spirits that exist. Some are very old, some very young, but all, to some degree, have an interest in the goings-on of mortal forms. They call it `The Game´ – or at least that is how my Patron described it to me. Some have played it since always. Others come and go. There are a few who choose to be merely spectators. They play to amuse themselves or to outdo or embarrass each other."

"How very childish of them."

"Do you play games?"

"I am not a god."

"It may shock you to know that gods are not all that different from you. Besides, not all of the mighty spirits are in it for the sport. Some try to help you. Of course, others always try to undo that help."

"So, we're pieces to them. Like chess."

"Not always, but in some ways, yes. My Patron says there was a time long ago – so long ago that saying *long ago* doesn't do it justice – that there was a time when The Game was different, and for reasons unknown to me, The Game became this. I've always gotten the impression that the change was not a unanimous decision."

"And what is your part in this?"

"I'm an agent of Charon. It's part of the rules of The Game. I act in his stead."

William grabs the sides of his head and cries out an annoyed grunt.

"This is," his hands suddenly dive into his satchel. "I've got to write some of this down. And Mym? Is she an agent as well? Are you real? What do you mean by `you act in his stead´? Do you have something specific you are here to do? Is it Mary? It must be Mary. You've been sent to stop Mary. And, and, this cult? How does this secret society fit into this ethereal pursuit? Is there an insignia I should be on the look out for?" He rattles off his questions as he pulls out a small ink bottle, quill, and parchment. He arranges himself on the cabin floor, using the seat as a desk.

I take a breath and release it slowly as I try to find answers to the deluge of questions. "The Cult works in the shadows with goals of their own design. Their patterns of action are how I recognize them. They have a sigil of sorts, but nothing you'll see in the open. They dress in robes and tabards of blue, black, and burgundy. For my part, I am real, though I don't know that I consider myself human anymore. Mary is who I am playing against. Though I did not know that at first."

"Why didn't you know?"

"It's part of the rules. We are tasked with being independent, though our Patrons' wishes guide us. She was sent on a mission, and I have come to realize that I have been sent to keep her from completing that mission."

"What's her mission?"

"I don't know. Something sinister. Something that will cause the deaths of many because that is what she always does – or tries to do."

William stops writing and looks at me.

I shrug sorrowfully. "I'm sorry. I don't know. She is searching for things. It turns out the Cult of Eleusis has been searching for the same things. That's probably why she is here. Her Patron became aware of what the Cult was doing and sent Mary to take it from them. That may also be the reason why they're so annoyed at me. Mary, apparently, has been nipping at their heels for a few years."

"You're guessing?" He turns around and begins writing again.

"Based on the facts at hand, yes."

"Could Mary be working with the Cult?"

"Possibly, but I don't think so. They seemed surprised to learn that I wasn't the one they were expecting. My attempt to get ahead of things at Saint Magnus did not go well, by the way."

"I noticed."

"They were there to do what I was there to do, which is very annoying. But they weren't expecting *me*, just one of us."

"One of us?"

"Like me. Like Mary. My other brothers and sisters."

"Agents like you?"

"Yes. Others who have been chosen to act in a Patron's name." I stop and watch him scribble furiously. "I have a friend, a brother-in-arms who is a lot like you. So many questions."

"Sounds like a capable and handsome chap."

"He's frustrating, but a good companion to have at your side in a fight."

"That seems to happen a lot. These fights behind the veil of civilization. Fights that determine our very existence."

"Not always. But yes. There are stretches of nothing. Just the passage of time. Then a rush of events, a puzzle to be solved, and then it's over, and I wait for my next mission."

The tip of his quill snaps, and still he keeps writing as best he can. I tap him on his shoulder. I gently pull him away from his task when he doesn't respond. "William, sit here, please."

"There's more?"

"There's always more. You, humans, you are – pieces, as you say – of interest for the task at hand. Most go about their lives never being involved in The Game or, if they were involved, never being aware that they were. Others, however, can become – noticed, and there are gods that take great offense at a human knowing of The Game. If the gods become aware of you, your skills, and your connections to others, you become useful to them as a sort of pseudo-agent. Or, at the very least, a target or catalyst for other things to happen."

He sighs. "Mary got me involved because I wrote that story about the Crusher?"

"You gained Mary's attention because of your story. Although, to her, you were just a loose end. She brought attention to herself, and that is something that is very against the rules. I think she figured getting rid of you would fix that."

"But, now I've been noticed?"

"Because of me. I put you on the board. And I'm sorry, I'm so sorry for that. I thought I was protecting you. If I had simply distracted Mary,"

"But then I insisted on coming along."

"I allowed you to come along. Yes."

"And that's why Charon pointed at me?"

"Yes," I say, hoping he doesn't pick up on the half-truth.

"But you must have suspected. You keep telling me my life is in danger."

"I feared. I hoped that even though you were with me, that if I kept you out of sight, you would continue to go unnoticed."

He slides back onto the floor of the cabin and continues to write. After a few lines, without looking up, he asks, "And Mym?"

"Mym is like you. She's a creature of this world." His quill stops moving and he looks back at me. "Oh yes. Your lore and mythology, some of that is just story, but some of it isn't. There are all manners of bumps in the night." It is my turn to smirk. He turns back to his writing. "There's more," I say.

"Isn't there always." He doesn't look up.

"I mentioned the rules. There are punishments when those rules are broken. And I think Mary has been naughty." He stops writing and turns to look at me. "I don't know what she's done, but Charon didn't appear simply to say hello. He gave me information I normally would have needed to figure out independently." I pull the journal and the page from my bag. "First off, the Key is not at the Natural History Museum. It is buried at the Chelsea Botanical Gardens. What's more, I know where in those gardens it is buried. I have a feeling Mary knows the Key is in the gardens, but not where -"

"Hence our need to move quickly."

"Yes. But I was given even more. It seems so obvious now." I laugh at myself.

"Hiding in plain sight can be very effective."

"In this case, it was. Look," I open the journal to a random page and slip the crumpled page in. The size is a perfect fit."

"That doesn't necessarily mean…" He reaches for the journal, and I allow him to take it. "But I've looked at this. There is no tear nor a breach in the binding," William examines the journal.

I give him a few minutes and then take the book. I open the front cover.

"I see it now, look. The wax was carefully, expertly melted. There, do you see it? Just enough to loosen the binding, and with some gentle tugging, the page came out."

"Why?"

"I don't know. The journal is old. Jane was using it, but it wasn't hers - not originally. Maybe she did it to hide the page."

"In plain sight."

"Indeed." William takes the page from me.

"But it's just a list of things and locations."

"There's more. So much more," I begin turning pages.

The *thump, thump* at the side of the cabin startles us both.

"Chelsea," the waterman calls out.

CHAPTER FIFTEEN

Though the sun drifts along above, the evening is on the cusp of folding in on the land. Standing at the docks, the touch of night's chill can already be felt. Up a slight rise is a stone path leading through a garden of rosemary bushes and lavender. The path comes to a wide archway built into the side of the tall brick walls surrounding the gardens' main grounds.

The wherry pulls away from the dock. The grizzled sailor gives a friendly wave as his ship finds the current and sails away. William, waiting for my cue, takes up a step behind me as I begin to march along the path. Having come from the city which is perpetually in motion, the quiet is odd. The sounds of nature aren't unsettling, just noticeable, and I can't help but wonder if such calm makes it easier or harder to sense each other. This thought tumbles in my mind as I reach out, waiting to feel the tingle in the back of my head that tells me one of my brothers or sisters is about. It's not always an accurate sensing as there are ways to hide, and

Mary has certainly learned how to evade the usual means of detection.

William clears his throat. "I'm sorry to interrupt," he whispers. "We are coming up to the back gate. I suspect we will still need to put forth the entry fee. And if you would like to blend with others…" he holds out his arm. As he does this, a thoughtful, almost troubled expression appears on his face.

"What?"

"I'm not really one to care about what people wear or how they look, but I wish we had the time to, ah, at least repair some of this," he nods at me.

I glance down at my bodice and skirt. My garments are torn, worn, and blood-spattered. "Am I unbecoming?"

He smirks. "You are a mess, my dear. But still, if I," he wraps my arm around his and presses in close. We move forward but at an angle with him slightly ahead. "If it were slightly darker," he mumbles.

As we approach, I spot a small damp boulder near the corner of the brick wall. "Mym."

"Do you see her?"

"Yes. And I think I have another idea. You continue on. I will meet you inside." I pat his hand and slip away.

I climb the slight rise, stepping between the rosemary and lavender. I rest a hand on Mym's wet, coarse surface. "Did you enjoy yourself?"

Rumble.

I find the hint of embarrassment adorable. "We need to get on the other side of this wall. Would you like me to give you a leg up?" She rolls forward a few inches. I give a quick glance around, and then, with Mym drawn between my chest and arm, I use gaps in the masonry and the ivy to climb. Part way up, I hear my skirt tear as it gets caught on something. "Merde." Mym is still chuckling as we reach the top.

I can see most of the gardens from this position about fifteen feet above the ground. There are two, one smaller than the other, but still large clusters of trees. I can see topiaries and paths winding around extensive herb gardens and rows of domestic and exotic flowers. Four large cedars also shade a central reflecting pond. I spy a few pedestrians, taking in the sweet odors and the safety of this natural environment. "Lovely," I whisper as I drop Mym - and promptly follow after her.

Our landing is not silent. The thump and rumble of our arrival, I'm sure, caused some alarm and certainly curiosity to be cast in our direction. Thankfully, we are not far from one of the wooded sections of the gardens. We dash between the trees, and I take a moment to collect my thoughts once out of sight. I see why Sir Sloane enjoyed this place. Only a few yards hidden among the trees, and I feel apart from the world. Crouched beside Mym, I glance around her through the trees. I can just spot the woodland path meandering through this section, and a little further afield behind us is where we landed near the wall. I close my eyes and replay Sir Sloane's words in my mind – *I know where to search*. I take a breath and try to track Mary again, but I get no sense of her.

"The Sloane key is here –"

Crackle.

"No. Not somewhere. Here. Among these trees or the other cluster, I'm sure of it."

Rumble.

"I'm sure Mary is also here."

Puff. Crackle. Rumble.

"As always, your pessimism is a delight." I'm about to stand when I spot through the trees, approaching our entry point, a lightly armored member of the city watch - spear in hand. He kicks at the disturbed earth and glances up at the brick wall's top. My ears twitch to the sound of footsteps behind me. I whirl around, morningstar in hand.

William manages to subdue his yelp behind his hand. He collects himself and whispers, "I heard a thump and assumed. Also, at least one member of the city watch is present. Perhaps on duty or here for fun, I don't know. A bit young. That may work in our favor."

I nod over my shoulder and press him into kneeling beside Mym. "Did you see us?"

"From the path? No. I didn't want to appear to be following the guard, so I came through the forest path and happened upon you."

I watch as the watchman inspects a small statue between the path and the wall, frowns at the placid face, and then moves along. I keep us crouched until I lose track of the watchman.

As we stand, William leans in and says, "I passed a few others, mostly couples walking about. There may be more, but I only spotted one groundskeeper on my way here. Oh, and the gates will be closed at sundown."

"Mary is here. I don't want her on alert any more than she may already be. You will stay here," I say to Mym. I'm about to address William when he holds up a finger.

"I know, my life is in danger. But if, as you say, I am now an active piece, Mary may already know that I am alive and assisting you."

"I -" I'm interrupted as he holds up another finger.

"I'm ever so good at skulking," he smirks.

I chew on my bottom lip and glance over my shoulder to see if that watchman has doubled back. "Skulk," I say reluctantly. "But stay hidden."

He nods, quite pleased with himself.

"There's a second woodland area. I'll search there. If you find anything, don't touch it. Find a safe place to hide and wait for me to find you."

"But if I'm hidden -"

"I'll find you," I almost snap – and mumble angrily as I step away. I follow the path to the main thoroughfare along the perimeter wall. I pass by a groundskeeper working among the perennial plants. She glances my way a second time before turning her back and continuing her work. William, apparently, wasn't simply jesting. I try to tuck and fold my garments, but hiding the wear is next to impossible. "Don't draw attention to yourself," I mutter to myself as I take a moment to nonchalantly lean against a cedar at the reflecting pond as I come to it. I notice a group of four on the other side of the pond conversing with each other. I also see the watchmen well across the various plots of flora, walking along a hedge wall that bisects the garden complex.

I pretend to inspect the cedar and the next one before continuing to the other wooded area. As I approach, I can see that this patch of trees is larger than the one where I left William and Mym. "This is going to take too long," I mutter as I set my feet upon the woodland path. But then I spot a tree that may offer some advantage. I approach the hawthorn. The season has brought out the small white flowers along the grey and twisting branches. Hawthorns are a favorite of fairies – or, as some rudely name them, pixies. They tend to build homes in them as the bluejay does. But this is a young tree and may not have drawn any settlers yet. I pull a small silver chain from my bag and drape it over one of the low branches, then knock on the tree three times.

Before anything can happen, I notice I won't be alone much longer. The group of four has broken up, and two have started to perambulate in this direction. Of more concern to me is the watchman continuing to meander towards this woodland area. I'm hardly a yard in among the trees, easily spotted from the main walk or the circuitous path through the woods. I crouch and pretend to be working the soil around the hawthorn, hoping my appearance passes for a groundskeeper.

I watch as the couple bypass the woodland path and continue on their way. I glance around, but I've lost sight of the guard. I stand up and notice the silver chain is missing. "Merde," I growl. I knock on the tree three more times. "Excuse me," I whisper. "I hope you enjoy the chain, but I'd like to ask you a question." I wait. "Hello?"

"Hello."

I hear the soft voice over my shoulder in the tree behind me. I don't turn for fear of scaring the creature off. "I'm looking for something."

"I'm always looking for something," the fairy giggles.

"There was a man -"

"Many men pass under these trees," it giggles again.

"And I'm sure they make for many shiny things."

"Oh, they do. My hoard is the biggest in the gardens."

Vampires always claim to be the oldest. Gods always claim to be the strongest. Fairies always claim to have the largest and shiniest hoards. "I'm sure it is. What can I call you?" I hear the faint flutter of light wings. A small creature with the features and appearance of a tiny, thin child lands on a branch of the hawthorn level with my eyes.

"You can call me Pebble." As Pebble says this, there's a soft pulse of the shimmery white aura surrounding the creature.

"Pebble, there was a man, gone now. He favored these woods. Maybe more so than most. He would walk among the trees, I guess, off the designated paths."

"You're not allowed off the paths. Only the caretakers and those invited can sample the trees, herbs, and flowers."

"He would have been allowed – though the caretakers may have privately griped about it. Sir Hans Sloane – have you heard that name mentioned?"

Pebble stands and begins to pace along the branch in thought. I begin losing hope as a minute and then another ticks by. Nervously, I glance over my shoulders and peer through the trees. Thankfully, we don't appear to be in danger of being interrupted. They are curious and observant creatures, but the problem with fairies is that they tend to focus on playful things – something shiny, wrestling, and dancing. It may be asking too much for Pebble to have noticed one man among many.

The fairy sighs and turns. "I'm sorry,"

I sigh, too. "He may have been troubled the last time he was here. A weight on his mind. He may have sat among the trees for a long time."

Pebble snaps their fingers. "The bench." Without another word, they streak away, by instinct becoming invisible.

I race after, come to the path, cross it, and enter the trees again, but nothing is left to follow. I proceed slowly in the same direction, hoping Pebble had flown in a straight line. I return to the path, which seems to curve back and forth in this section. Pebble appears in front of my face.

"This way, silly." They point and flutter away – becoming invisible again.

I follow in the direction indicated, leaving the path once more. I travel through the trees for several yards before finding the path again. Here I stop. I hear a woman's laughter from ahead, through the trees, and to the left. "Pebble," I strain a whisper. "Pebble."

"Here," the fairy waves from about a stone's throw into the trees ahead of me. "Not far," and flutters away.

I enter a slightly thicker section of these woods. After traveling several paces, I spot a small stone bench with a plinth and statue next to it. Pebble makes themselves known, appearing with legs dangling off the side of the bench.

"The bench," they say proudly. "The caretakers don't like it here but have left it."

Perhaps it was in Sir Sloane's will that the bench be left. "Thank you, Pebble. This has helped me a great deal." My hand digs around in my satchel, and I pull out a small silver ring. I watch as Pebble's eyes open wide. I leave the anticipation for a moment and then hand the ring over. "For your hoard." There's no thank you. The white aura glows brightly briefly, and then they're gone. I step back from the bench and quickly switch my attention to one of the trees as I notice footsteps along the path. Through the branches, I see the puffy white sleeves and parasol of the woman enjoying the scenic walk with her man. The path must pass through this area in a wide loop because, for an annoying amount of time, they are always just within eyesight of me and I of them. Though, unless they chose to peer this deeply into the trees, I doubt they would see me. As they begin to move away, I don't wait any longer. I turn back to the bench.

"I hoped that the purity of those grounds would hide the key," I mutter Sir Sloane's words. "Purity," I utter and turn my attention to the statue. A grey cherub sits atop a sturdy plinth. Both bench and plinth have been here for a while, but neither, I would guess - based on the other benches and statues I've passed - started here. "Purity," I mutter again. "Purity would hide the key." I glance down at the base of the plinth and poke at the soil with my boot.

I glance up at the sound of more footsteps. Through the trees, I spot the watchman coming in this direction. I step away from the bench and plinth and reprise my performance as a groundskeeper. I hear footsteps and the rapid cracking of twigs behind me. As I turn, I see William's face for just a moment before he tackles me to the ground.

CHAPTER SIXTEEN

"It's her. The guard — it's her. She's him — he's her," William pants.

Prone on my back, I crane my head as best I can. Night comes early when you're under trees, but plenty can still be seen by the ebbing light. Mym, however, is now in my way. She is slowly rolling to her right, presumably keeping pace with Mary as she walks the path. "Mym, I can't see. And you, get off."

Rumble.

"My apologies," William says as he slides off. He slinks close to the ground, keeping behind Mym.

I roll onto my stomach. About forty yards of trees separate us from the figure strolling the path. It's difficult to discern details through the trees, but it looks like a guard dressed in the typical padded leather of their station and carrying a spear. The gait suggests a man — and a curious one at that, for he keeps stopping to gaze around. I can sense William and Mym tense as the figure turns our way. But nothing happens and, after a moment, the guard continues along the path.

"One of you better explain yourselves."

"There's a body. I found a body. Over there," William begins to raise his hand but thinks better of making sudden movements and slowly lowers it. "It was partially hidden," his voice is even more of a whisper. "Covered enough to be overlooked, but it won't remain that way for long."

My attention shifts to the guard slowly moving away. "Are you sure? You need to be sure."

"I'm sure. It is that guard there. The same young man. And more, the body had two puncture marks in the neck."

"Like the courier," I say and William nods. On elbows and knees, I crawl a little closer toward the path. William follows. Despite our awkward conveyance, I hear William's breathing begin to steady. By the time I come to a stop, his flushed face has returned to his normal shade. I hold a finger to my lips as I face him before returning my attention to the guard. A few seconds later, William taps me on the shoulder but doesn't wait for me to turn to him.

"There is something that gives me pause," he whispers.

"Lost your confidence?"

"Not entirely. I admit my excitement got the better of me, but having a moment to breathe has allowed me to recall something you said earlier. You said I needed to be careful because Mary could have any woman's face."

"A false assumption on my part," I say and crawl a little further over grass and soil. I can better see the guard now – he's perhaps twenty yards ahead. He's walked a few paces into the trees on the other side of the path. I watch as, his back to me, he pokes around several trees with the point of his spear. A slight rustle of clothing scraping against dirt and twigs tells me William has crawled up behind me. Without looking back, I say to him, "I've known her for a very long time. Without knowing it, *you* picked the perfect name for her – Crusher. She doesn't look at the world around her as objects to interact with; she sees them as obstacles in her way. You see, she hates everything - with a special place carved out for those of your ilk."

"Some specific oppression handed down by a man in her life. A father figure?"

I glance over my shoulder at him. "Are you looking for a sympathetic understanding?"

William looks past me, over the path, to the trees on the other side. I follow his eyes as we watch the guard walk further under the trees. "We are all responsible for our own actions," he finally says, "but thought and action can be manipulated for a purpose. Even when such manipulation isn't the intent, our thoughts and actions are, to some degree, the product of what we perceive of the world. So, I just wonder what Mary has perceived to have her act in such a monstrous way?"

"I can't say what went on in Mary's world before she was chosen." I can't help but feel the wisps of my own childhood fogging my mind. "But I mean it when I say she hates everyone. She hates the young for their youthfulness and vitality. She hates the old because of their frailty. She finds women to be vapid. She despises men because they see her as one of those thoughtless women she hates. She doesn't want to rule over any of them. She doesn't want to change anything. She just wants to burn it all down."

"Anger personified. Is that why she was chosen?"

"I think it is what her Patron was looking for, yes. The gods' field of vision is wide, but they are not everywhere all the time. I can't say when Thanatos took an interest in Mary, but I believe he waited until the perfect moment before harvesting her. Her disguises may have prevented you from seeing this, but she is of a mature body. Her mind is convinced she can do it better than everyone else. And her soul is a pit of jealousy that twists and writhes in the presence of any she deems having something she wants." We flatten ourselves even further against the ground as the guard emerges from the trees. Knowing now that it is her, I'm reluctant to let her out of my sight. I glance back at William, grinding my teeth against a decision I'm not happy about making.

"Do you think she knows you are here?" William asks in such a low whisper that I'm not sure if he fears asking the question or the answer more.

I stare, watching and waiting for some indication, but I think she is well-focused on her task and not me. "There are ways for my kind to detect each other… I'm not sure. Mary is crafty." I wait until the guard has turned his back on us to speak again. "Get back to Mym as quietly as you can. Somewhere around that bench will be the Key. Find it and then run."

He nods his understanding and then crawls away.

"Alright, Mary," I whisper after William has gone. "Let's you and I have some words." I creep over to the path and begin following the guard at a distance. The idle stroll of the young guard becomes a bit of a stomp the further we move along the path. After a few minutes, he – she – stops and breaks away, stepping once more into the tree line. Mary – *if this is Mary* – is drawn to a copse of trees with shredded bark, almost as if they're covered in wooden strands of hair. She ducks and bends around the trunks and branches. There's an air of confidence as she moves among the cluster of odd trees and pokes at their roots. She doesn't notice me standing at the edge of the path, perhaps thirty feet behind her. I'm about to interrupt when she growls with angry passion and plunges her spear into the earth. She turns sharply and walks about ten feet in my direction before abruptly stopping.

"Come to gloat?" she sneers as she reaches back to pull the spear from the ground.

The young man's voice coming out of a mouth behind which somewhere hides the true Mary is disturbing, to say the least. "Wearing a man's clothes, I never thought I'd see the day."

"It seemed the least likely to gain attention."

Mary jabs at the ground with the butt of her spear in an irritated fashion, but does not approach. She glances left and then right - *keeping an eye out*. "How odd," I say as I begin to walk toward her.

"Odd?" she asks.

"Looking like a man. Talking like a man." I shrug with a disinterested frown, "What I find odd - amusing even - is not the disguise, but you, by all appearances, acting the part of a scared and subdued puppy."

The strike was expected, though it comes without warning. Suddenly, a spear is streaking at my head. I deflect the projectile easily with my morningstar and match Mary's charge. She swoops in under my arching swing and rams her shoulder into my chest. I lose my footing and stumble back a few steps. She takes the moment to pull the stolen, thin, black dagger, its edges tinted in green, from a secret sheath.

Mary lunges forward, the razor's edge slicing toward me.

I bend back as I step forward with my swing, falling to my knees and sliding under her attack.

We spin to face one another, pressing in once more.

Mary jabs.

I sidestep, moving around her, the points of my morningstar arcing towards the small of her back.

Mary reaches up and taking hold of a sturdy branch, lifts herself out of danger – tossing a small glass vial as she flips to perch atop the branch.

The vial cracks against the back of my hand. My flesh sizzles and burns. I cry out and lose the grip on my weapon as I step into another swing. The morningstar leaves my hands and thumps into a tree trunk with shredded bark.

We stare at each other – each at the ready. It is off putting to see her so tame. No theatrics. No threats. The growing tickle in the back of my mind is perhaps one reason. There is a slight breeze, but the air feels thick and heavy. We have the attention of more than the usual few gods for this fight. I can tell Mary is aware of this as well. She's paranoid by nature, and the feeling of so many watching has her attention shifting. "You seem nervous." I verbally jab at her.

"You are unusually talkative. Am I keeping you from something?"

"You have my full attention."

She chuckles and smiles. "Where's Mym?"

I don't answer.

"Found it, have you?" She laughs a bitter chuckle and sighs. "All that for nothing," she says to herself. "Do you have it on you, or is your dog guarding it?" Mary peers over my shoulder, scanning the trees behind me. "Or have you set the beast to digging it up? That's a laugh. Round and round she spins. No hands. She'll be like a wheel in the mud." Mary laughs. "It is an amusing image." She leaps down from the branch, landing with the grace of a cat.

"She's nearby, if that's what you're asking." We take a few steps toward each other.

"I'm too smart for your ambushes. I think our history has proven that." Giving nothing away, Mary jabs at me with the dagger.

I press forward with a side block and backfist her face.

She steps back, blood trickling from her lip. She smiles and charges forward with a series of quick slashes.

I back up with each slice, then spin low with a tripping attack.

Mary jumps my legs, coming down with the point of the dagger aimed at my shoulder.

I roll out of the way, coming to my feet and taking several large strides to give myself some distance – and reclaim my morningstar.

Mary is on my heels. Almost a blur, the hand holding the dagger jabs and slices – her attacks clinking off the metal of my mace.

I backflip as Mary's attack presses forward, shifting the fight to the path. As I land on my feet, my mind relaxes as I exert my will. I take another couple of steps back.

"Hold still," Mary growls.

Within a couple of quick steps, Mary's dagger is driving toward my chest when her wrist is forced back at a painful angle. "Ahhh!" Mary cries as the dagger falls to the ground. She stumbles back, cradling her arm.

I step around the tree that now becomes visible to Mary. "Leaping before looking, as always." I'm surprised when Mary begins to laugh. I see her hand reaching into a pouch and brace for her next attack.

At the same time, we hear footsteps upon the gravel of the path coming towards us.

Mary puts her back to the tree of flaking bark, striking a resting pose.

I turn my back to the path and fall to my knees, pretending to tend to the soil around a neighboring tree. I'm ready to leap to the defense of the civilians slowly approaching us. The couple, a middle-aged man and woman, pass by, nodding to the guard they see. "Evening, watchman," the man says.

Mary nods in return, but only calls out to them once they've taken several steps away. "Don't be caught here after dark."

The man half turns with a wave. "Don't ye worry, watchman. We were just taking one last pass through the trees on our way to the gate."

I hear Mary's attention shift back to me as I begin to chuckle. "You must have done something very naughty." I continue to poke at the ground as the couple moves away. I can feel Mary's eyes on me – and the fire of hatred behind them. I hear her shift away as she checks on the couple.

"I saw what they did to you at the church. Saw you run away with your tail between your legs."

I don't respond.

"They're quick, I must admit. Moving like a bunch of angry ants. I thought I had the time. And you - after what I did to your friend, I thought you would be stuck in the mud."

She doesn't see my smile - *she doesn't know William is still alive.*

"By the time I located the Jar, it was gone. I went to the church, but they and you were already there. So I jumped ahead to the Key - or at least where I thought the Key was - but the Cult was there too. It surprises me that they surprised you. I saw them right away. They're predictable. Though, slightly better at laying traps than you. Obviously."

I bite my tongue and give a side glance - the couple is almost out of sight.

Mary sighs. "Impatient. I'm impatient. I admit it. The museum is a big place and guarded. So many hiding places -"

"So, you broke the rules," I say.

"I know of certain gateways that have no psychopomps." she delights in mentioning. "Having one as mighty as Thanatos as your Patron, rather than a simple ferryman, has its advantages. Sloane was… made available. He gave me enough to let me know that the Key wasn't at the museum."

"You're not supposed to use a god's power or knowledge."

"Well, that's our little secret."

"But it isn't, is it?" I laugh. "You got caught." I don't have to reach out to sense *Them* watching – I almost feel *Them* leaning in expectantly. As Mary's eyes dart back and forth, I can tell that she is also very aware of the scrutiny. "And now here you are. Declawed. Defanged. Sheepishly poking at rocks and turning over leaves." I leap at her, but her knee is there first – apparently, I made her a little too angry. I'm stunned and tumble back onto my rear end.

Before she can scoop up her dagger, Mary is sent flying as a small boulder slams into her. She somersaults but can't save the landing and skids into a tree. She scrambles to her feet, scowling at Mym. Completely distracted, she doesn't see, but I do. Further along, I watch William dash across the path. The tails of his blue coat flap in the wind as he vanishes among the trees.

Mary taunts Mym, but Mym doesn't pursue. Instead, Mym slowly, deliberately, spins back and forth in place - pushing down with such force that she digs herself a little into the pathway. The grinding of metal under rock can be clearly heard.

Waves of anger wash over Mary's face. "I rather enjoyed that dagger." Mary takes a step. Instead of backing away, Mym pushes up with a puff of steam and slams down on the dagger. I'm amused by this and react too late to Mary pulling out another vial. As she reaches back to throw it, a small dirt-stained box, being wielded as an inadequate club, knocks the vial from Mary's hand. Mary turns and comes face to face with William.

On puffs of nervous breaths, William says, "Hello. We haven't been formally introduced -"

Mary backhands William.

William's head snaps back with such force that he tumbles through the air, feet over head. The box drops. A shoe flings away. His satchel falls from his shoulder. William hits the graveled pathway with a groan and then lays silent.

Mary brings her arm up in time to block my morningstar from striking her skull. I hear the crack of bone and see the splash of blood as the strike sends Mary crashing to the ground. She rolls away from my follow-up assault, and as she rises to her feet, she's holding the dirt-stained box. As she backs away, she shakes it tauntingly. I rush forward a few steps – she sprints back an equal amount. She produces another vial.

"Trees burn so easily. Maybe it's against the rules, maybe it's not. I'm willing to take the chance. Are you?"

I don't press.

"Maybe he's really dead this time. I'm sure you'll let me know." Mary turns and runs away.

CHAPTER SEVENTEEN

An unsettling juxtaposition descends upon me as my mind is pressed between what is around and within me. The sweet smells of blossoms and herbs. The gentle breeze. The peacefulness of the tree menagerie. The rage boiling up from the pits of my soul. The flutter of concern in my chest. The swirl of guilt I feel for all of this — everything. I take a step — away from William. And then one more before turning around. "Merde." I don't move. "Merde!" I stomp toward Mym. "Take a look around. She is gone, but just in case. Be sneaky." As Mym rolls away, I feel the presence of the Patrons' prying eyes lift. Undoubtedly, others still watch, but it would seem the lure for their full attention has passed. So I turn toward William.

Before kneeling beside him, I watch his chest. The rise and fall are encouraging. Less encouraging is the blood smeared across his face. The split lip and his swollen nose. I give him a gentle shove. He groans. "William," I say. "William, open your eyes so I can yell at you." His eyes open. "I said run."

"You did, but Mym was very persuasive." His voice is nasal. The broken and swollen nose muffles his words.

"She spoke to you? You understood her?"

"A puff of flame erupted from her. It was very inspiring," he says, gently rubbing the sides of his head.

"I do not need you rushing to my rescue."

He blinks several times as he tries to focus on me. "I would never presume such a thing." His lips lift into a smirk, and his tone becomes playful. "Did you happen to notice her expression when she saw me? I don't think I've ever seen such irritation."

"At any time, did you take a moment to consider the pseudonym you bestowed on her?"

"Ah, yes. An unfortunate oversight." William closes his eyes. "I know there is a great rush, but if I could just lie here for a moment more?"

I sigh and lift my face to the darkening sky in a silent shout. I take a step away and then return, lowering myself to my back as I lay next to him. "You're a bloody mess."

"I feel it," he mumbles.

"And now Mary has the Key. Based on your investigations, I gather Mary has a Cup and Dagger important to her task. We know she has the Ring from the courier. And now she has the Key."

"By my count," William begins, his voice edged with pain. "The Cult has the Bone from Saint Magnus and the Jar from the Art Society. As I recall, there was also a Diadem on the list. It wasn't crossed out, however."

"Neither were the Bone and the Jar, and now they are in the hands of the Cult."

William gives a defeated sigh. "Maybe they will find and destroy each other."

His words roll around in my mind – there is a certain appeal to the notion. I shake my head. "No. One would survive, and then they would have everything." A defeated malaise befalls us. Several seconds pass before I hear him speak again.

"You're wrong about something."

"What is that?" I ask with a little bit of heat. I don't want his words of encouragement. I don't want him to make a heartfelt yet misguided attempt to minimize the dire situation. I don't want to hear a chipper human saying about never giving up or that it

263

can't be as bad as it sounds. *It is as bad as it sounds!* Words to dismiss him are already forming in my mind.

"The Key. Mary doesn't have it."

"I saw the box. She has it."

"She has the box. Not the Key."

"Where's the Key?" I prop myself up on my elbows and stare at him.

His hand drifts down and searches his side. After a few pats at his frayed clothing and the ground at his side, his eyes spring open. "Where is it?"

"I asked you…"

"Where is it?" Energized by his distress, William sits up. "My satchel, do you see it?"

"It was thrown from you when you were hit." I scan around for the discarded item. "It can't be too far." I help him to his feet.

As we search, I come upon the Cult dagger Mym had destroyed. The shards of black metal are partially embedded in the gravel path. I squat and examine the pieces – though I'm hesitant to touch them. Among the metal are tiny slivers of green crystal. I get down onto hands and knees, my face hovering a few inches above the shattered weapon. I notice the crystal, where it hasn't been broken from the metal blade, is fused with the metal itself like a sheath of hardened resin. I pull a silk scarf out of my bag and, with great care, place the shards into it and fold it up. I turn at the sound of several items tumbling onto the path.

I approach William. He's on his knees, staring at a small pile of things, his satchel crumpled, lying at his side. "It's not here," he says.

I scan the objects over his shoulder. Among the items I'm familiar with him carrying – his quill, ink bottle, notebook, coin purse – I spot a small metallic key. "You do have it," I scoop up the Key.

William slides out from under the grateful hand I lay on his shoulder and limps away. His eyes cast downward, searching along the edges of the path and into the trees.

"What are you looking for?" I ask, but he doesn't seem to hear me. His search becomes more frantic. I step toward him, but I am stopped by the faint flutter of wings and an almost imperceptible amount of pressure on my shoulder. Even though I know a fairy has landed there, I do not see it. "Hello," I say.

"Hello," it's Pebble's voice. "Has something happened?"

"It has," they say and become visible. "We saw the fight. We felt," their words tremble some as their eyes dart upward. "*Them*," they say in a whisper.

I understand the anxiety. Fairies tend to be chaotic. They aren't evil, as so many seem to portray them. They are mischievous and drawn to shiny things. Just by the nature of being themselves, they have occasionally unintentionally ruined celestial machinations. "Yes," I say, "but *They* are gone." It was close enough to the truth. "Besides, I would not allow any of *Them* to harass you."

Pebble looks over their shoulder and sticks a tongue out, seemingly at thin air. "I told the others you would not bring harm to us."

"Please, tell the others that the danger has passed. There is nothing to fear."

A soft-white glow encompasses Pebble as their wings begin to flutter. "Not all the danger. He seems very concerned," they say, floating beside me.

"William," I call out to him. He finally recognizes my voice and turns slowly in response.

He's struck by a moment of awe as he sees the small hovering figure next to me. He blinks and takes an unconscious step forward before shaking his head. "Please, help me find it," he says to me.

"I have the Key," I say.

"To Hell with your blasted Key," William snaps. He takes a breath and calms himself. "It's a small crystal orb." He cups his hands, approximating the size of the item.

"Oh," Pebble exclaims and vanishes.

"William," I say, stepping over to him. Pebble reappears before I can say anything further.

"This is Bitter," Pebble says.

On wings gently fluttering in rhythm with Pebble's is a second fairy – a faint yellow aura around them. Clutched to Bitter's chest is a crystal orb that nearly obscures them. Their reluctance is apparent.

William stutters forward, hand out, but Bitter withdraws.

Pebble pushes their hand into Bitter's back and presses them forward. "I promised something in trade."

"Whatever. Anything." William says, his hand still outstretched, though maintaining the distance.

Bitter hesitates momentarily and then does a quick flyby, dropping the orb in William's hand as they pass.

Pebble dashes forward, landing with Bitter at William's bag, just before four other fairies land to pick over the spilled contents. Pebble slaps the hand of one and pushes another, all the while displaying a stern face. "I said wait," Pebble utters angrily.

The other fairies accept the order and wait while Bitter tiptoes among the various items. Bitter kicks aside the broken quill. They don't give the journal a second glance. At the coin purse they spend time untying the leather cord holding the pouch shut, though after examining the coins, they decide not to take one. Bitter stops at the glass ink bottle. They lift the copper stopper and seem pleased that some ink remains. Bitter wraps both arms around the bottle and vanishes with it.

William witnesses none of this as he'd limped over to and sat under one of the shredded bark trees. His eyes mournful as they gaze upon the orb cupped in his hands. As I approach, he speaks without looking up.

"I can't write about any of this, can I?"

Standing over him but looking back in the direction of his bag, I spot a few more fairies buzzing around his satchel. "It would be a fanciful tale. Not really fitting with the current mood of literature as I am aware of it."

"Literary sentiment shifts," he says.

"It does."

William closes his eyes and rests his head against the tree.

"Don't get too comfortable. I think it best we move from this place."

"Yes, I agree that would be prudent. Although getting a carriage in this state will be more difficult."

I leave his side and gather up his belongings. As I am doing this, I hear Mym approaching. She is in no rush, so I assume all is clear. "We are leaving," I say to her.

"I am not looking forward to the walk back to London," William says as he limps in our direction.

"There are other means of travel that I'm more willing to avail myself of at this time." I toss his bag at him. "Stand close to Mym," I order, and then make a rough circle with my foot around them in the gravel path. I quickly draw out the necessary arcane

269

symbols and step into the circle. As
the ground under us begins to swirl,
flashes of electrical energy crackle
away from the edges of the circle. I
clear my throat nervously. "I'm not
very practiced in the art of directed
magic," I make a show of crossing my
fingers. "Oh, and take a deep breath,"
I say as we sink into the swirl of
gravel and soil.

We drop from ceiling to bed. By
some miracle, the frame holds as our
combined weight sinks into the soft
mattress. Mym immediately rolls from
the bed, thumping onto the floor. Wood
creaks under her as she rolls to a spot
near the door. I would have been
worried about her noisy movement, but
the whole building is rattling and
creaking. The swirl above unwinds,
returning the natural wood to its usual
state. It takes a few seconds more for
the flashes of arcane energy to
dissipate.

There is a brief moment of quiet
before the building is alive with
movement. Thankfully, the evening is
still young. I guess the number of
people who have witnessed the building
shaking will be minimal. I sigh and
allow my head to press into the pillow.

William coughs and takes a deep breath. "My word, that squeezed the air right out of me." He coughs again. "Investigator. Warrior. Practitioner. Your talents know no bounds."

"I much prefer my morningstar."

"And yet you have safely deposited us," he pauses to look around. "Oh, we're in my chambers." With some effort, William gets to his feet, rubbing his neck. He lights a lamp by the bedside and then sets a small fire to burn in the fireplace. He limps over to the window and stares out.

I notice him absently rolling the small crystal sphere in his hand. It reminds me of what I'm holding. I squeeze the Key. I'm too afraid to set it down. "You switched out the Key, for…?"

"Another key."

"You happened to have another key on you? Oh, not your door key?"

William gestures to the armoire. "We found the box in a shallow – grave – under the statue plinth. As we were running –"

"Not away," I cut in. I notice his soft chuckle.

"As we were running, I had a thought. What if Mary *thought* she had the Key? So, I dirtied up the armoire key, switched it out, and hoped Mary would be pleased or distracted enough not to look too closely until much later." He lifts the orb to eye level for a long look before slipping it into his bag. He places his bag on the dresser and flops into his high-backed chair. He exhales slowly as he nestles into the cushioned fabric.

"We have things to discuss," I say.

"To business," he says with some forced enthusiasm.

"Actually, I need to know you are alright."

"Are you referring to my bloody face or my limp? Either way, I assure you, I am fit as a fiddle."

"I'm referring to the crystal orb." My statement hangs in the air for several heartbeats before I hear the slow intake of air and a sigh.

"There was a fire. I was returning home – by the time I arrived…" he clears his throat. "I stood there. I stood there for a long time. Frozen by the terror of it. And then, much too late, I ran into the house. I knew it was too late, even before kicking down the front door – I knew. I dashed upstairs, but the smoke – there was so much smoke. I opened a window, and there was this explosion. I was found in the garden some time later."

William falls quiet, and I can't tell if it is emotion or his swollen nose giving his words a heavy element of sorrow. In the pause, I slide from the bed and move to stand next to him.

"There wasn't much left. A few trinkets. The orb was the first gift I ever gave to her. It had this lovely wooden base," he smiles. "She would handle it like a toy. I'd chide her and playfully threaten to take it away. But near the end… she had gotten rather good at rolling it around between her hands."

He falls silent again, and I'm not sure he will say much more this evening, so I pat his shoulder and step away. I'd already gleaned some of what he had just related to me from our first meeting. His scars. The silver hand mirror. A missing woman in his life. But to hear it – I know the feeling of having one's family ripped away. At the window, I glance across the street to a small gathering of friends outside the theater. *Happy and sad. Devastated and gleeful. All within shouting distance of each other. I can't help but wonder, if humans were able to comprehend the emotional state*

of those around them, would it be
progressive understanding or disaster?
Would it pop their insulated bubbles or
expand them? I hear the clink of
bottles as William bends in search of
one still containing liquid. A small
slosh and a triumphant grunt let me
know he's found his prey.

"I feel we both need a change of
clothes before our next adventure. If
you open the right door of the armoire,
you'll find some clothing I think will
suit you."

As I step over to the armoire, I
drop the Key into my bag. On this side
of the closet, there are two sets of
clothing. The first is a simple dress,
something that might be worn for a walk
or around the house. It's a dark shade
of blue with tiny embroidered yellow
flowers and a pleated skirt. The second
is a fancy blue and white gown. "These
were your wife's?"

"Yes and no," William empties the
bottle into his mouth and then drops it
to the floor. "The armoire and the
dresses were meant to be her birthday
present. I had them hidden in an
outbuilding."

I don't press further. I nod and
say, "Thank you. They are lovely." I
hold the dark blue dress up to myself

but set it down right away when I hear William stumble getting up from the chair. "You need tending to."

"And yet, *I* get chastised for the appearance of coming to your rescue."

I lay him out on the bed. "Do not make me insult you." I pull from my bag the crystal bottle of oil I'd applied to his wounds the last time we were in this room.

"This seems familiar," he smirks.

"Stop getting hurt." I shake the bottle. "This is the last of this, and I'm not sure when I'll get more." I apply the oil to my hands. "This will hurt," I say as I rub at his face and around his neck. Almost instantly, there is some knitting of the cut to his upper lip, and the swelling of his nose reduces. I tear a bit of the cloth from my ruined skirt and, with the help of a few dribbles of alcohol, wipe away most of the blood on his face. "I'm not rubbing your leg. That you will just have to put up with."

He gently touches his face as I step away. "Ah, oh well. You didn't get my shirt off this time."

"That is rude and unbecoming."

"I do apologize."

"Besides," I say, "You were shirtless even before I arrived." I hide my smile by looking away, and I notice a few folded pieces of paper by the door. "These didn't just arrive, did they?" I ask Mym as I retrieve the paper.

Crackle.

"I thought for a moment they were notes from his landlady regarding our rather noisy entrance." I unfold the first sheet.

"At least read my correspondence out loud," William says from the bed.

"`My Friend,`" I begin, "`I have not heard from you, and I have dreadful news. The Crusher – it's a woman. You must come see me. Respectfully, William`. There is another as well. `William` – with an exclamation point – `whether convenient or not, you must come see me. Respectfully, William.`"

"Mary's been to see him. That is worrying." William tries to get up.

"Stay," I order in a calm tone. "I don't think it was Mary. It was me, I'm not sorry to say."

"Oh?"

"I don't like your friend William. I may have threatened him."

William chuckles. "He probably deserved it. I don't understand him. Well-read. Born to an almost penniless family. Worked himself into a respectable position. Progressive, and yet he has this unctuous way about him. He's off-putting."

"To put it mildly." I crumple the notes and drop them. However, they do bring to mind another note and the new information I was given. I pull the crumpled page from my bag and approach the fireplace.

"Is that the journal page?" William shifts.

"Stay," I order absently as I turn the page back and forth in my hand. "There are secret ways of writing," I mutter as I hold the paper as near to the fire as I dare. I watch Jane's handwriting fade a few breaths later, and another artful script appears.

"Don't leave me in suspense."

"There is new writing. It is an older dialect of English and seems to be describing something even older. The author is unnamed, but the intent is clear. This journal is meant to hold everything undertaken in search of the Ritual of Solomon."

"A magical rite?"

My attention cannot be pulled to answer him. The words I read are wonderous and terrifying. I clear my throat in an attempt to quash the flutter of anxiety in my stomach. "It is only a brief description. Thoughtful guesses based on a few unaccounted-for sources." My mouth is dry. "If I'm reading this correctly, they were in search of something that they believed would be a weapon."

"A weapon? A new type of musket?"

"Not as such, no."

"What type of weapon, then?"

I clear my throat. "The type that `unmakes´ things."

"That's what it says, `unmake things´?" William's words drift from his lips, only lightly tethered to such an incomprehensible thought.

"The written words are unimportant —"

"What do they say?"

I consider lying but choose not to. "As written — `Rip asunder all creation, be it made by man or god.´"

William is silent.

I step back from the fire. As the page cools, the ancient writing vanishes and is replaced once more by Jane's scribbles.

Rumble.

I pat Mym as I pass on my way to the empty side of the bed. "Colorful, but you are not wrong."

William turns his head as I lay down next to him. "In my world, such a thing would have been impossible a few days ago. Standing in your world, as I do now, I see that nothing is impossible. Your world is very scary."

"Yes, it is." I close my eyes. I hear William lean over and snuff out the lamp. I listen to our breathing and the crackle coming from the fireplace. Our bedtime story was not one that readily brings on slumber.

CHAPTER EIGHTEEN

It is still dark when I awake. William remains sound asleep in the bed next to me. My eyes will no longer close, however. The fire has gone out, but I stoke it back to life. By the light of the fireplace, I change out of my ruined clothing and into the dark blue dress from the armoire and then clean myself with what is available from the tray William had produced during our last morning in this room. With fresh eyes and an idea of what I'm now looking for, thanks to the information provided to me by my Patron, the rest of the night is spent carefully studying the books and notebook I'd taken from the Wren house.

The writing, a jumbled mess that my brain could hardly discern but a few words, now opens up to me. I discover that the ritual is named only once in all these pages – and that page had been torn out to help hide it. The authors of this journal were committed and secretive. There are many notes from one contributor to the next. Bits of conversations held over time. It appears the founding authors were not well received within the Cult. There seems to have been opposition to the use of such power – many in the Cult feared it would taint their human purity. As I read through the pages, it's interesting to see the transition from hiding on the fringe to begrudging acceptance. There is certainly a bolder rendering of information in the later pages. There are even descriptions of each item and rough guesses as to when and where those items had been held and moved to and fro.

All the items appear to be mortal creations – although the gods may have touched one. These items were scattered over time and regions until the reign of Liu Bei, a warlord and later emperor of China. I learn that under "divine inspiration," he constructed the Jar. Because of that Jar, he became aware of a formula – a collection of items that could unmake creation. Horrified by this, he tried to destroy the Jar and could not. His only option was to hide it – hide all knowledge of it.

The original author cited this story as the muse that whispered in her ear. She passed this story on to the others who would follow her – each hoping to accumulate enough evidence to force the Cult to accept this new weapon. All of the objects, those that came before the Jar and those that came after, bounced around in history. Buried, unburied, forgotten, hidden, passed down as heirlooms and trinkets until, by some design, they were all within reach.

The Stone Dagger is listed as existing before history – though it eventually found itself in the collection of a wealthy family in Kent.

The Ring was apparently forged from stardust by a magi. The magi advised King Solomon, hence the name. It was seen for the powerful artifact it was and passed down between kings and queens. However, there is no mention of how it ended up in a pawn shop in Mykonos.

The Finger Bone is not a saintly artifact but from a scribe named Issit, who existed during the reign of the Pharoah Ibi. Its existence was relatively easy to track as it passed from temple to temple and church to church.

The Bronze Key wasn't always a key. It began as a sword of Assyrian origins. It was the most difficult to track down as it was "Reshaped in the forges of Hephaestus."

The Diadem is written as "A gift from Jayapala," but the "A" and the word "from" have been scratched out, so the entry now reads, "The Gift of Jayapala." Another item passed down through royal lineage.

The Cup is noted as having had Boudica's lips upon it. It was uncovered by a farmer about twenty years ago. The family of which was recently murdered by Mary.

The Jar made all of this possible. It didn't remain hidden. At some point, it was found, and someone wrote down the vision they saw. The authors of the journal discovered that list and have been working toward building this weapon. "All before my time. Hidden, discovered, hidden again – someone's been playing a long game. I feel these items have brought many clashes of my brothers and sisters," I say to myself. I set the books aside and stretch out on the floor. I arch my back and neck. I welcome the pop of joints. "All before my time," I mutter. Time is not something I think about. But the past does come to mind more often than I'd like. There are gods who have existed before time. The Game has been played for almost as long. My Patron – Charon by name, but his existence is greater than that designation. He's as old as a mountain and has witnessed the rise and fall of several civilizations. *I can't be his first champion, can I?* And that is the fear. It is a mighty link in the chains that keep us devoted to our Patrons.

We are threatened. Punished. The Rules applied without mercy. We know, we all know, that we can be replaced for we are told this often. We all ask, *what happens when our Patron grows too tired of us?* Is there an ethereal prison? Do we cease to exist? Are we sent to the Beyond? "Will I see my family again?" I mutter. I try not to think about it. *The mission is what matters.* I hear William take in a deep breath and yawn.

I quickly clean up my studies and stand. "We must move. Mary will be looking for revenge, and staying too long in one place will give her opportunity."

"Plan as we go, or have you our next step?"

"Get dressed," I say as I move to the door and pick Mym up. I don't look back as I leave him to his privacy. Once outside, I set Mym down. Even at this early hour, with the sun just casting shadows, there is plenty of motion along the street. I lean against Mym in the shadow of the boarding house and watch a cluster of young men chatting energetically as they move past on their way north along Tottingham.

"I tell you, I read it," one of the young men says, jabbing at the paper in his hand.

"I tell you, reading is nothing but trouble," the oldest-looking man in the group grumbles.

"Probably just a story to keep the streets clear at night," a third says.

Crackle.

Before responding, I wait for the group to be a little further along the road. "Young men are usually very excitable. Though I don't think without reason in this case." I continue to watch them. The one with the paper remains agitated. "There is fear there."

The door of the boarding house opens, and William steps out. He takes in a deep breath and slaps his hands together. "Our victory has made me very hungry." There's a jaunty energy to his steps. "There's this wonderful pub just up the lane there," he points, but his joy falters as he stares at my placid face.

"Victory?"

"Well, yes. You have the Key. No unmaking of creation." He lifts his eyebrows and tries to smile.

"According to Jane's books, the ritual must be done with precision. The proper words at the proper time. They will be panicking now. Desperate. They've been waiting for this moment in time. This year. This equinox. Their door is closing, and I guess it will not open again for many years."

"The equinox?" His eyes narrow as he thinks. "That's a few days away. I think a pleasant place to wait them out is this pub -"

"Two days, William. Two days for them to do something desperate. They will act, I assure you."

He frowns. "So, no pub then?"

"And Mary is still out there. Her plans unfulfilled, and seeking revenge."

He sighs. "Right. No pub. What's your plan?"

I turn to the sound of a street crier. The lyrical chant sounds again. I take William's hand and exert my will. "Heel," I say - the command is more than enough for Mym to understand. I steer them towards a stout woman with a basket balanced on her head.

"Little pastries, all hot!" she calls out. Her smile brightens as she sees us approaching. "Pastry, Ma'am?"

"Yes, please. Two," I say sweetly.

"A quick drink as well?" the vendor asks. She pats the small keg hanging at her side. "A sweet wine. A perfect pairing."

I nod.

The vendor expertly retrieves two pastries and fills two small tin cups with the raspberry-colored wine from the tiny barrel.

I accept the tasty-smelling confections and cups with another nod as William sets a few coins into her open palm.

"Little pastries, all hot!" the vendor calls out as she moves away.

I pass the food and drink to William as we continue our journey in the opposite direction. I allow him a few minutes to munch while we walk. A sorrowful sigh eventually disrupts the chewing.

"Oh."

"Oh?" I ask as he unfolds the paper the pastries had come wrapped in.

"Well, that's humbling," he says. He wipes a bit of cream away and points at the page. "The newspaper I write for. Yesterday's edition."

I glance at him. He's intently scanning the page. "Well, consider this a form of advertising." He's unmoved by my comment. His pace slows. "William, this is not the time for such vanity."

"William – the other William – has written his own article about the Crusher. Only, he doesn't describe Mary. He describes you in detail. He goes on to say that this Crusher is actually a spy that has yet to be caught. He's refined the drawing I based on the descriptions I received from the people at the almshouse."

"Of me."

"Yes," he says with regret. "It looks a lot more like you,"

He hands me the paper. The article is very unflattering and much longer than the one William had posted. "Rather inflammatory. His prose lacks your flow and descriptive flourish, however." We've come to a complete stop now. Without looking up from the page, I can feel William's nervousness. The shifting of his clothing suggests he is casting looks about us. "Calm yourself," I command, "You will draw attention to us. At the moment, we are a couple out for a walk with our dog."

"Yes, of course," he whispers and then laughs aloud. He clears his throat. "Sorry, I was trying to -"

"Yes, I know what you were trying to do." I tug his arm, and we begin walking again. His eyes, however, dart about, and I feel him tense when we pass a member of the city watch.

"I should go to William. I need to clear this up," William leans in and whispers.

"I am not concerned about William."

"It could make things more difficult. Besides, for all his bluster, he is a friend - sort of."

I don't care about the article and am unconcerned about the city watch and Other William. But such dismissal has in the past soured William's mood. I need to get him to focus. "I was thinking about something you had said before. About Mary and the Princess."

"You said there was a good chance the Diadem may already be in one of their hands," William says, his head still swiveling.

"Not my exact words, but yes. However, I was thinking about the series of events and felt there may be more truth to your suggestion. The Princess has something Mary and the

Cult want, and I think now that it might be the last item unclaimed. It is probably the hardest item to collect. It is probably the item they were leaving until last for this reason. As I said, they will be desperate. If they don't have it, they will make an attempt for it, and there is a good chance they will not be subtle about it."

"With rumors of a spy about and tension with France already high, any violent action taken against the royal family might just reignite war."

"That might also be part of their plan."

"You could be right. Their desperation might be an opportunity for us." He takes a deep breath.

I see the tension in his shoulders ease. I find it interesting that replacing one set of problems with another has had such a rapid and positive effect. *Humans are funny creatures*. "Princess Louisa is part of the extended family, correct?"

"Yes. The granddaughter of King George. She's in residence at Carlton House, where part of the art exhibition was held on the garden grounds of that estate. Let us hope for the Cult over Mary."

I grin. "Has Mary rattled you too many times?"

"No. Well, yes. But what I mean is, the Cult will be easier to spot. You say they operate in dark robes…"

Something about this statement has him trailing off in thought. "I'm pretty sure the cloaks and robes are official uniforms. For something like this, they'll probably be less conspicuous." I say.

"Hmm, robes?"

I give him a moment, and when he continues to be silent, I say, "William, I read people, not minds."

"Yes, of course. My mind is working on a nugget of a memory," he taps his lip in thought. "You said the robes are more for official use," he taps at his lips for a few more steps and then says, almost to himself, "Robes in the night. A few years ago. There was mention of a secret society. The Princess also mentioned a secret gathering. Something she'd been recently invited to and was rather insistent that I would enjoy myself as well." He grumbles in frustration and rubs his forehead. He then chuckles to himself. "I feel I am jumping at shadows. Forgive me."

"Wheels are turning," I mutter. "In my experience, the gods will shoot an arrow into a storm, by all accounts losing that arrow, but in truth, they know the direction of every gust and which of those gusts will take that arrow and see it to its target. Robes in the night, you say. Do you have notes? You said a nugget of a memory. Do you have notes that would enlighten you further?"

"It's an old story. I wasn't able to get much on it. I keep all my old story notes at the printing room." He shrugs. "It would seem that a trip to see William is inevitable."

I step away from William and wave frantically at a passing carriage driver. William and Mym climb aboard without being told or asked while I speak to the driver. "Saint Paul's, Sir. As fast as you like." I receive a brusque nod and then find my seat.

"Explaining the company I keep to William may be difficult."

"I will be unnoticed. Mym will wait outside. I would also wait outside, but things are moving very fast at this time, and I don't want you left unguarded." My head tilts and my jaw clenches at the sight of his smirk.

My irritation only seems to urge the corners of his mouth even higher.

"I rather like having a personal guard."

CHAPTER NINETEEN

I directed our driver to Pater-Noster Row as we approached Saint Paul's Cathedral. I glance at William as we pass by the enormity of the religious edifice – there's a whisper of a smile on his face. Although I haven't considered myself human for many years, I am not immune to the beauty and pleasure of their world. As the carriage turns, I gain a better view of the colossal building. The brilliance of the Portland stone. The masterful stonework. The flawless weave of geometric and organic lines. The spires. The dome. It is a piece of art. However, I can't help the ever-present thought when admiring such massive feats of human engineering and architecture. *Why?*

Art doesn't need a reason. Art has existed for as long as there have been people. Even in the harshest of environments, when food is a daily challenge, art stands side by side with other basic needs of survival. Art, maybe more so than anything else, says "we were here, and this is what was happening." Art reflects those moments. No different from music or a painting.

Architecture is art. All of it small, captured moments in time, and yet, as I stare at this massive building, I do ask – *Why?* How many smaller buildings could have been built? How many people and families could have been helped by the money spent? *Perhaps I'm too practical to be a true art lover.* I feel William's hand on my arm and look at him.

"We're here," he says with a raised eyebrow.

"I am aware," I shake my trance and step from the carriage. William speaks briefly with the driver while I quietly help Mym to the street. The Row is busy and full of life. I spot the bakery and the bookstore and, now that I know where to look for it, I can see the edge of The Globe. There is a member of the city watch. I can just make out the tip of his spear further along the street, past the pub with the backroom printing house. I look at William, but in that moment of hesitation between deciding to distract him or point out the guard to him, he also spots the spear tip. His face changes – it's subtle, but I notice. Wrinkle lines on his forehead shift, going from planning to worrying. I grip his hand. "Remember, we're two people out for a walk with our dog." He nods, but I'm not entirely sure he heard me. This is his home, probably more so than his room. These are his people. He has spent a great deal of time here. And yet, he has all the bearing of a thief about to rob his first house. "William?" He nods again, though this time it is followed by words.

"There's an alley just past the bakery. It's narrow and dark even when the sun is fully up, but it will take us to the little courtyard behind The Globe." He looks down at Mym, "Might be a tight fit."

"She will manage. Lead on." I give him a little shove.

We make our way through the small crowd, pass the bakery, and step into the narrow alley. William was not exaggerating. The walls press in on my shoulders, and I hear Mym scraping against the bricks. She can't decide if moving fast or slow is better or stealthier. "Will you try and be a little quiet?" I cock my head over my shoulder and say to her. I wonder if she can sense my smirk and quicken my pace a little just in case she decides to ram into me as either jest or retribution. The light of the small courtyard is ahead and William pulls off to the side as he steps into it.

"William, the other William, must be working," he whispers.

"I know who you are and who he is. So unless you start speaking in the third person, you don't have to specify which William."

"Right. Right." He nervously glances at the door. He clears his throat. "We usually keep that door bolted shut unless one of us is working. If you'll excuse the intensive, it gets bloody warm in there otherwise."

He glances back at the door. The day is comfortable, but I see sweat on his brow. "This is just another day, William, and you must act the part. Take a breath and get in there. I want to be away while we still have the lead."

"Just another day," he whispers to himself and crosses to the open door.

I turn to Mym, "Stay here."

Crackle. Puff.

"I don't know," I say, hating the unusual feeling of uncertainty. "Follow, don't engage. This place is too crowded for a brawl." As I approach the door, I see William knocking on the desk and waking William Arnall.

"William!" Arnall exclaims as he stands. The two embrace.

This Arnall is vastly different from the one I had met before. His hair is uncombed, and he wears only his breeches and a simple linen shirt – no shoes. He looks unrested.

"William, my dear friend. I thought…"

William, reading his friend's expression of dread, smiles warmly. "Not yet. Listen, Will -"

"I haven't received any replies to my notes. I even called on you a few times. Where have you been?! Sit. I can order us some tea."

"William, stop. Wait."

"I thought the Crusher had gotten you," Arnall says, running his hands through his hair. "She was here," he whispers. "Right here. She, she threatened me." Arnall begins to absently wander the small printing room. "She was looking for you, and I," he gulps, "and then I -" he runs his hands through his hair again and steps back over to William. "I'm so sorry, my friend."

William is caught between his friend's distress and the urgency of the matter at hand. He places a firm hand on Arnall's shoulder. "I am well, my friend. I've been following a story. You know, as I do. Before I get into any of that, I saw the article you wrote. You've got some stuff wrong, my friend." William chuckles.

"You saw that I wrote about that spy – The Crusher," Arnall says, stepping away from William. "Is that why you are here?"

No, you wrote about me and that's why we're here – but I keep the angry statement internal.

"In part, yes. In part, to see you. And, in part, to look over some of my old notes."

Arnall wags a finger at William. "I knew you'd notice. I said the article would get your attention." Arnall places his hands on the wooden beams of his printing press. "I thought people should know. I thought we should get the word out. I thought – I don't know what I thought. I don't know what I was thinking. I'm sorry my initial response to this story of yours was to dismiss it."

"Maybe you should sit," William laughs and pulls the chair out for Arnall.

"Why was the Crusher looking for you? Was it the article? Or something else?"

"I think I've uncovered something exceptional, if that's what you're asking," William smirks.

"I see. Of course," Arnall laughs. He strides over to William and embraces him once more. "Who knew this would be such a dangerous undertaking? Sit. Sit," Arnall insists and even directs William to the desk chair. "I'll get us some tea, and then we can talk."

Arnall is gone before William can say anything further. As the door closes, I take a step toward William, and from his perspective, appear from a shadow. I ignore the slight jump. "He seems nervous."

"William? He hasn't been sleeping by the look of him. Besides, he did say he's been worried. Worried could pass for nervous."

We both stare at the door for a few seconds before I turn to him and say, "Notes."

"Right." William begins inspecting the various cubbyholes and drawers.

As he's looking, I spot a drawing in one of the drawers and stop him from closing it. I reach in and pick up the small drawing. The sketch is of a woman seated in a chair with the faint outline of a fireplace behind her. She's wearing a simple but elegant dress, and he's drawn her with a warm smile. "She was lovely."

"She was," he says after a moment.

His focus on finding his notes becomes even more intense. "I'm sorry for your loss." His search slows to a halt. He doesn't turn to me, but that doesn't stop me from spotting the slumped shoulders. "I understand how hollow those words can sound. So unmeaningful. It's what you say when you don't know what to say. Call it a failure of language. But please know this. I say them with understanding. I know what it is like to have your family taken from you in an instant. And I know the struggle to overcome such an event."

He turns to face me. "There is a long conversation I wish to have with you when all of this is concluded. Questions I hope you'll do me the honor of answering without deflection."

I find myself smiling, "But not today." I indicate the desk with my eyes.

"Right." He begins to shuffle papers and peek into drawers again. "Ah," he says in triumph. He pulls a small leather-bound notebook from under a ledger. He flips through several pages before stopping. "Yes. Here." He sets the book on the desk, his finger pressed against his handwriting. "Cloaked and hooded figures in the night. So much of what I catch wind of is whispers and rumors. About half the time, that's all it is. I gave up the chase on this because I thought that's all it was. But," he turns the page, "here is a list of places and times when these hooded figures were spotted. There's even a chap who was spooked by a dark carriage being driven by a heavily cloaked and hooded fellow."

I scan the notes. "Not much here," I mutter. "A handful of comments. Sightings that cluster around the middle of a few months. Most of these sightings are in Wycombe." I shake my head. "I'm not sure there's anything for us here. The Cult isn't going to be gallivanting around for all to see."

I see him shaking his head, too. "I'm sorry. There's less here than I remembered." He sighs, flips a page, and then goes back again. "About ten years ago there's a smattering of appearances in Wycombe. But then almost nothing until about five years ago when similar stories began popping up again. Several in Medmenham. All of these notes date back only two years, however. That's when I caught wind of this. Lots of running around and carriages for nothing, I'm afraid. I suppose looking back, with my mind and eyes of today, I'd find the dismissiveness I mistook at the time for annoyance as very odd, but I'm not sure that's really enough to go on. Again, sorry. I was sure I had something on the Cult." He grows silent, a slight mumble from time to time as he rereads his notes.

There's something here, I think as I join his eyes on the pages. I feel there should be something here. *Hooded figures* - it isn't mere coincidence that he has these notes. There must be something here. I find myself drawn to the repeated words `hooded figures´ every time William lists a sighting.

"Although…" His finger begins tapping the page, but he says nothing further.

I'm too wrapped up in my own thoughts to ask about his. *Why would they be in Wycombe? Why allow themselves to be seen? Though, I doubt it was a purposeful act. Mistakes were made, the Cult isn't flawless. Did they settle in Wycombe? They found a safe place, some hidden away spot, from which they venture out in search of artifacts.*

William brushes his shoulder against mine. "You found something, didn't you?"

I turn my head slightly, just enough to see the smile on his face. I return the gesture – he'd earned it. "I think, on retrospect, that we may have found their nest."

"Well done, us. In addition, I think I have an idea on where we might more easily pilfer the Diadem, assuming the Cult hasn't gotten to it first." He taps the open page of his notes.

I glance down. "Who is Lady Elizabeth?"

"Lady Elizabeth is an inn. A rather comfortable place to stay while in Medmenham. It was the last place I went when I was sniffing around these sightings. It's owned by the Braddock family. I spoke with," he pauses as he scans his notes. "Haley Braddock," his finger comes down on the name. "She and her husband, Harry. The inn is named after her grandmother - Elizabeth Braddock. As I recall, the story is that King George, the first of his name, stayed at the inn on two separate occasions. He was so taken by his treatment that he bestowed the honorary title of Lady on Elizabeth. The family still has the documentation. And, more

pressing to our current situation,
Princess Louisa invited me to this
gathering that may take place there.
Some sort of association she's
nominally a part of – though, Mister
Walpole was a bit put off when it was
brought up. They have an odd
relationship. Respectful, yet somewhat
contentious –"

"William!" I snap. "What about
it?"

"Right. If I was interested, the
Princess said she would meet me at this
inn. From what I found out during my
time with her, she's never without that
particular decoration. I suspect she'll
have it with her when she travels."

"When are you meant to meet her?"

William pauses as he recalls the
conversation. "Tomorrow evening."

"The equinox," we say at the same
time.

The door opens behind us. We
assume it's Arnall and don't turn until
a hand clamps onto William's wrist.
"William Monkton, you will come with
us."

My head snaps up, coming nearly
face-to-face with the blonde hair and
fair features of the young city
watchman Mary had taken as a disguise.

More guardsmen enter the room, both from the courtyard and from the doorway to the pub. Four plus Mary now fill the small printing room.

"You said you just wanted to ask him some questions!" Arnall's voice shouts from just beyond the doorway to the pub. "You said you wouldn't hurt him!"

The guards ignore the outcry and pull William away from the desk. His hands are forcefully yanked behind his back.

"What is the meaning of this?" William demands.

"Cavorting with a suspected spy and murderer. The Magistrate wants a word with you," one of the guards says as he pushes William through the doorway into the pub area.

"You have a job to do," William says to Arnall, though I suspect the message is meant for me. I listen as Arnall follows the guards out. His occasional disagreement with their heavy-handed tactics is ignored.

The guard that is Mary lingers at the doorway. She doesn't turn around. "I wonder if the Cult is watching. If they are, I wonder what they'll do now that William is in the open. Hmm." She walks away.

CHAPTER TWENTY

I should go.

I will not give in to Mary's transparent plan to distract me, slow me down, and pit me against the Cult while she conducts herself freely.

I should go.

I have what I need. I know where the Princess will be. The Diadem is in her possession. It's not a coincidence that she will be in that location during the equinox. Save the Princess, save the world.

I should go.

Mary wants a fight between the Cult and me. But I'll fight on my terms. They'll be after the Princess. I follow the Princess, and I'll find the Cult.

I should go.

I hear Mym race over to the open door to the courtyard. She stops with a crunching slide. **Rumble. Puff.**

I don't move.

Arnall enters the printing room from the open door to the pub.

I'm in motion. I grab and hoist him up, kick the door closed, and slam him to the wooden planks. "You lured

him here! Why?" It takes him a moment
to collect himself.

Cowering behind his hands, he
says, "I wasn't trying to lure him. I
was trying to remind him, to warn him,"
his eyes peek around his fingers, and
an expression of brave resolution forms
on his face, "Warn him about you."

"I am not the Crusher, and I'm not
a spy." I thump him against the floor.
"All you have done is put him in more
danger."

"I was trying to save him. I don't
know who you are, but you're dangerous.
William is drawn to that like a moth to
a flame. I wasn't sure at first, but
then he vanished without even a note.
And then that guard showed up asking
questions about him."

I thump him against the floor
again. "Where are they taking him?" He
doesn't answer, so I raise a fist.

"The watchhouse!" he says as he
covers his face. "They'll take him to
the watchhouse. Portugal Street, by the
new churchyard." His hands muffle the
words.

I walk away.

"It is to my great shame that my
concern led to matters becoming worse
for William," Arnall says from the

floor. "By what excuse have your intentions brought him to this point?"

I don't look back as I step into the courtyard.

With Mym behind me, scraping along the bricks of the narrow alleyway, I race toward Pater-Noster Row. *What do I know? What can I presume?* "At least four guards, plus Mary," I say out loud for Mym and my sake. "They'll put him in a cage-cart. The streets will be crowded. I don't think he'll live to see the Magistrate."

Rumble. Rumble.

"One way or the other, yes." I slow my pace and stop as we reach the bakery. A small crowd had gathered and is still dispersing. I glance around and spot the back of the cage-cart turning the corner out of sight. I run in that direction. I don't have to shift perception away from me – the gossip mill has everyone's attention. However, as I move away from Pater-Noster Row, I do catch glimpses of more than a few eyes shifting in my direction as I race along the street trying to catch up to the cart.

Rumble. Rumble.

Right. The drawing of me. In this instance, I think she be correct – *I might be drawing more attention than the boulder it appears as if I'm running from.* I reluctantly slow my pace, allowing Mym to come alongside. "Portugal Street? Where's Portugal Street?" I pace back and forth. I mentally trudge through memories of London streets about sixty years out of date.

Rumble.

My eyes flick up. "Yes, I see them." I catch some glances moving away from me. There was more than simply noticing me in those looks. "Walk. Try not to draw any more attention."

Rumble.

"I don't know. Walk casual." I exert my will. We follow in the direction of the cart, but after two more streets, it is well out of sight.

Rumble. Crackle.

I glance up. "Yes, that is possible. A rooftop run might be faster," I say, but then spot something easier. "Mym, barking dog." Without question, Mym rolls out into the street, blocking a carriage and causing the horse to rear up.

"Mym, you bad beast. Come back here!" I shout as I run over to the carriage. I open the door for Mym and then hoist myself onto the Driver's perch.

"Miss, this isn't -"

"Sorry," I say with sincerity as I shove the Driver off the carriage. I give the reins a flick. The cage-cart was traveling west, so that's the direction I maintain. I turn onto Fleet Street. No one along the wide and busy thoroughfare is surprised by another carriage. Even if they look in my direction, they'll only see a driver no more interesting than any other. Despite some hands waving for me to stop, I press on. We pass taverns and coffeehouses, gathering spots not unlike The Globe, where writers and thinkers come to share and boast. There are printing houses as well, some – most – far larger than the printing room at The Globe. I begin to see legal buildings as we approach The Temple – several carriages are here. Some privately owned, others - like the one I now drive - public conveyances. I slow and pull alongside another carriage.

"Good, Sir," I say as I incline my head and touch the tip of the nonexistent tricorn the driver of the other carriage sees. I clear my throat and lean in with a partial whisper. "I've got a fare. They're looking for Portugal Street,"

"Memory not what it used to be, old timer?" The Driver gives a good-natured chuckle. He leans in and says, "Take this next lane. Follow that to Carey Street. You should find your way from there."

"My thanks," I say and twitch the reins. I follow the directions and find myself on Portugal Street after a few more minutes. I spot the churchyard nearly right away. Like much of the public land in London, this plot of land has undergone several lifestyle changes. It seems to have begun as a cemetery – the short iron fence still separates those original internments from the rest of the open area. A public park must have come next, for there are worn resting areas. Lately, it seems as though sections have been sold off, for housing has begun to creep along the edges of this open area.

At the southwestern corner of this plot is a squat, round building. A converted watchtower, now the home of the city watch for this parish. There's an attached carriage house and a walled-off courtyard at the back, with a wide set of stairs leading up to a large front door. At the moment, there doesn't seem to be anything out of the ordinary going on. I pass the watchhouse at a steady but slow pace – I spot the cage-cart in the carriage house. I abandon my carriage at the side of the road and make my way back to the watchhouse on foot with Mym at my side. "There won't be a trial," I say as we skulk in the shadows of the alley across the way from the watchhouse. "When the Magistrate gets here, questions will be asked that William won't be able to answer. And that's all assuming the guards don't decide to have a little fun with him before that."

Crackle. Rumble.

"That's not helping." A member of the city watch approaches the watchhouse, and I crouch a little lower. "I can get in. It's getting him out which may be the problem. This isn't some drunk they've picked up after curfew. They're going to notice if he goes missing." I wait a few more seconds for the guard to get a little closer. "Get yourself across the street and wait for me near the stairs." The guard begins to walk up the stairs to the door of the watchhouse. I dash across the road and slip in behind him as he enters.

The large wooden hall beyond the front door is poorly lit and filled with several people, some seated, others pacing. The two rows of benches to one side of the chamber hold a family of three — a mother and two little ones, all with tear-streaked faces. There's also an older woman dressed in a black dress suitable for mourning. The last citizen is a young man leaning against the wall, nervously chewing on his fingernails. At the center of the room is a small desk with a seated man behind it. He's not dressed in a guard's armor — he has the appearance of an overworked, underpaid clerk. His nose is about an inch above a bit of paper on which he's writing. The scratch of the quill rises above the soft sniffles, the shuffling feet, and the hushed words between guards. Along the opposite wall are a couple of racks of weapons and three watchmen, one standing guard over the weaponry while the other two exchange words. There are some narrow stone stairs beside a stout door at the far end of this round room.

I remind myself that heightened emotions can make it challenging to stay unnoticed, so I press forward steadily, crossing the room as quickly and quietly as possible. Oddly, the man at the desk appears to be the only one to sense me as I pass him by.

"Name," he says as he briefly looks up. He rubs his eyes and then returns his attention to scribbling.

The watchman standing guard turns his head to the clerk as he speaks but quickly returns his attention to eavesdropping on the conversation between the other two watchmen.

At the door I'm thrilled to see that there is no lock. There is a bar to secure the door, but the beam is currently leaning against the wall, doing nothing. I reach for the handle, focusing all my will on masking my next action. I can hide myself from the humans, but for my kind, I'm lit up like a bonfire. I can feel the ripples of magic pulse away from me, hitting the air like bubbles breaking the surface of a still lake. And then my hand stops. I hear footsteps and voices from behind the door. I quickly back away as the door opens.

"If he's not awake when the Magistrate gets here -"

"He'll wake up quick enough when a bucket of piss is dumped on him."

Their laughter boils my blood. I slip behind them and through as the door is slowly closed. The smell is apparent immediately and only worsens with each step along the stone hallway and down the stairs. A ripe swirl of sweat, vomit, urine, and excrement. There are two torches down here, neither working too hard to drive back the dark. I see a door at the far end with a heavy lock and a large open crate next to it. There's a pit with a heavy iron grate across it, which reminds me very much of the oubliettes of my homeland, and four gaols with doors reinforced with heavy fittings.

My Patron has never punished me, but I've heard the stories. I know of one of my brothers who was kept in an oubliette for a hundred years - buried alive. There is an unease in my stomach as I lightly step around the pit to get to the doors. I check each, peering through the small barred window in each door. These are small rooms, hardly big enough for two people, and in the first there are three. Somewhat respectable clothing, but each with scuff marks and one with a bloody nose. The next has a single occupant, an older man with neat white hair. He is kneeling in prayer - the smell of alcohol was prevalent. In the third, I find William. There is no use trying to get his attention because he is unconscious on the floor.

I step away and check the locked door at the end of the room. I gently slide the small window partition aside. On the other side of the door, stairs lead up to an archway. The sounds drifting down from above suggest the carriage house. I glance down at the crate as I step away from the barred door. Several discarded items are within. A book. A few daggers. A bottle. Several personal items, such as lockets and rings. A couple of satchels – one of which I recognize. I pull William's bag from the crate and examine it. It seems intact, the contents undisturbed. I assume the items will be divided among the watchmen after sentencing. I'm surprised there's enough discipline to wait – not that it's ever a long wait.

I pull William's bag over my shoulder and peek into his small room. It's already well into the afternoon and I have no idea how much longer it will be before the Magistrate arrives. I examine the door, it won't take much effort to bring it down. I examine the door leading to the carriage house. It will require a little more effort - time enough for the other watchmen to

arrive. *Perhaps a more subtle approach?*
I examine the locks on each of the
doors. There are ways to pick these
locks, both physical and arcane, but I
haven't enough skills in either to make
that happen. I return to thoughts of
forcing the doors open. *I could open
his and then cloak us both. It would be
difficult, and Mary would have no
trouble sensing it if she is nearby.*

*If? Mary is absolutely nearby.
Watching and mocking me. Watching and
waiting. And the Cult.* My mind stops,
suddenly frozen. *The Cult? What is the
Cult going to do?* Mary is not wrong;
they will come for him if they think
him unprotected. They may come for him
regardless, and they will not care how
many watchmen and citizens die in the
effort. Objects have been taken from
them. Although I only have the one,
they are of the mind, it would seem,
that I am the only one hunting and
stealing from them. *They will come.*

The door to the carriage house
opens in, so I slide the crate over.
That's about all I can do to slow down
anyone trying to get to William.
Perhaps they'll make enough noise that
the guards will be alerted. In the
meantime, I make my way back up the
stairs and push the door wide as if a

gust of wind caught it. The moment of fright as the door swings wide and thuds against the wall is an opening to slide left and press myself against the wall. There are shouts and cries of surprise, but no one is the wiser. One of the watchmen is even laughing as he comes to shut the door. He doesn't notice me as he returns to his post by the weapon racks.

I need to figure out what the Cult will do. It's the middle of the day. I have to assume they'll sneak in, overpower the guards, and leave before anyone notices. There's a second and third level, a front and back door. Somewhere, there's a door to the walled courtyard. *Too many ways in. I can't guard them all.*

The front door opens quickly, and a watchman steps half in and shouts, "Lads, to-arms!" He points at the citizens. "You lot, out now. Run." No one moves. "Run! Now!"

Everyone is in motion. I quickly get to the front door and slip out. I can hear shouting heading in this direction. "Hiding in a mob. An interesting choice," I mutter as the first of the small groups settles in front of the watchhouse, hurling angry words. By twos, threes, and another small group of five, the mob grows to about fifty faces. I scan the crowd - plenty of men, a handful of women. Some of those women a bit cleaner than the others. The Cult is good at using society to destroy itself but less so at blending with said society. It's a distraction. I turn, not caring if I'm noticed opening the door, but that's when the crowd surges forward.

"Bring him out!"

"Murderer!"

"Turncoat!"

"Spy!"

Some in the crowd stutter-step as the mob moves forward - causing confusion - as I allow myself to be noticed. Those looking toward the door of the watchhouse suddenly became aware of a tall, broad-in-the-shoulders woman wearing a blue dress. Some don't know what to think. Others balk as if my sudden appearance is ghostly. But not everyone; plenty are entirely focused on the guards. And that's when I hear the click of a pistol hammer being pulled back - it's a woman near the stairs to my left. She's a member of the Cult, using another member to hide behind while she uses their shoulder to steady her aim.

I don't think she sees me until I
move toward them. Her eyes flick to the
sudden movement. There's a hint of
surprise, and then the pistol shifts
target to me. She'll fire before I can
get there. Or she would have, if not
for Mym suddenly appearing at ramming
speed. Both women tumble sideways, the
former landing in a crouching stance,
the pistol wielder landing on her side.
The pistol goes off. The pockets of
shouting come to a halt as the cries of
a butcherman screech out above the
noise. Attention shifts from the man
holding his wounded shoulder to the
guards – despite none of the guards
holding muskets or pistols, the crowd
assumes the shot came from them.

There's fresh panic in the crowd,
followed by chaos as some push forward
and others run. Seeing the panic, the
watchmen rush into the crowd, using
spears and halberds to shove and bash.

I leap over Mym and slam my foot
into the head of the crouching Cult
member and my fist into the one getting
to her feet. "Circle around. If a
civilian wants to flee, discourage
anyone from following them. There have
been enough victims of the Cult."

Mym rolls away.

I rush forward three steps and
then spin-kick to my left and clobber
the Cult member coming up behind one of
the watchmen.

She stumbles but recovers and
draws a green-tipped dagger.

I recognize her. I fought her at
the church. She's a member of the
Sisters of Hera. Trained to fight my
kind. Not trained to fight in a crowd.
She takes too wide a stance and is
almost immediately jostled into as the
crowd ebbs and flows - accidentally
tripping a civilian backing away from a
watchman. Off balance, she lunges
forward with a dagger.

I flick up my skirt, flaring it
out like a cloak. The heavy fabric
catches the dagger and draws it down,
giving me an opening to step forward
and drive my fist into her face.

I duck and weave, moving low
around people in the crowd as they move
in response to their own fear and
determination. Two Sisters come up on
me, pushing through the crowd, daggers
low and ready. I back up. They swipe
and then kick, but I am already
spinning around a large man smelling of
sweat and sawdust - a woodcutter. They
miss him with their daggers but hit him
with their sidekicks. He stumbles

forward a step with a cry of pain. He turns sharply, his anger blunted as he comes face to face with two women.

"I'll not hit a woman. But I will push one. Get out of here and take your friend with you."

As he reaches for them, I grab his shoulders, leap over, and then use his broad chest to launch myself at the two Cult members. The woodcutter falls backward into a group of three crowd members pressing in on a guard. The whole group tumbles to the street as I fly into the two Cult members. I elbow one in the nose. The other puts up a fight. We struggle as we come to our knees. A green-tipped dagger comes at me, but I catch her wrist. The acolyte drops the dagger and grabs it with the other hand, but again, I'm too quick and pull her friend between us as the dagger plunges. I shove forward, using the body of the acolyte as a shield, into the other Cult member, all three of us toppling to the ground. I roll off them, grabbing the arm of an innocent woman shouting at the guards.

"Bring him out!" She yells as I take her arm, pulling her into the tangle of Cult members I'd left on the ground.

"Sorry," I say as I dash away.

The crowd thickens at the stairs where many have gathered to push against the two watchmen guarding the way into the watchhouse. Two Sisters of Hera are at the back of the cluster offering encouraging shouts to enflame the fear and anger of the crowd. Before I can get to them, I hear someone in the chaos shout a warning.

"The Watch! More are coming!"

The mood shifts as self-preservation takes over. The crowd scatters. Through the fleeing mob, I spot Mary, in the guise of that young guard, dragging a member of the Cult into an alleyway. I dash in her direction, but my haste gets the better of my judgment, and a body I assumed dead reaches out for me. My ankle is caught, and I trip. I roll and save myself from fresh scrapes and bruises and turn to my attacker, a mere child dressed in the white and burgundy of an acolyte. There's little to fear. She has managed to get herself over onto her front, but there she stays, struggling to move any further. I glance back. Mary is gone. "Merde!"

I sit for a moment and allow my will to wash over me. The watchmen have gained control of the situation, and they don't notice me as they begin to

chase after the dispersing mob.
Hopefully, Mym will do what she can to
allow most of them to escape. The
passions of those poor citizens were
obviously whipped into a frenzy by the
Cult. All used as a distraction to get
to William – *to get to me.*

The head of the Cult member tilts
up. Blood from her still bleeding nose
smears her face. There's also blood on
the street from where a wound in her
back bled - and probably continues to
bleed. She's young. Perhaps sixteen.
Too young to be a member of a group of
assassins and thieves. Too young to be
dying on the streets. She tries to
speak, but instead she coughs up blood.

"They left you to die," I say.

"Th-they left me to give you a
message. We have him," she struggles to
say.

"It doesn't have to be like this,"
I sigh.

"It will always be like this,
Avatar. Always,"

I'm surprised at the strength with
which she says that. "You'll gain
nothing from this." Her responding
smile is even more irritating than
William's smirk.

"You will bring what you have taken. You will bring the Princess. You will do this, or your pet dies."

"The Princess? Not just the Diadem? What do you want with the Princess?" There's no reply. She lowers her head and is gone.

CHAPTER TWENTY-ONE

I scan the vicinity. The watch has scared off the mob. The Cult had indeed left this acolyte to die - none of them are to be seen either. "Message received," I mumble as I get to my feet. Mary's plan worked – the truth of that is embarrassing. She wanted the Cult and I to fight. To either kill or hinder each other while she captured one of them to torture for information. With less embarrassment and more anger, I realize that the Cult also got what they wanted. The Cult wanted William. They wanted to give me that message. "What do they want with the Princess?" I rub the back of my head in thought. *They want the Diadem, so why not take it at this point?* I hear Mym roll up alongside me as thoughts spin in my head. "I'm getting really tired of being behind on this." I can feel the anger in my throat. The taste of it in my mouth. The twisting in my gut.

Rumble.

"Then no more following the trail," I say as I scoop Mym up and run. I'm not going to deliver the Princess to them. They want her, but can't get to her, and they think they can manipulate me into getting her for them. I'll not jump at their bait. *Time to kick in a door*. I think about retrieving the carriage I stole, but I need a guide and someone better capable of coaxing speed out of a horse. We're not far from the streets William said McAllister frequented with his carriage.

It takes me twenty minutes to find him. He's at the next corner, a fare exiting his carriage. I run up to him. "Sir," I say as I come up on him.

Despite the cool spring evening, I'm sweating from the trouble to find him. His eyebrows go up upon seeing the sight of me, but he doesn't speak on my disheveled appearance. "About finished for the night, Miss, oh —" He recognizes me and tips his tricorne.

"Mister McAllister, I need your expertise again," I say, reaching into William's bag and finding his purse full of money. I take a fist full and press it into McAllister's hand. "Wycombe, if you please. As fast as you can."

"I know the way, Ma'am, but," he pauses to look around, "Mister Monkton?"

I squeeze his fist around the money I had given him. "As fast as you

can, if you please," I whisper. He
nods, and Mym and I get into the
carriage.

Much to my frustration, we travel
at a steady pace through the streets of
London as we make our way north and
west toward the city outskirts. But,
once on the open road, McAllister is
not shy about calling for speed from
his steed. Through the night, he
presses his horse. It is still dark by
the time we roll into Wycombe - driver
and horse exhausted. "It is the hour of
the bread makers, as William would put
it," I say to Mym. I hang my head out
the window. The carriage trundles down
the High Street of this thriving
village, coming to a large and
prominent medieval timber-framed
building along the road. The sign
hanging from the wall claims this to be
The Wheatsheaf Pub & Inn. A much older
sign, a bit lower, names the place The
Gathering Hall.

I exit the carriage, helping Mym
down - who rolls over and settles in
along the wall. I step over to the
Driver's perch and extend my hand.
"Come along, Mister McAllister. You'll
be having a room and some food, and
I'll hear nothing about it." His smile
lights up his tired face. I help him

down and walk ahead of him into the tavern. It is mostly dark but for a couple of candle sconces. An older woman appears from a back room. She looks at us and then around us to the carriage through the window.

"Welcome, travelers. I'm afraid the kitchen won't be available for a bit yet, but I can get you something to drink."

"An ale, a room, and food when it is available for my friend here. And care for the horse if you're amenable." McAllister sits at a table as the woman disappears into the back room. I pace the room, returning my attention to the woman as she reappears.

"Just the one ale?" she says as she sets down the drink.

"Yes, and some information, Madam." I set some money on the table.

"You have my attention," she smiles and slides the money into her apron pocket. "And you can call me Molly, young miss."

"Persephone. And that gentleman is McAllister." They exchange smiles and nods. "I'm looking for someone - or possibly a group."

She laughs and takes a seat at the table with McAllister. I'm not sure what creaks more, the chair or her bones. "That don't narrow it down. But I know most people around the village."

"These would be strange people, may even be strangers. Perhaps there are rumors of shadows moving in the night that you associate with robed figures."

Molly nods and sighs as she scratches her chin. She sighs again as she gets up. "I'll get you another," she smiles at McAllister and makes her way toward the backroom. I follow and give her a bit of a shock as she comes back into the main room.

"Forgive my forwardness, but a friend is in need, and any information you have will help."

She purses her lips and gives me a disapproving look before moving around me. She sets the mug down and then lowers herself into a chair. "I'll not have you stirring things up again."

"I assure you, I'm only here to help a friend." I take a seat at the table.

"Maybe you are, and maybe you're not," Molly rubs her face.

As the awkward silence lingers, McAllister raises his mug and says, "The ale's very nice,"

With an irritated grumble, Molly leans forward and shakes a bony finger at me. "Sir Dashwood is a good man. A scoundrel for sure, but a good man. When hard times have come, he's not like these other lords who shutter indoors. He's out with his money, coming up with some work to be done to keep the lads busy. You'll not find many 'round here to speak ill of him."

The name Dashwood means nothing to me. I don't recall seeing it among William's notes. As I recall, William said he spent most of his time investigating the more recent rumors. If this Dashwood was an early puppet of the Cult… *I think I'm finally where I need to be*. It's a moment before I realize I'm staring. I watch Molly's expression change from irritation to regret.

"I've said too much." She tries to get up, but I stop her.

"Or not enough. Please, I'm not interested in Sir Dashwood. I'm just trying to help a friend." I don't remove my hand from her forearm, as I feel it's the only thing keeping her in that chair. *I really don't want to hurt you, but I am in a bit of a rush*, I think and somehow manage not to say it out loud.

"He's a good man, Ma'am," McAllister says. "If he's in trouble, you'll not dishonor anyone by helping this lady."

Molly takes comfort in those words. I feel her relax and pull my hand back. "You're here about those rumors. You'd probably find out sooner or later, anyway. They all lead back to Sir Dashwood's – meetings. Gatherings of his friends. There's some unsavory talk about what they'd get up to. Debauchery and such. Mind, I serve spirits, and there are plenty who come here, so I'm not exactly sure what all the fuss was,"

"Was?" I ask.

"Yes. Been a few years now since there's been any talk of his gatherings. At least 'round here. Very respectable now."

They moved! I shout in my head. *Why? Is Dashwood still involved?* But I don't press her on those questions. I don't want her thinking my focus is Dashwood. *I just need to know what he knows.* "I think Sir Dashwood may know how to help my friend. I'd like to call on him…"

Molly purses her lips again and glances at McAllister, who nods reassuringly. She looks back at me. "North of the village, a short walk up into the hills. Lovely estate with a lake."

I rise and McAllister begins too as well. "No, Mister McAllister. You've done more than enough. Pay me no more mind. I will find my way back to London if I have need. Please stay, rest, and keep enjoying this fine woman's hospitality." I pull William's purse out of his bag, set it on the table, and then leave.

As directed, I travel north from the village center, moving along a country road. The air is cool and sweet. Soothing insect noises accompany me – and are only partially drowned out by Mym crunching through the soil and gravel as she rolls alongside me. The sky is dark, with only the faintest hues beginning to appear on the eastern horizon.

Crackle. Puff. Rumble.

"I have a plan."

Rumble.

"No, I'm not kicking down the front door." *Not anymore*, I mentally stick out my tongue. Unfortunately, the all too familiar sense of uncertainty fills my mind. I try to reassure myself that this could still be the Cult stronghold. *If Dashwood is in charge of*

*keeping things quiet, he just might be
doing a better job of it these days.*

We travel through some woods along
the country road, across a narrow river
in the lull of two shallow hills, and
as we crest the subsequent rise, we
find ourselves at the country estate of
Sir Dashwood. It is a somewhat muted
architectural style compared to other
grand homes of the upper class I've
seen. Of Dutch influence, if I'm not
mistaken. The structure is all straight
lines with a simple facade reminiscent
of more classical Roman inspirations.
The large building has two wings with
most of the house having a view of the
lake. We approach slowly, mainly so I
can formulate a new plan.

I haven't decided what to do by
the time we reach an east-facing
portico. Before stepping onto the
porch, I tap Mym but can't find the
words. I don't want to admit that this
is yet another mistake. That this is
more wasted time. But I don't have to
say any of that. I sense understanding,
as she rolls away without comment. I
press forward and am not entirely
surprised to find this side door
unlocked. I enter into a music room. A
lively fresco occupies the walls here,
depicting the gods at a banquet. I see

several familiar faces but no Charon. "He doesn't really like his family anyway," I mutter as I slowly crack the door. I hear movement. The house staff is about. "But probably not the Master," I say, slipping into the corridor.

Rather than tiptoeing about, I shift eyes away from me as I move through the house. I pass a small study, a drawing room, through the main hall and the salon, checking behind doors for the bed chamber of Sir Dashwood. Off the main hall are stairs to the second floor, but I decided to finish my tour of the main ground level. Each room is furnished in tasteful luxury. Statues, busts, paintings, plants, tapestries, fine rugs, marvelously carved clocks, frescos, all of it happy and light, giving this beacon of wealth a very warm, homey feeling. However, as I pass yet another statue of two nude figures intertwined and still more paintings of revelry, I get a more unmistakable impression of the Master of the House.

I've almost walked from wing to wing when the snort of someone sleeping catches my ear. I press my ear to the door. Whoever is on the other side is most definitely asleep. I creep into the chamber and spy two individuals on a sizable bed. Despite knowing that her Ladyship sleeping on the right side of the bed could be a Cult member as Jane was to Robert Wren, the only thing I know for certain is Dashwood's involvement. I move to the left side of the bed. Dashwood is on his back. I stare at his plump face, prominent nose, and small eyes. *Still no plan.*

And then his eyes blink open.

My hand is faster than his scream, "Shhhh." For good measure, I pull my morningstar over my shoulder and lay the pointy bits on his chest. "I don't want to disturb your lovely wife." His eyes dart sideways to the woman sleeping on her side, facing away from us. "Do you believe I can do you a great deal of harm?"

He nods.

"Do you believe I have any reason to lie to you?"

He thinks about this and then shakes his head.

"Good. Come with me. Stay silent. Do as I say, and no one will get hurt."

He slowly gets up from his bed. He's dressed in a heavy nightshirt, and as he's reaching for his bedrobe and slippers, I give him a quiet growl. His

hand darts back to his side, and he
joins me by the door.

I hear footsteps in the corridor
and wait for silence before pushing Sir
Dashwood out of the room. I gamble on
the symmetry of the house and continue
along the corridor. Thankfully, we come
to a vestibule and a glass door that
leads out onto the western-facing
portico. "Keep walking," I nudge him as
we step onto the grass.

As we arrive at the lake, I notice
that the morning dew has thoroughly
soaked his feet, ankles, and the hem of
his nightshirt. He lifts his dirty
feet, inspects them, and almost loses
his balance as he rubs a sore spot on
the ball of his foot. I spot Mym about
fifty feet away under a large tree. She
begins to roll toward me, but I hold up
a hand, asking her to wait for now.

"I have questions," I say.

"So do I," he says – with a rather
bold tone. He catches my raised eyebrow
and squares his shoulders. "I have
traveled. I have seen. I have
experienced," he says with a chuckle.
"I have lived a life, and although I
feel I have more that I can do, I am
ready to face my death with dignity,"
he says and then glances down at his
nightshirt with a bit of embarrassment.

"There are scandalous rumors about you."

"All true," he says with a smile. "I have, in fact, had many a flight of fancy regarding a maiden, such as yourself, sneaking into my bed chamber." He clears his throat, becoming more serious. "But, come now, it is plain to see that you are not the type to sneak into a gentleman's bed chamber for fancy or on rumor. Speak plainly."

"Cloaks and hoods in the night. Strangers coming and going. I ask you, Sir Dashwood, to which cult do you belong?"

He chuckles, then, seeing my sincere expression, he rubs his smile away. "Not here on rumor, but I see your information isn't completely accurate. I am not part of a cult."

I sigh inwardly. I feel my attempt to get ahead evaporating and the sudden weight of time wasted.

"I'm not ashamed to say I am the leader of a gathering of like-minded individuals. Or used to be. I've stepped back in recent years."

He interprets my silence as reason to continue.

He clears his throat. "I had the pleasure of being a spiritual successor to Duke Wharton and his group. Thinkers and satirists. People who find social normality to be subjective. People who are smart enough to know how things could be done better, but sadly cowardly enough only to gripe about it among the like-minded."

"And these are the people dashing about with hoods up."

"Well, yes and no. As the group I established became a known secret amongst certain levels of society, we began to attract a number of members. It became prudent to move to more established surroundings. I have some natural chalk caves right here on these grounds. I had them expanded and made habitable. We were the Knights of Saint Francis," he smiles broadly. "We joked about society. Read poetry and books deemed unsavory. We partook of exotics. Ideas were shared. Meaningful arguments had. All opinions were welcome. There was freedom of mind and body for all. But," he scratches at the back of his head and looks away.

"But?"

"My life's story… this seems a rather unbecoming reason to jostle a man from his bed."

"Talk, Dashwood," I poke him with my morningstar.

He sighs and takes a breath. "You see, my social stature and political standing have waxed and waned – mostly due to my own doings. But, recently, my star is in ascension. I'm up for a seat. I thought I'd try some of this being respectable business. Rather than *talking* about helping and change, you know, actually *doing* it."

His words have the tone of truth, but there is more. There's something he's not saying. I step toward him, and he throws his hands between us.

"You have to understand," he blurts, "my wife, a wonderful woman, is also a prudish woman. She's lovely enough to ignore or at least tolerate my excesses, but she is a woman of station, so… I had the group moved again." He is saddened by this – embarrassed and regretful. "As I said, we attracted all sorts. There was obviously a bit of scrutiny to join, but in the end," he shrugs, "*Fay ce que Voudras* – do what thou wilt. That philosophy binds me, and so too all our Knights. A few eventually joined – Bates, Whitehead, oh, and what was his name? Thompson, I think. They had partners who, well, at times they would make me blush. Suggestions and demands began to be made…"

"What suggestions?"

"I'm all for making fun of Crown and Church, and we played at all sorts of mockery, but these new women were suggesting odd rituals and demanding The Temple – that's what we called our main meeting area – be expanded. Something about the drawings they showed me unsettled my spirit. I politely declined to pay for such an expansion. Not that it mattered much," his words drift off.

Dashwood glances over his shoulder, I think not looking for help. His eyes are those of a man not wanting to be overheard. He begins to fidget with his fingers.

"Ah,"

"Ah?"

"You're full of regret, Sir Dashwood, and I don't mean about your hedonistic life. You made a decision to do something, and you've been unhappy with it. Your wife asked you to do something – no… you did something for your wife," I pause as my thoughts solidify. "It *didn't matter* because you weren't making decisions for the group anymore, or seldom so. Soon after these new members came around, your political appeal improved. You were spending less and less time with your Knights. Your wife, a woman of station, would rather have you with a seat in parliament than as a scoundrel philosopher. So, you had the group moved again."

"Yes," he breathes a heavy sigh. "She grew more and more angry and ashamed of the things she was hearing about my gatherings. As my respectability flourished, she became obsessed with the idea that the Knights would end us. So, I did what I had to do." He takes a breath and utters a regretful groan as he turns to look toward a mausoleum. "One does miss one's youth and vigor, though. And one does feel as if one has abandoned his friends." His mind drifts away.

"Where?" I snap.

Dashwood blinks at my outburst and stammers. "Medmenham. I have an architect friend, a member of our group. He has this property with a defunct abbey along the Thames. I rented the land from him and handled most expenses while he and his friends renovated and excavated. I mean, I had my suggestions and directions - you know how it is, things I'd learned from expanding these caves I made sure were implemented at the new site. However, my duties elsewhere kept most of the leadership in the hands of others.

They've been calling themselves the Monks of Medmenham."

We stare at each other for several moments as I try to put pieces together in my mind.

"I must admit. I find myself very attracted to your strength and intelligence -"

He's cut off as I take a step into him.

"Well put - wrong time for such statements," he nervously clears his throat.

I step away from Dashwood. I turn to the lake, casting my eyes out over the water as my mind sinks inward. They didn't need *Dashwood*. They needed his money and influence. I thought this to be the base from which they spread their fear. But ultimately, it didn't fit their liking. The ritual needs to be enacted at certain places at certain times. *The abbey*. They weren't spotted while searching for artifacts. They were spotted searching for the proper ritual location. They needed a legitimate reason to be at that abbey. They required a willing group. They distracted Dashwood with other priorities and used him to build them exactly what they needed. The Cult wants change and will use murder and mayhem for that end – and I think now I know who they're going to start with.

"Are – are we finished? It's just, well, my feet are cold and wet, and I'd rather not catch my death."

I turn to him. "What changes did you insist upon?"

"To the caves? Air vents and a secondary egress. It can get a little stuffy down there when all are in attendance."

Secondary egress – another way in, perhaps a forgotten or neglected way in. That feeling that I had wasted my time in coming here lifts. "Tell me about this secondary egress."

A prideful smile springs to his lips. "Rather proud of it, I must say. It's disguised as an old well, off in the wood near the abbey. Has a capstone to keep the curious from getting into it. Can only be opened from the inside."

I stare at him with a placid expression while my mind works – I enjoy the way he awkwardly looks away. I need to get to the abbey fast… *but portals are so noisy*. The Cult won't know. *Mary will*. But Mary is probably already there with a plan. Already there waiting for me to attack the Cult and allow her to sneak in during the chaos. *I have no frame of reference to even form a portal to Medmenham.* I tap at my bag, very much aware that Sir Dashwood is staring again. *I need to get there, but I think I really do need to save a Princess first.* My ears catch the sound of someone calling for Sir Dashwood from the house. I snap my fingers. I hear Mym churning the ground under her as she races towards me.

"By Heaven!" Dashwood exclaims and stumbles backward, falling onto his rear end.

"Calm yourself, Dashwood. You are going to live yet." I use the chalk from my satchel to draw the circle and runes of a portal. It only takes a moment and then Mym and I step into the swirl of grass that forms. "You're sleep walking, Sir Dashwood. For your sanity and peace of mind, I suggest you believe that."

CHAPTER TWENTY-TWO

Mym and I drop softly into the grass of the Spring Gardens. The crackle of energy in the air surrounds us. I watch the small bolts of jagged magic spread over the ground and even up a tree, causing leaves to shake loose. The rumble dissipates as my eyes scan for anyone who might have heard or seen our arrival. The tents of the art show are still up, and I wonder if there is anything exciting planned for this last day. At the moment, however, the grounds are clear and quiet. I know this public land, and at this hour, even with the art show, I think it is the closest and emptiest place to our destination.

Carlton House.

With its gardens buttressed up against the public lands, the mansion looms ahead of me up a small rise. The building is set on a slope, with this end of the house much higher than the front street side. I was here just after it was built, chasing a demon through its pristine corridors. I can tell there have been some renovations since then. However, the principal courtyard is still there and, as I recall, guarded by red coats. In comparison to the city watch, the red coats are better trained, have better instincts, and are better disciplined. A greater concern, but getting past them won't be an issue.

Rumble.

"No, not this time. Maybe the Cult has been here. Maybe they haven't. They gave me a message after the watchhouse fight - bring the Princess. For whatever reason, they are reluctant or blocked from getting to her on their own. I suspect a trap. Stay close, we may need to leave in a hurry."

We move up the grassy rise, using trees and bushes when available - but with haste, as time is not in our favor. I can tell by the light in the sky and the shifting shadows that the sun has fully peaked above the horizon. If the Princess is here and still alone, catching her in her bed chamber will be my best chance of controlling the conversation.

I slow to a walk as I spot the first of the red coats pacing the front of the courtyard. The problem with a good guard is that they'll be on alert. It makes it very difficult to shift their attention away from me. Even if they don't register me, they will detect a presence approaching on them. I crouch down behind a row of hedges about fifty feet from the soldier. "The thing about good guards is that their greatest strength is also their greatest weakness," I whisper to Mym. It's not hard to find a suitable stone around the base of the hedge. I grip the stone tightly and judge its weight. "They'll respond to a disturbance. It's an old trick, but it works almost every time."

I wait for my moment. As the red coat turns towards me, I launch my projectile, striking him square in the forehead. His musket drops as he doubles over. His cry of pain echoes off the walls of the courtyard, drawing the attention of several other soldiers.

"Who threw that?!" the bloodied soldier yells, his voice colored a bit more with anger than pain.

There's some light chuckling from the other guards as the injury is inspected.

And, while they are distracted, my will is sufficient enough to allow Mym and myself to pass into the courtyard unnoticed. I take the first turn down a wide archway and brick tunnel leading to a second, more secluded courtyard.

From here I have my choice of several doors to enter the house. "There are bedrooms on the top floor. I believe this door will bring us close to the library. As I recall, there's a staircase in the hall beyond that."

I help Mym up the stairs to the side door. We enter into a small drawing room, currently being redecorated. Thankfully, the workers have yet to report for duty. We do pass into a library next. Here, we find two servants facing the window, watching the ruckus I had left behind. As I remembered, beyond the library is a small hall with a staircase. As we start up, a young man comes racing down. I grab Mym and hold her above my head, pressing myself as far against the wall as possible. I'm not sure what he sees, but there are mutterings about "More odd art."

Arriving on the top floor, I find myself in a split corridor, with a branch ahead of me and another to my left. Each direction has several doors and archways, but the path ahead has tarps, scaffolding, and a crew of workers. "I don't think a Princess would allow herself to sleep beside such noise."

Crackle.

"If you like, we can call it fate. I'm allowing my instincts to carry me."

Crackle.

"I think it's a fair guess based on what I see."

Crackle.

"Call it whatever you want. We're going this way."

Whoever sleeps in the first bedroom is up and about already, as two chambermaids are fluffing and resetting the room.

We pass a small sitting room next and see a single couch, a small table with a white and blue vase, and a maid dusting some shelves.

The next room is brightly painted and the heavy curtains are pulled open, but the room feels empty despite the light. Paintings are on the walls, and the room has the necessities for sleeping, but it feels cold and unlived in. My eyes are drawn to scratch marks on the floor. My feet follow my eyes, and I find myself gliding my fingertips over the slashes in the wood. I glance up. There is a fireplace, and above the fireplace, a pair of crossed swords. I suspect the room once belonged to someone who practiced their swordplay in secret but didn't have the strength or proper training to prevent the tip of the blade from catching the floor. With thoughts falling into place inside my mind, I back out of the room and close the door. I turn to the door behind me. "It will be this one."

I crack the door. There's a soft but distinct patter of feet and then silence. The room is dark, but enough light creeps around the curtains to keep me from bumping into anything as I step inside. I can see someone on the bed – unfortunately, that's about all I can see clearly. By the slight shifting and general body language, I get the sense that despite their prone position, this person is not asleep. Mym at my side, we move to the bedside. "Princess," I say to the small body under the duvet.

There's a moment of silence, and then, "Yes." The defeated reply, is followed by a sigh and the covers are pulled down. The small face stares up at me – squints, trying to see through the dark - and then the mouth goes slack, and the eyes open wider. "You're not Abigail."

I shake my head.

"Are you here to kill me?"

This strikes me as a very odd question. *Are there that many assassins who wait to speak to their victims before murdering them?* I shake my head.

Her eyes dart away from me in the direction of Mym. "Are you going to smash me with that rock?"

"I just said I wasn't here to kill you."

"You didn't say anything. You just shook your head."

I fight the urge to smash her with Mym. "I'm a friend. I'm here to tell you that you are in danger."

She sighs again as she pulls the covers off to reveal her traveling clothes. "Father says I'm always in danger. There are always people ready to murder me."

I step out of the way as the Princess gets down from the bed and moves toward the window. "I don't know about always, but there is a real threat against you at the moment."

Princess Louisa pulls back the curtains, letting in a flood of light. "Well, come on then." She picks up a satchel from the window cushion.

"I don't understand."

"My father sent you, didn't he? To replace that old stick in the mud, Walpole, since he's abandoned me. I must say, you're better than the ten soldiers Father threatened to shackle me to."

"Your Highness," I say as I come around the bed, "I'm not here to replace anyone. And if you're implying that you are under orders to stay put, then I'm here to say, follow those orders."

"So, my father didn't send you," Louisa is struck by a coughing fit, which she muffles by quickly placing a small pillow from the window seat over her face.

I wait and feel somewhat concerned when the pillow comes away from her face, and there's a moment when the Princess has trouble breathing. When this passes, I speak. "I'm not here to kill you, and I'm not here to take you anywhere. I'm here to make sure you are safe. Stay here. In fact, have your father post those ten soldiers right here in your room."

"Oh my," she giggles and turns to face the window. "No, we can't have that."

It's my turn to sigh. I step toward her, my eyes playing around the room as I contemplate tying her up and taking her someplace safe until all of this is over. Now that the curtains have been pulled, I can see the room is decorated in reds and yellows. A bit austere. Not the room I pictured for such an adventurous young woman. Perhaps a temporary lodging, or maybe something she would grow into. *Or maybe more of a place of honor.* As my eyes come back to the Princess, I find her staring at me - sad eyes, with just a hint of a snarl to her upper lip. As she recognizes me looking at her, her face becomes more placid.

"This isn't my room - well, it is, I suppose - but I never think of it as such. This was my sister's room when we stayed at Carlton House. This might be the longest I've ever spent in one location." Louisa steps away from the window. "She died."

"I'm aware of the passing, Your Highness."

"Passing," Louisa scoffs. "She was murdered, and I think me as well." She coughs, though the fit is much shorter this time. "Weak, sickly - Father has tried to marry me off, but there aren't many willing to go through with such a feat once they've heard me cough a few times."

"And the sneaking out is to prove you are vibrant and adventurous."

"I've always been adventurous. The sneaking out is just fun."

"Sneaking out is dangerous."

"Just so," Louisa smiles. "You sound like her - like Elizabeth. I think she enjoyed Father's rules and the rules of society. I think she liked knowing what she could and couldn't do. She certainly enjoyed telling me what I could and couldn't do. She never allowed me to play with her things – her dresses and jewelry," Louisa stares longingly at the armoire. "I think I miss her telling me to stop touching things." She shakes off her mournful expression and looks at me. "Come on then," she walks back over to the window. "I would have liked to have been off during the night, but on such short notice, it took a bit to pull the things I would need together."

"I'm not taking you anywhere, Your Highness."

"Ugh! You're as useless as that old goat."

"Walpole?"

"Who else? My shadow. Father says I can sneak out, but Walpole goes with me. I've often wondered about the weight of the favor owed for Walpole, a crafter of words, to put up with such a command."

"And he is no longer your escort?"

"Oh, he may well be again. Tomorrow perhaps. I'm told he has been called away, though I overheard he got himself into some trouble. A fight, if you can believe it. Anyway, by tomorrow, it will be too late."

"Too late?"

Louisa clears her throat. "Coming?" She turns to the window.

"Louisa," I snap. I'm pleased by the sheepish demeanor that befalls her. "I am about to make a ruckus that will draw attention."

"You said you weren't going to kill me."

"I'm not. But I am going to draw the guards. I may even allow them to see me before I go. Either way, I'm sure there will be many eyes on you to keep you safe after I've gone." I say sternly. I walk up to her, take her hand — there's a slight flinch - and then gently, as if perambulating around a garden, I lead her back to her bed and sit her upon it. "Stay here. Be a child. Play with your sister's things. Keep it all in this room. Be safe." I can tell by her expression that she is not pleased. I'm struck by a memory of myself at this age and suddenly feel like a hypocrite. *But this needs to be done*. I sigh. "Would you like to help me with something fun?"

Despite the squinting uncertainty, she says, "Yes."

I give her the chalk from my bag. "I'm going to instruct you to draw a picture."

"And this will be fun?"

"Let's find out." I step back and gesture to the floor. Louisa gives me a begrudging shrug and gets on her hands and knees. "Where were you sneaking off to?"

"A place."

Don't crush her with Mym – I think this hard enough that I'm pretty sure Mym picks up on the thought, but I don't say it. Instead, I tell her, "That's alright. You don't have to tell me. Picture it. Picture it in as much detail as you can and draw the symbols as I instruct you."

"Picture a place, but draw symbols?"

"It's a trick. Trust me. If you concentrate hard enough, the symbols will become the picture in your mind."

Louisa shrugs but obeys as I have her draw a circle and the symbols around it. I could have done this much faster, but I need her memory. *She won't know where the Cult Stronghold*

358

*is, but If I'm correct, this will
hopefully send me to the Lady Elizabeth
inn. I think this will work. I hope
this works.* As she finishes, I ask her
to stand over by the bed. When she
steps away, I kneel and place my hands
upon the runes in front of me at the
edge of the circle she drew. *Open*, I
think with quiet intensity. The magic
spreads through the runes into the
circle, and I feel the connection as
the ethereal pathway is created. Louisa
jumps onto the bed. "Mym," I call out.
She rolls around the bed. Louisa
watches, not with fear but with
intrigue and astonishment. I step with
Mym into the swirl of wood as it forms.
"This is all a dream. Stay."

Louisa nods.

Then, as we sink into the floor,
"Surprise!" Louisa leaps at me,
clinging to my chest.

CHAPTER TWENTY-THREE

There's a difference between the skills necessary to wield a weapon and those necessary for arcane usage. I've always envisioned it as the difference between a savory item and a sweet treat. When you cook a steak or roast some vegetables - a little under, a little over, it doesn't matter. Dash it with spice. Maybe a cream sauce. Depending on your skill and imagination, you can pivot to fix the problem. When you bake a cake, the measurements need to be precise. Too many eggs, bake it for too long, too little flour, too much flour, switching salt and sugar - you get inedible mush or an inedible brick.

These are my thoughts as I'm flung from the portal about twenty feet above the ground and at an angle. I hit the tall grass, skid, tumble, and roll into the side of a building. There's a crack and the faint sound of a crash, as if something has been knocked from the other side of the wall I'm now leaning against.

The rumble of the portal dissipates just as I hear a creak and the groan of a heavy door opening. Footsteps follow, and the mumble of voices. I slide down the wall until I'm lying low among the grass.

"The whole building shook. Someone fired a cannon," a man speaks.

"It did not, and I see no cannon. Thunder, perhaps," another man responds.

"Out of a clear sky?"

"Maybe these grounds have decided they take issue with what we do here." There's a chuckle.

"These grounds have had more than enough time to object to our presence. It's rather rude to be making a fuss now."

"Come on. We've got a whole other cart to unload."

"The whole building shook."

"A story we can tell the others when they arrive."

The two men retreat. I hear the heavy door close. I wait a few seconds more. My senses have almost fully returned, but the ache in my shoulder where I slammed into the building needs a few moments more. With my eyes cast upward as I lay in the grass, I notice the sky is fully alight. *It is much later in the day*, I think with some distress. "I hope it's the same day," I

say as I strain to get to my feet. I
lean on the side of the building as I
get to my feet. The portal has taken a
lot out of me. I meant it only for Mym
and myself – the addition of the
Princess threw off a great many things.
The portal needed more energy to
stabilize, and I was the only spring to
draw from. *I don't think it would have
drawn from Mym.* I look around, but
other than the building, all I see is
tall grass and woods.

Mym? I project as best I can with
my foggy mind. I don't get a sense of
her. But she's not the one I'm worried
about. "The Princess," I mutter with
irritation and concern. I step away
from the building, and only just
realize my morningstar had been pulled
from its sheath at my back. It seems to
have cracked a stone as it landed. As I
lean in to pick up my trusted weapon, I
see that it isn't a broken stone but a
grave marker. Weathered and forgotten,
but it is not alone. There are several
scattered through the tall grass. I
take a step back and glance up at the
building.

I'm not sure how it is possible. A
mix of what the Princess was thinking
and what I was thinking – *the arcane is
a strange and wild beast.* "The Abbey.

Surely, it must be. At least I know where I am," I say as I begin to circumnavigate the structure. It's larger than I imagined. From what I can see, the roof has been worked on extensively, but the walls and other stonework have been left with their rustic appearance. *For ambiance or a purpose?* I wonder. I make my way around to the front of the structure and stand in awe of the pleasant landscape. The Thames is within walking distance. There's a lovely field. "I wonder if she landed in the river?" I smirk but quickly chastise myself, "The brazen youth might not be able to swim." I stare at the river momentarily and then shrug, "Well, we can at least hope she is soggy." I say out loud, forgetting that Mym isn't by my side.

I must allow the moment of tranquility to pass. There is a mission to complete and less time to do so now. I'm not sure how much, but it would seem the time I had hoped to gain with a quick portal jump has been lost. *And my arrival has certainly made some noise.* Part of me wishes I had retained Mister McAllister's employment. But I recall those men had mentioned unloading a wagon. *Preparations are still being made.*

I backtrack to where I had landed and sneak to the door the two men had come through. I ease the door open but stop when I hear, "You didn't latch the door -"

"Maybe *you* didn't latch the door. Worry about it later. Help me with this."

I push the door open a bit more and slip into the open courtyard beyond. I watch the two men disappear through an archway on my left. I gather from the smell that it is the stables. There's a well at the center of this courtyard, but as it is not in the woods near the abbey and lacks a capstone, I assume it is not the secondary egress Dashwood was so proud of designing. Across the yard, I see a stout door that must lead into the abbey. I make my way to the right and reach a broken wall where a door used to be. Through the hole, I see the dilapidated remains of a chapel.

I see the two men reappear, carrying a crate between them. "You sure this is safe?"

"Would you rather heave all this stuff up and down those stairs? Nothing to worry about. A bit of a splash. Thomas is down there with one of the boats. He'll collect everything before it gets soggy."

A voice echoes up from the well. It is too distorted for me to understand from where I'm standing, but the two men laugh and drop the crate down the well. I hear the splash and more words from the man below.

"What did he say?"

"Thomas wants to know if you want to trade. Do you?"

"What? Punt around in one of those boats? Nay. I'm not too fond of the water. Can't swim."

"No!" The other man leans over the side of the well and yells. "You're doing fine, my lad. More to come." The two men return to the stables. From that direction I also hear other voices – it would seem the *others* are arriving. I don't see who has arrived, but one of the men calls over his shoulder as he returns to the courtyard, "About an hour. Everything will be in order, don't you worry."

I step over the rocky threshold into the forgotten chapel. *Do these men work for the Cult, or are they here for the gathering the Princess was eager to join?* As my thoughts collect around that question, I quickly inspect my surroundings. Although the roof has been repaired, the chapel has, for the most part, been left unattended. A cracked and uneven floor. There are weather-worn benches. Dust and debris blown in from the nearby woods cover most surfaces. I see no footsteps or signs that anyone has been here for some time. I check my own path to make sure I am leaving no trail.

"That's the last of it!" I hear outside.

I turn to watch the two men walk in this direction. They don't enter the chapel but instead open the other door leading into the abbey. I listen, but no one approaches from either the hole in the wall or the half-open door ahead of me. I stealthly move toward that door, and as I do, I answer my earlier question. *There's every chance they work for the Cult and don't even realize it. I would say that's the game here. The Cult wormed its way into this gathering and has manipulated things to fit their needs. These people are being used – metaphorically digging their own graves.*

I can hear the voices of a few different people drifting this way as I approach the door. I peek through the ajar door into a hall – a statuary. I see beautiful polished black stone floors and cobbled walls leading to a vaulted ceiling. At the center, arranged in a circle, are six statues. I see Zeus, Hera, Poseidon, Aphrodite, Athena, and Dionysus - all nudes. It's not all that different from seeing one's parents naked. My eyes flinch away but are drawn back by laughter among the men assembled near the statues. From my vantage point, I don't see much besides a narrow archway along the wall to my right and a pair of large doors across the hall from me, which I guess is the main entrance.

They share a few more minutes of idle talk before moving in the direction of and passing through the narrow archway. Soon after, I hear the footsteps of others arriving - three women. They enter the statuary by way of an entrance or a corridor I cannot see and make their way to whatever is beyond the narrow archway. Over the next several minutes, two other small groups arrive. These members come dressed in hooded robes, attire that very much fits the surroundings, though I doubt any of them have taken monastic orders. Those in the hooded robes wait and are soon joined by a line of similarly dressed people entering the hall from the archway. Every other person in this line carries a lantern.

"Brothers, Sisters," A man at the front of the line says warmly as he approaches the group at the statues, "Welcome. Do we have any novices? Any nuns among us during this hallowed gathering?"

Two hands go up.

"Welcome to you as well. Follow the Brothers and Sisters. They will guide you. I say to you, our new members, our nuns, that you must nay speak what ye are about to witness. Great evil will befall ye if you have thoughts to betray us."

With everyone having their hoods drawn up, I can't see faces, but despite the dire way those words are said, I detect a few soft snickers. After a dramatic pause, that same man speaks more.

"Your reverence will be useful. Your wit and good nature will be necessary. Now – let us begin." The group shuffles around, forming a circle within the circle of statues. "We –" the speaker stops abruptly. A new robed figure arrives and squeezes themselves into the circle. "Sorry" is mumbled a few times, and then the man leading the ritual nods and begins again. "We gather here under the watchful eyes of our benefactors. In the presence of all the demons and denizens of Hell. In the name of the Lord, amen."

"Amen," is echoed by those around the circle.

"In his name, we welcome darkness. Our Father, who is somewhere," the speaker shrugs, "Hollow is thy name. Thy will is cruelly implemented by those who withhold bread from others. We trespass against you and hope to be led into temptation. Amen."

"Amen," the group repeats.

"Produce the artifacts!" The speaker's voice echoes around the chamber.

From under robes, several objects are pulled and held aloft. I spot a crown, a scepter, a chalice, a leather-bound book, and a metal cross.

"*Fay ce que Voudras*," everyone says at once.

The phrase is repeated.

Repeated.

Repeated.

Each time, said louder as those holding objects slowly raise those items above their heads.

Above the chant of *Fay ce que Voudras,* the speaker shouts in a robust

and forceful voice, "Cast down
mediocrity!"

Book, chalice, cross, scepter, and
crown are thrown against the floor. The
thump of the book and the clatter of
the metallic objects reverberate around
the chamber, bringing the chanting to
an end.

The speaker flips back his hood.
He's a man of at least fifty with a
flat-bridged Roman nose, high
cheekbones, and a beaming smile. "To
the banquet. Let us feast upon food,
conversation, poetry, and love."

"Hear. Hear."

"Food and Love."

"Well said, Paul."

While they celebrate their opening
ceremony, I sense the arrival of
ethereal presences. The light cast
through the windows seems to dim, and
the air becomes thick and heavy, which
is a telltale sign that more than one
has come to watch. Perhaps it is
coincidental, given the invocation, or
they know the Endgame is afoot. In
either case, I feel as if the attention
is less focused on what the gathering
is doing and more on what I'm going to
do. I'm distracted by this and don't
notice at first as the gathering begins
to move.

The group forms into a two-by-two line and shuffles in my direction. I back up behind the chapel door and watch them approach with hardly a sliver of my face exposed. The speaker is last to take up a position in line. He touches the base of the statue of Athena as he passes. In that instant, there's a clank and something heavy slides beneath the stone I stand upon. The floor a few feet in front of the door to the chapel lifts. My view is blocked, but I hear them begin a descent upon stone steps. I listen for the last person to pass into the secret tunnel, but before I can move to follow, the floor begins to sink and settles back into place.

"Clever," I say, pacing over the hidden doorway. "Or maybe not clever enough. They'll hear if I try to open the way now. I have to find Dashwood's well." I race back into the chapel and recognize the familiar sound of sand and stone grinding under Mym. "Where have you been?" I fire at her as I step through the hole in the chapel wall.

Rumble. Rumble.

"That far. Interesting."

Rumble.

"No. I didn't see him."

Rumble.

"Talkative. Do I sense a little excitement?"

Rumble. Rumble. Crackle. Puff.

"Alright. Alright. No, I don't know what happened. The Princess threw off the spell. No. I haven't seen her either. But I'm not looking for her. I'm looking for Dashwood's well. It will be in the woods nearby."

Rumble.

"You do? Show me."

Mym leads me away from the abbey. The well is hidden among the trees not far from the abbey. It has a capstone and some extra deterrent in the form of bramble bushes.

Rumble.

"I'm certain the Cult is here. I feel it," I say as I inspect the well. "At this point, Mary is not my focus. My fight is with the Cult. When I defeat them, Mary's mission will end in failure." I test the weight of the capstone by pushing against it. "A strong door, but not, I think, made with me in mind." I push with some more effort. I hear the locking mechanism snap, and the capstone pivots on an unseen fulcrum.

I look over the rim of the well and see a spiral staircase.

CHAPTER TWENTY-FOUR

Before venturing into the unknown, I cast my senses out around me. Mary is undoubtedly around, watching - probably close by and knowing that when she is changed, I can't sense her. However, her lack of patience has resulted in her giving herself away several times. For better or worse, I don't see her. "Mary is not my focus," I say to myself. *A mantra I should have been paying attention to earlier.*

I return my attention to the spiral staircase. There is no light beyond the first few steps. I pick Mym up and take my first step down into the dark. After several turns, I hear voices and the clatter of dishes. When I arrive at the bottom, flickering dim light creeps around the edges of a door - no, not a door, but two large crates. I set Mym down and listen. Perceiving it safe, I gently shove the crates, just a little at first, enough to get my head around. I'm in a storage room. There are burlap sacks, baskets, crates, and chests. There's no door. It's more like a deep alcove with a forgotten statue at the back. "Janus, if I'm not mistaken," I whisper to Mym as I push the crates a little more and slip into the room.

The tunnel off this storage area is dark but for a few lanterns set on the ground at somewhat regular spacing. To the right, the tunnel opens into a larger chamber that is much better lit. By the sound of it, that is where the Monks of Medmenham have gathered for their banquet. *I'll peek in on them later.* Before stepping away, I glance up the stairs and then down at Mym. "Please guard this spot. And make haste if I have need of you elsewhere." Getting a notion of something without any sound from her is always strange. I distinctly sense the determined head nod and resolute attitude in this case. I smile and pat her surface before moving left down the tunnel, passing several larger alcoves with statues of greater and lesser technique. There's also graffiti and crude drawings – some excellently worked with charcoal. As I come to a side tunnel, I listen but hear nothing that gains my attention, so I press ahead. I arrive at a narrow, pebbly beach and an underground lake. A single shaft of light pours in from what I presume to be the abbey well-head. There are several boats pulled ashore here. I can see an island with a

grotesque idol upon it. The iconography
is so overwhelming as to be purposeful.
Deamons with enormous genitalia. Carnal
entwining. Skulls and bones. Symbols of
crown and church. "They are not shy
about their mockery," I mutter.

I backtrack along the tunnel and
take the side passage. There's only one
lantern in this corridor, but through
it, I come to a large round chamber
with a sunken floor, lit by candles and
lanterns. Flickering shadows highlight
the statues, chains, and manacles that
decorate the surrounding wall. There
are two archways – through the one to
my right, I hear the sounds of the
banquet. As I cross the room, each step
taken with care, my eyes and ears ready
to catch a hidden member of the Cult, I
notice an image. It's painted in red
and gold on the floor at the center of
the room. A swirl of color perhaps
representing the sun or maybe an
explosion, with lines or rays of light
of different lengths coming away from
it. The faded color and scuff marks
suggest it was put in when the room was
dug out and seemingly forgotten about.
I continue to investigate ahead. I
leave the round chamber and reach a
narrow river and a small stone bridge.

Beyond this are switchback stairs leading up.

"I don't like this. No guards. I don't understand. Is the banquet poisoned? Is the Cult simply waiting for them all to tire themselves?" I glance through the darkness in the direction of the round chamber. On the drift of air, I catch the sounds of the gathering – and then a scream. I rush forward, mentally tallying what I have in my satchel. *I have nothing to handle this many suffering from poison.* I place a hand against William's bag, trying to sense what he may have within, but I doubt there's anything for the task at hand.

As I arrive at the banquet hall, I press myself against the wall just outside and exert my will. The room is roughly triangular, with a large table that matches the shape of the room. At almost a right angle from my position is the tunnel with the storage area where I left Mym to guard. Even though there's plenty of space for all, a few small groups are spread throughout the chamber. I can't see everyone's face, but I do recognize a few from my ordeal at Saint Magnus and again at the watchhouse. However, I sense nothing sinister and only hear laughter and pleasant conversations. Whatever the reason for the scream, it seems to have been good-natured.

I remain vigilant. The scream that drew my attention might have been innoxious, but that doesn't change the fact that these people are in a great deal of danger. I want to warn them, but appearing now would be difficult to explain, and I feel would diminish my warning. This is Endgame, I'm certain. But I need to find my opportunity.

I shift from faces and interactions to the food. I have a hunch these people are necessary for the Cult's plans. The Cult is patient and more likely to allow these revelers to walk into the trap rather than push them. *It must be in the food*. Plates of cheese, fruit, and sliced meat. Jugs of wine and ale. I sniff for odd odors. I scrutinize the glistening meals, trying to judge natural juices from a glaze of deadly poison, but I'm too concerned about being noticed to venture further in for a better view. I fear if I wait any longer, it will be too late – *it may already be too late*.

My foot slides forward but halts. I hear the motion of the gears first, but slowly, the chamber goes silent as everyone looks in my direction. The unmistakable sound of the hidden entrance opening and then closing rumbles through the tunnels. Expressions of curiosity and some of concern dance over the faces of the gathering. For what it's worth, the Cult members mixed among the revelers are equally perplexed.

Marching along the tunnel, lit periodically by the evenly spaced lanterns, is the Princess. The light and shadow play off her features. I see a torn skirt and dirt on her sleeves – I am disappointed that she seems relatively dry. She reaches up to pat down a few stray strands of hair and then reaches into her bag. My level of agitation rises as I see her pull out the Diadem and affix it to her head. But it's not only the Diadem that draws my eyes to her face. There's something in how her eyes are suddenly and steadfastly focused forward, purposefully unmoving, unblinking.

There's a roar of celebration and laughter from the banquet hall. Several shout, "Princess!"

A smile breaks upon her face as she enters the chamber. "I am under the impression, Mister Whitehead, that there are no titles here. No age. No gender."

Laughing, the speaker steps forward. "Of course. Forgive us, but you have surprised us. Louisa, please come in. Join the revelry. I've never known you and your escort to arrive separately."

As with all the others, the man who steps forward is dressed in monk's robes. He's of average height and thin, with a round face, a long nose, and lively eyes that narrow inquisitively as he looks this way.

"Mister Walpole," the Princess says in surprise.

"Louisa? I was notified that you would remain at Carlton House this evening."

"Well," Louisa says with a chipper exasperation, "after my ill-fated travel, I wish I had. And you, Mister Walpole, I thought I'd overheard you'd been in a fight."

Walpole bristles at her words and takes a step back. "Well – an exaggeration, I assure you."

"Oh, happy days. Two stories of mystery and mayhem. Sit and tell us your tales," Mister Whitehead says as he gestures to two empty seats at the table.

I anxiously watch as the Princess is drawn into the crowded room. The

Cult members quietly break from where
they were seated and standing and begin
to make their way toward the table –
though none but I find this suspect, as
several others do the same. *I need to
move now.*

I take a step, and as if I'm
moving out of shadow, several in the
banquet hall take notice of me. There's
a gasp and several surprised
expressions – but neither the Princess
nor Walpole flinches, and suddenly I
feel as if I'm the one walking into a
trap.

"My word!" Mister Whitehead
exclaims.

"Your Highness," I nod. "You were
so excited to be a part of this that
you've gone and left me in the dark
back there."

"Oh! Yes. Of course. Please
forgive me –" Louisa's words stutter to
a stop as she realizes she has no idea
what my name is. "Yes, come in. I have
forgotten myself. Brothers and Sisters,
this is Sophia. A friend I met at an
art showing, and I just knew she would
fit in with us. Please forgive the
state of our clothing. We had the most
exciting time getting here."

"Sophia!" Several cups are raised.

"Come, sit by me. I was just about to tell them the story of what we had to go through to get here." The Princess takes a seat, and I take the one next to her – the one meant for Walpole, but another is made available further along the table for him. "There I was, scaling the side of Carlton House. My skirt in the wind for all to see,"

"Scandalous."

I don't see who said this, but it elicits a round of laughter.

"Rather," Louisa smiles. "I tell you, I nearly lost my stomach a few times. But it was easy going until, just near the end, the ledge gave way, and I fell. I can't say how I managed not to scream –"

"A will of iron. You'll make a fine queen one day," Whitehead shares.

"To the queen," the toast is taken up by several others.

"Anyway, there I was falling through the air – and Sophia caught me. Can you believe it? Swooped in under me. We both fell to the ground, laughing into each other's arms. Scared and relieved."

"S'at so, Sophia?" a man across the table slurs at me.

"It was terrifying, I assure you. And I hurt my shoulder."

A round of applause follows.

"Were that the end of it. Then we found a carriage. He weren't too happy about the distance, but we paid him well. Though, that ride," Louisa covers her face as she laughs. "That ride. How did we survive? He hit every bump in the road. My hand to our patrons," she says, looking at me. "We were flung from the carriage, and he just kept driving. I rolled down a hill, nearly into the Thames. It took me the longest time to get my breath back. We got separated -"

I take Louisa's arm and squeeze it - somewhat friendly. "Oh, but we found each other."

"So we did. So we did." Louisa dabs at her face with a silk napkin. "Telling the story has made me all flushed. Perhaps someone else would like a chance at attention. Mister Walpole, you had a story."

"Horace always has a story," a few of the ladies twitter and a few laughs circle the table.

"Not much to tell, I'm afraid. There was a beggar boy. He attacked me. If not for the timely arrival of a watchman, I say I would not be seated here now."

Those at the table and standing around it wait on bated breath for more. When none comes, curious glances are cast about.

"We need reform. Relief for the poorest of us all. If something were in place to turn that unfortunate's life around, he might not have resorted to violence. Perhaps our Founder's new respectability will bring some of that to parliament." Mister Whitehead claps Walpole on the back.

"Well said, Paul. Well said," someone in the crowd says, and several others drink to it.

The conversation drifts away from Louisa and Walpole as more philosophical discussions develop. More wine and ale are served, and food from the platters is taken without regard for station. I've come to be an expert on poison. Its scents. The color. How it changes the texture and taste of drink and food. The signs upon the flesh and how it can alter a person's functionality. But I decide the meal is clean, and judging by the amount of alcohol being consumed, I now understand why the Cult felt no need to hinder these people.

My attention switches to the faces
and body language of the group. There
are Cult members in this room and we
are very much aware of each other. *Will
they strike now? What are they waiting
for?* But other than some intense side
eye cast in my direction, they remain
engrossed in their conversations with
others. The trap does not spring – the
gathering remains friendly and
wholesome. However, the satirical
comments, words and attitudes, and
jokes and puns usually involving
genitalia and bodily functions that are
spoken would be considered blasphemous
by many. Despite the level of danger I
sense, time passes with nothing to
prove my anxiousness.

As the night progresses, my
attention shifts to Walpole. I notice
surprise in a few others as they try to
engage him in conversation only to draw
but a few words or none at all from
him. I also notice his drumming fingers
and constant glances at the Princess.
There's irritation there and some
disapproval – though that particular
disdain appears more often during the
furtive glances at me. Although there
is danger here, I feel more than ever
that the gathering is just the lure. *I
need to find the hunter before the trap*

is closed. I glance over my shoulder at the tunnel where Mym waits and then at the tunnel to the round chamber. I need to be moving, searching. *Too much waiting*. Before I can find an excuse to leave, the Princess suddenly rises from her seat. The action entices the Cult members and Walpole to shift as if making ready to stand themselves. However, she is only leaning forward a little to speak with a man across the table.

They told me to bring her. Is it that simple? Is the answer for them indulging in this gathering simply a matter of waiting for an opportunity to grab her? The Princess catches me as my eyes linger on the Diadem. "Princess," I lean in and say.

"Louisa, please."

"Louisa, is this a place for such finery? It strikes me as out of place. Perhaps tucking it away would be better."

"My circlet? No. It is far from out of place. This was my sister's. Her favorite. I wear it and, and it feels as if she is near. I wear it here because she enjoyed these gatherings as much as I've come to enjoy them."

"She was a member?"

"I believe she was considered a `Nun´. A partial participant. Whereas they see you as a `novice´. Someone here, but who will probably not come back."

Those words convey a hint of venom, and I notice a shift in her gaze – perhaps unconscious. Behind me, further along the table, is a Cult member. I don't have eyes in the back of my head, but I feel the Princess' change in focus was meant for that person.

My eyes remain fixed on hers, and I play into the curiosity of the conversation. "Did she sneak out as well?"

"No. Father is a Brother, though much like Dashwood, he hasn't been present for some time. But, there was a time when he came to these monthly gatherings, and he would bring Elizabeth with him. She was older than I am now. Perhaps that is the difference."

"And when he stopped attending?"

"She did as well," she looks away from me. "And then she got sick. And then she –" the Princess clears her throat and looks at me again, smiling. "And then I allowed my curiosity to get the better of me, and I followed Father on one of his last outings to this place. I love it here." She stands and raises her cup high. "I love you all!"

"And we, you." I'm noticing several fighting their drooping eyes.

She sits, her smile dropping away as she stares into her cup. "Father wasn't pleased. I don't know why. He never felt the need to explain it to me. He only said I was to stay away. He was rather cross when he found out about my continued escapades. Though Mister Walpole has curtailed many of those actions since becoming my shadow."

"Mister Walpole protects you?"

"As much as an old goat can. He ruins a lot of fun, that's for certain."

I glance over to Walpole again, but he's gone. *Did he need to relieve himself? Did someone pull him away and I didn't see it? He was acting strange – does this have something to do with that?* I pass my eyes over the crowded room. *Is anyone else missing?* With alarm, I note that one of the Cult members is missing. I count again. *One. Two. Three. Number four is gone.* I try to stand but find the Princess's hand on my arm.

"Please stay." Her whisper is insistent. "I'm sorry to have taken your warning so lightly. I feel eyes on me. I am unsettled."

I don't know what to do. *How long has Mister Walpole been missing?* I glance across the table to the nearest Cult member masquerading as a Monk of Medmenham. She was separated from Walpole by one seated person and probably saw him get up. I shift, ready to stand, but I remember the hand on my forearm. I lean to whisper to the Princess, when I see one of the other Cult members stand. The one across the table from me and this one whisper into each other's ears. They smile and giggle, and then move through the archway into the tunnel leading to the round chamber.

I can leave the Princess with one Cult member and a room full of people, right? Things are moving fast – very fast, too fast to worry about one human's safety. *Would you think that if this was William?* The shock of that thought makes me blink as if swallowing a bad taste. I look at the Princess. I see the creases of fear on her forehead. I see her hand on my forearm. I see her other hand fidgeting with the fabric of her dress. I see her eyes. I look into them. Eyes that have probably shed many a tear – and not always honestly. I'm sure of it. "Princess – I mean, Louisa. I need to find a chamber pot, if you please. The matter is quite urgent. If you wish, sit by Mister Whitehead." However, as I reach to take the Princess' hand from my arm, the two Cult members return. They take seats next to each other – with one taking the seat Mister Walpole had been using – and in unison, nod to someone, but I don't see who.

They'd been gone only a few minutes. Long enough to kill Mister Walpole. *Is that what they're saying by taking his seat? And what was the nod for?* I feel like I'm on a cart racing down a hill and I'm struggling to keep in control. I push the Princess from my arm and stand, but as I do, there's a thump at the table.

Mister Whitehead stands. "Come. Our revelry has ended. Up, you dirty bastards. Why did we go to the expense of making the cloisters comfortable just to always fall asleep down here? To our beds and what fun may follow there." Whitehead nudges the few around him, rousing one from snoring.

"Mister Whitehead," the Princess says as she stands, "if I may. The happenings of the cloister are not of interest to me, as you know. I would like to remain behind for a few minutes to give my friend a proper tour of all the nooks and art we have tucked away around here."

"Lamp and candle drift to sleep as well, Louisa. Mind your step," Whitehead nods and then continues to usher the gathering from the banquet hall.

Within moments, we are alone. "I wish I had the wisdom to know if you'd be safer with them or me."

"It is an ill wind that blows nobody any good," the Princess says with a shrug. "There is always trouble to be had. This way. There's a spot I like to tuck myself away in. No one knows about it." She steps away, moving into the tunnel toward the round chamber.

I don't want her to get too far ahead, but I need a moment to speak with Mym. I lean into the tunnel with the storage nook. "The wind is shifting, my friend. Be ready."

I catch up to the Princess as she steps into the round chamber. The candles have mostly gone out, but the lamps are still burning. She looks back and reaches a hand out for me to take.

She smiles as I do and gently pulls me into the room.

"There's a lovely echo here. Listen - Oooh!" Her voice bounces off the walls, fading as the sound travels down the tunnels. "Oooh!" she says again. She shapes her lips to do it again when we both turn to the sound of Mister Walpole entering from the tunnel leading down to the lake.

He has shed his monk's robes, now appearing in a suit of brown and red with an elaborately inlaid waistcoat. "That's enough of that, Your Highness." He stomps toward us as another figure takes shape in the tunnel archway.

It's a woman in the autumn of her years dressed in a flowing wrap-skirt and wide-sleeved shirt of blue and black. *A Priestess!* I reach back to draw my morningstar when I'm startled by the Princess choking on her words.

"Mister Walp -"

"Much better," Walpole says with his hand around the throat of the young Princess.

I take a step back and finish drawing my weapon. "That's enough, Mary." Still with Walpole's face, she turns to me. "I said -" I'm silenced by a finger in my face irritatingly twitching back and forth.

"Stay," Mister Walpole orders. His grip around the Princess' throat tightens – hardly a squeak escapes her lips. "You're too late. We've made a deal. Haven't we?" Walpole calls out.

My jaw clenches. "You're a fool, Mary. The Cult of Eleusis doesn't make deals."

"I have everything they want," Mary, in Mister Walpole's voice, says to me.

My eyes open wide. "You didn't. Tell me you didn't bring everything you've taken from them here."

"Did you bring the Key?"

"That is but one item. You are about to deliver all of the items to them."

"And steal it away later," Mary smirks, and then, with her head cocked over her shoulder she says to the Priestess, "Do you really want the Princess? Or is it just the Diadem?" With that, Mary snatches the circlet from the Princess and tosses it toward the Priestess.

As the Diadem clatters to the floor, three other Cult members - wraps and shirts of white, burgundy, and gray – step up behind the Priestess. "No deal if anything is missing."

"I assure you. Everything you want is right here. Do what you want with -"

Mary's words are stopped short by the *thwip* of something small and thin striking her neck. The Princess is dropped to the ground where she gasps for air. Mary pulls a tiny dart from her neck, the tip of which is covered in green crystal. "If you think -" She's cut off again as four more *thwips* foretell four more dart strikes. "Deal's off," Mary growls. Her hand dives into her pocket but, as she takes a step, she stiffens with a grunt. This time I hear the blade pulled and then plunged once more into Mary's back. She takes a step and falls flat on her face.

There's no time to enjoy the moment. I take another step away from the Princess.

"I really hope that wasn't the real Mister Walpole. You knew?" Louisa asks sweetly, the dagger she used to stab Mary lightly held in her hand.

"That that wasn't Mister Walpole? I had my doubts. I gathered he was acting strangely, but was that because of his own suspicions or because he wasn't Mister Walpole?"

"And me?"

"I suspected. You're not much of an actor." I glance up at the tunnel archway as more Cult members enter and begin to encircle the room. The first *thwip* comes from behind me. I turn and deflect the in coming dart. I rush the Cult member. They try to dodge, but I'm faster.

Thwip

I sidestep the dart and hear it strike the wall. I dash at the next Cult member, but this one rolls forward under my swing.

Thwip. Thwip

I deflect one, but the second bites into my shoulder. *There are too many. Too spread out.* I try for surprise with a standing leap to about the center of the room and charge at the Cult members across from me.

Thwip. Thwip. Thwip. Thwip.

Dodge. Duck. Dip. Deflect.

I swing at the nearest Cult member. They move to block. I shift my forward momentum, spin, and bring my morningstar around behind them. I hear their shoulder crack and see the well-spring of blood staining their shirt.

Thwip.

I feel a sting in my neck.

Thwip.

This time the bite is at my back.

I stumble forward but remain on my feet. It's difficult to lift my head, but I do as I hear the churning of gravel beneath an angry rolling boulder.

Coming up behind them, from the lake tunnel, Mym slams into one of the acolytes, sending her clear across the room. Mym shifts and crushes another against the wall. As she shifts again, this time targeting the Priestess, a net made of thick chains falls from the ceiling. Four acolytes with large hammers fall half a second behind the net. There's an echoing, sickly clang of heavy metal on stone floor as the net drapes over Mym. As the four acolytes land, they are already in mid-swing – the heads of their hammers glowing a bright orange. Nearly in unison, the hammers fall on the net's four corners, welding it with the stone. Mym tries to move but manages hardly an inch in any direction.

My knees give out as the darts do their work. I feel my morningstar slip from my hand. I'm vaguely aware of the Priestess coming toward me.

"The Sisters of Hera are more than prepared for the likes of you, Avatar."

CHAPTER TWENTY-FIVE

I awake in chains.

I'm alone in the round chamber but for two unconscious bodies. By the flickering light of several new candles and lamps with refreshed oil, I see that one of those bodies is Mary - chained to the floor and wall as I am - and William, who is crumpled on his side several feet from me. It would seem the chains and manacles which I thought were decorative, are in fact very functional. I test my range and the strength of the chains. My arms are heavy, and it's not just the weight of the thick metal. I can lift my arms, but I can't fully extend them. My legs have even less range; the cuffs around my ankles allow me only a few inches of movement. I'm dizzy from moving my head around and need to take a moment to rest it against the wall. The resin, that coats the ends of the Cult's daggers, their darts, and which I also see on these manacles, is potent.

I tap my head against the wall. "Never chase two rabbits." I bang my head harder against the wall.

"What is that you are mewling about?" Mary's groggy voice grumbles.

"A tactical error. A wildly stupid tactical error." I don't bother to hide my irritation and embarrassment. "I was too concerned about you. Too distracted. So, congratulations. The same with the Cult. Back and forth. Back and forth. My eyes and attention. Now, here I sit." I rattle my chains. I tilt my head so I can look at her. She's herself again. Long, gray, coarse hair tumbles over and blocks her face. Her hands are wrinkled and blotched with dark spots. She's fit but stocky, with an ample bosom. The clothes of Mister Walpole ill-fit her – tight in places and baggy in others. She's a rumpled mess. There's no dignity in what I see. I can't help the derisive chuckle. She looks like someone's mother, well into her cups, who has forgotten how to dress herself.

"Thanks for the warning, by the way." She begins to laugh. "Your arrival was not quiet. Ah," Mary goes quiet as she contemplates a fresh thought. "I am a fool. Was that on purpose? The ripple was intense, but the echo of it covered a wide area. I tried looking for you and almost didn't make it back here in time. I was hoping to lead you away, do the old double-back. Hopefully you'd be distracted long enough to keep you from ruining my plans. Was that your intent as well? To keep me distracted?" She pauses, leaning her head back against the wall. "You ruined them, by the way - my plans - by showing up with the Princess. So, congratulations to you as well." Mary proceeds to test the strength of her chains.

"That won't work," I say.

"Then you're not trying hard enough." She grunts and pulls even harder - her effort gaining nothing. She drops her arms in frustration. "Your pet rock is equally trapped, but your human lies there. Tell it to come over here and free us."

I hold up the manacle. "We need a key." I let my hand noisily drop.

Mary stretches to her left, straining for every inch as she tries to peek around Mym into the tunnel through which lies the underground lake.

"Mary," I say, but she ignores me. "Mary, we need to work together. Do you have anything, see anything, that we might be able to use?"

She sighs. "Why did you bring the Princess? She's important to their plans, far beyond that bobble she wears."

"Why did you try to make a deal with the Cult?" I snap back.

"I wasn't going to make a deal. I was going to steal it."

"It's not an it, you fool. They're not building something. They're going to conduct a ritual. It will kill everything, including us."

"Kill everything, you say," Mary settles back against the wall.

"This is no time for your machinations. Do you have anything to help?"

Mary searches her clothing. "They took all of my vials."

I glance around and notice a small pile of discarded items to my right. I spot my bag – the items tumbled carelessly on the ground. The same with the collection of things from William's bag, my morningstar, and several glass vials. "They certainly have the Key and the Wren journal," I mutter.

"They have everything."

Something in Mary's tone catches my attention. I turn to face her. "If you have anything - anything at all - now is the time."

"There's nothing to help us because you've given them everything. I have nothing for you," she growls at me.

"I was once told by a tutor, `When you want to catch a rabbit, don't set one trap; set five.´" We hear the words of the Princess as she steps into the chamber from the tunnel that leads to the switchback stairs. "Not what I expected from exalted beings. Spying. Thievery. Such tasks seem unbecoming of creatures such as yourselves." She approaches but stays well back. "And murder," her voice trembles a bit as she says this. "We have plenty who do that among us. Why stoop to such actions?" She's looking at, and speaking directly to, me.

"I didn't kill your sister. She did." I nod to my left.

Mary wiggles a few fingers in a haphazard attempt at a wave.

This statement confuses the Princess. She switches her attention between Mary and me as a coughing fit takes her. "No matter. Whoever you are, whoever she is, you're both guilty. I'm sure of it." She scowls at me before making an abrupt turn and walking away. She steps to the center of the room, glancing down at the painting on the floor as she tiptoes along the different lengths of the rays. "I knew it was you. I knew it was you the whole time."

"No, you didn't," I say.

"I did."

"You didn't," both Mary and I say at the same time.

She scoops up a pebble and throws it at us – missing. "I knew when you made the floor begin to swirl. I knew you were the one the Priestess had told me about. I knew then that you had killed my sister."

I sigh but decide not to argue.

"I know you've been following me around."

"I haven't been following you around."

"You have! I saw you –"

"At the art showing." Watching the Princess' lips purse together and her nostrils flare as I finish her statement is almost amusing.

"You think you were hiding –"

"In the tunnel outside the banquet hall." This time, her hands ball into little fists. "It's the Diadem, isn't it? It allows you to see things. Could you see that it wasn't Mister Walpole?"

The Princess' anger melts away as she cocks her head to the side and takes on a sly grin. "You don't know how it works. Would you like me to tell you?" With some of her confidence returned, the Princess takes several steps closer. "It tells me when someone is lying. It shows me truth. It -"

"I think that is all you need say, Louisa." The Priestess enters the chamber carrying a wooden box carved to resemble a small stone house with a thatched roof. Several other Cult members stream in behind her, spreading out to either side. Entering behind them is Mister Whitehead, who stands near the archway holding a small crate. Last to come into the round chamber is a tall woman dressed in a black robe with her hood up. She says nothing and stands at the lip where the floor sinks into the shallow pit with the sun painting.

The Cultist standing nearest to where we are chained is a young acolyte, about the same age as the one left to die in the streets outside the watchhouse. She pays us no attention, staring fixedly at the woman in the black robe. Dangling from a leather strap, with obvious intent, is a single key. They want to watch us hopelessly pull against our chains like wild animals. I will not give them the satisfaction. Mary, however, chooses a different path.

"Step closer, you infantile brat! Face me!" Mary claws at the air and spits as she shouts.

Annoying as her useless outburst is, it does have the added effect of causing William to stir. He takes a slow breath, jolting for a moment as he becomes aware of his surroundings, but I don't think anyone else notices. His head subtly shifts as he takes in what he can see of the room – pausing as he spots the acolyte with the key, and then again when he sees me. He smiles. It isn't easy to smile back. His left eye is swollen, and there is bruising on his face. He places his head back in its original position and then very slowly, pausing for several seconds between pushes, begins to slide in my direction. I'm unsure if he has a plan or if his goal is simply to move closer so we may speak without being detected. His approach is stealthy, but I think some further distraction will help.

I shift forward as much as my chains will allow. I'm about to call out to the Priestess when she sets down the box she had carried in and opens it. There's an odd sensation as I look at the small crystal orb on a velvet pillow. It has a transparent shell, but the center is smokey. The whisps become denser the deeper you gaze until you are staring at a white core. The object is about the size of a large fist, but it has the presence of something bigger that I can't put my finger on.

The Priestess reverently reaches in, gently placing a palm on the orb and closing her eyes. Several soft beams of light appear, terminating at the near walls and floor. From those points of light, objects begin to take shape. Within seconds, there are three bookshelves against the chamber wall, a chest, a stand displaying a longsword, and a table. "Bring the artifacts," she calls out.

Mister Whitehead steps forward. He sets the crate next to the table and pulls out a Jar with the Eye floating at its center. He sets a Fingerbone on the table next, followed by a Stone Dagger, a Wooden Cup, a Silver Ring, the Metal Key, and the Diadem. As the Priestess comes forward, Mister Whitehead steps back.

There is silence as the Priestess inspects each artifact.

"What's going on?" I call out.

The Priestess sets down the Diadem and turns to face me, "An end and a beginning. Amazing, isn't it?"

"It is," I say, and I can tell she wasn't prepared for that. "I've never seen such - such -"

"Power," the Priestess says. "Such control of the ethereal. And I include both of you avatars in that."

"Obviously," I lift my chains.

"Look at you."

And everyone does. Everyone is looking at me, and to a lesser extent, the Priestess - even Mary. And no one sees William inch closer. *Pandering will be too obvious*. "I will stop you. Whatever it is you are planning to do. I will stop you."

The Priestess laughs - a soft chuckle spreads through the acolytes in the room. Even the Princess and Mister Whitehead laugh. Only the woman in black remains silent. "You and your kind are a perversion. You are the untrained hounds of the former masters of this house."

"Untrained?" Mary scoffs, "Trained enough to best you on several occasions."

"And yet you are there," the Priestess points. She returns to the table and the artifacts. "Witness your demise," she says over her shoulder.

"Witness what?" I call out, trying to get her attention. "Witness what?!"

The Priestess sets down the Wooden Cup and turns to me. "What do you see here?"

"The library of a mad woman."

The Priestess raises her arms. "I see hundreds of years of hard work and dedication to a renewed beginning. The culmination of years of study and convincing the Superiors to use your own powers against you." She hikes up the hem of her skirt to move faster and races over to one of the bookshelves. "The packing spell," she pulls out a thin tome and slaps it down on the table so hard that the objects rattle. "The poison resin," she pulls another book. "Observations on your kind," her finger slides along several spines. "Even treatises on war so that we may train our acolytes. This is your doom. This has allowed us to give birth to the Sisters of Hera," she says, as the acolytes around the chamber stand straighter. "This has allowed us to defeat you."

"That's enough!" the woman in the black hooded robe commands. "Stop showing off, Priestess. Time is almost upon us. You have convinced the Superiors of this foolhardy dabble into the arcane, and I am here to see to it that you honor your bold statements. Proceed with the ritual."

The Priestess bows. "Of course, Mother Superior." She continues her inspection of the artifacts. There's silence until she steps back. "Add the Artifacts to the ritual circle." She steps away as the acolytes move to the table – including the one nearest to me, the one with the key. Under the direction of the Priestess, artifacts are placed at the terminus of particular rays.

"Hey," William whispers. "You have a plan, right? You and Mym?"

I can't look at him – out of fear it will draw attention, but also because of the shame.

"Persephone?"

I close my eyes. When I open them, I'm staring at him. He smirks.

"He did point at me, didn't he?"

I don't know what to say, but I can't look away. I'm cold. But it's more than that. It's as if an arctic breeze has blown through this chamber. A powerful presence has arrived – my guess, more than one. I can see Mary shivering out of the corner of my eye as she switches her gaze from William to me and then back to William.

"William," I'm barely able to form the word.

With only the slightest motion, he shakes his head – that smirk still on his face. "Well then, to it." William groans, rolls slightly from side to side, and staggers to his feet. "What's going on? Excuse me? Could I get a drink?" He stumbles forward.

"Silence him," Mother Superior orders.

An acolyte – the acolyte guarding us – turns from the ritual. Her face is picturesque anger.

"Yes, hello," William says, holding the side of his head as he steps up to her. "I was hoping –" A punch to his gut doubles him over. The high front-kick snaps his head back and sends him reeling. He falls flat on his back, crying out in pain – although I'm partially certain at least some of his volume is exaggerated. The acolyte draws her fist back to punch him again, but William covers his face and calls out, "I yield. I yield."

It's not so much William's pleas as the *woosh* of air drawn into the center of the room that takes the acolyte's attention away. Fire springs to life around the ritual circle, shooting up to the ceiling in a wall of flame. The room fills with the brightness of day, but the light shifts and a sickly green glow falls upon the room. The fire is not like fire but like liquid. It is as if the murky water of a swamp or stagnant pond has suddenly been transformed into green flame.

"The sword," the Priestess calls out. An acolyte brings the weapon to her outstretched hand. The Priestess takes a front stance and readies to thrust the sword into the green flames. "We are the makers of our own destinies," she says – the roar of fire almost masking her words. The tip of the sword begins to glow an intense white. "We are the makers of the world." She pushes forward, sinking the now glowing blade into the flames. "We are the destroyers and builders of creation." She struggles to hold the blade in the flames, but an almost giddy expression appears on her face as the white glow of the blade becomes green to match the circle of flame.

The Priestess withdraws the sword, not enflamed but glowing green with a pulsing energy. She holds the weapon high before turning to approach me. I hear Mym pulling and pushing against the heavy metal net she's trapped under. I watch William scramble to his feet, only to be held tight by acolytes and the Princess. I see Mary slide back as much as her chains will allow. I feel the eyes of all on me.

"Nothing in all our research tells us by what method to distribute the unmaking," the Priestess says. "But I do enjoy a well-made sword." She twirls the blade around and thrusts it backward into William.

Other than his shocked expression at having a blade sunk into his chest, William makes no sound.

The Princess and acolytes holding him step back as the Priestess slowly pulls the sword from William's chest – the green glow of the sword transfers to him. Like the tendrils of an angry octopus, the energy spreads out from the wound until he is completely covered.

He struggles to remain standing and falls to his knees. His head droops but comes up again. Our eyes entwine. "There's no pain," he manages to say. His form becomes a pulsing beacon of green energy that fades into nothingness.

There's an awed silence for several seconds broken only by the crackle of the ritual flames as they intensify.

I can't see the smile on the Priestess' face, but I can hear it in her tone.

"Yes. Yes. Yes. Yes. By all my sisters, it worked."

"Why did you not kill one of the avatars?" Mother Superior, standing across the room, demands to know.

"The flames will need to be fed," the menacing delight of the Priestess is highlighted by the eerie glow of orange and green bathing the surfaces of this chamber. "We have a few more sacrifices to make, and then it will be strong enough to consume our enemies. Trust me, Mother Superior, all preparations have been made." The Priestess raises her hand to point at the Princess. "The Princess first. Her lineage will give the fire much to feed upon."

The Princess backs away from the acolytes. "No. You said – you said – my sister, I'd be able to - you said," she kicks the nearest acolyte in the shin and breaks for the archway leading to the switchback stairs. Several acolytes chase after her.

"The man will do, for now." Mother Superior flicks a hand in Mister

Whitehead's direction as the Priestess
gets back into position.

"What? No. I embrace you. I
believe in you."

The acolytes are quicker this
time, and there is nowhere for Mister
Whitehead to run.

"I support you. You don't have to
do this. Upstairs, there are plenty
upstairs!"

I'm vaguely aware of a movement as
my numb mind takes in the actions
around me. The acolytes as they drag
Mister Whitehead toward the center of
the chamber. The sounds of Mym's
burning exterior sizzling against the
metal net. The grinding of stone under
Mym as she spins in place. Mary
aggressively shaking her head and
saying, "No. I don't care. No," as she
bounces up and down. More than the
rest, this odd behavior calls to my
curiosity, and I turn to look at her. I
watch as a small vial begins to poke
out from between her breasts. She bends
her head down, pulls off the stopper,
and proceeds to contort herself into
such a position as to allow the vial's
contents to drip into her mouth.

I watch as there's a shimmer of
light around her. Her features shift
from Mary to the likeness of the

courier boy I found several days ago in that small forgotten storage room under the furniture factory. With some effort, Mary, now much reduced in shape and size, can pull her hands free of the manacles. Clutching the still ill-fitting clothes to his body, Mary says in that young man's voice. "You crept in through some back entrance, right?"

I say nothing. I do nothing.

She grimaces. "Fine. I'll find it myself."

I hear Mary vault over Mym and the sound of her naked feet slapping against the stone floor, vanishing in the distance as she escapes down the tunnel toward the lake. The cry of alarm a few seconds later snaps me back.

"One of the avatars has gone!" an acolyte holding Whitehead points as she shouts.

All eyes focus on the empty spot between me and the tunnel leading to the lake.

"Find her!" Mother Superior shouts. "Find her and bring her back!" Unadulterated anger spews from her. "I'll have the head of every member of this cohort if she isn't found!" She steps closer to the ritual, grabbing the Priestess by the elbow. "Get on with it!" She shoves the Priestess. "Slay that beast first. I'm tired of its wailing."

I glance to my side. I can hear Mym grinding against stone and metal. Sparks and stones spray into the round chamber.

The Priestess begins the ritual of bathing the sword in the flame again – only this time, there are no words as the fountain of energy has already been prepared. She takes a strong front stance and slowly slides the blade into the liquid flame, waiting for the fire to mesh with the metal, and then slowly withdraws the sword, now pulsing green. She turns and walks toward Mym.

I see the crack in her composure. She's not sure this will work against Mym. She'd rather feed the flames with a few more not-so-innocent humans first before trying this. I watch as she approaches, my hands moving in my lap as quickly and subtly as I can manage. What no one saw, what no one suspected, was that William had taken the key from that acolyte. When that acolyte punched him, he leaned forward, anticipating what would happen next, grabbed ahold of the leather cord, and yanked when he was sent flying. He tossed the key backward, keeping attention on him by wailing.

But she is too near now – I can't find the key in the folds of fabric.

And then I feel the heat. A wave of intensely hot air washes into the chamber, and those chips and chunks of stone spraying into the room change to molten drops splashing onto the stone floor.

The Priestess tucks her head, trying to press on against the hot air and melted earth pelting her. She looks up after a few paces as the ground shakes and the grinding stops. With the sword still in hand, she takes on a defensive stance. "Where did that beast go!" she yells at me.

The ground shakes again. "Get ready for a surprise," I say. As the Priestess turns around, I abandon all subterfuge and find the key.

The floor about halfway between the wall and the fountain of energy cracks, and steam spills forth. We all feel the rumble of the earth hardly a few seconds before that spot erupts in a fiery explosion of molten stone and a flaming boulder.

Mym arcs up and comes crashing down through the circle of flame. She crushes the Ring beneath her. A

415

dazzling, intensely hot burst of light shines so brightly and with such heat that it makes my skin burn. There is no choice but to look away.

When the light fades, Mym stands at the center of the room. The fountain of energy is gone. Everything flammable is charred and smoking – even my own clothes. Mother Superior struggles to get to her feet – I can tell she's having trouble seeing. "Attack! Attack!" she calls out, but no one rushes to answer the order as they are still recovering. Whitehead, equally struggling to see, takes his chance and runs in the direction of the switchback stairs.

I allow the chains to drop noisily.

The Priestess, the no longer glowing sword at her side, turns to the sound. She looks up at me. "No. No, that's impossible. Impossible," she says.

Impossible things sometimes cause us to freeze – and she does. Eyes locked on me as I approach, she doesn't even have the good sense to raise a hand in defense as I jab upward with the palm of my hand. I snatch the sword as it drops. I spin and slice – her head comes free of her body.

I stand there, not staring at the lifeless form of the decapitated Priestess but at the spot where William had fallen. I'm unaware of the sword slipping from my hand until I hear the clatter of it striking the ground. My eyes still on that spot, I whisper as Mym rolls up alongside me, "Mym, bad dog."

Mym immediately erupts into renewed flame and slams into the far wall like a cannonball. She rebounds, sailing across the room, striking the wall with such force that she buries herself several feet into it. She blasts away from that wall, this time pulverizing an acolyte en route to the archway leading to the lake.

The ground shakes and rumbles. Large chunks of stone begin to fall. I look up from my vigil over William's last moment of existence to the sound of a scream and the crash of stone. Mother Superior is trapped under several pieces of large stone. Acolytes rush to her aide, but as more ceiling falls, they abandon their efforts and run. With walls tumbling around me and flames spreading from smashed oil lamps, I walk over to the table. A heavy chunk of ceiling has smashed it, and nearly all the bookshelves have toppled. I kick some stones away and push the chunk from the table. There isn't time to properly search, but those two books the Priestess had kindly pointed out are right here. I grab them and then decide there are other things I should grab.

The artifacts have been scattered but are all within reach, except the Jar with the Eye. It is buried under several feet of rubble. "I know where it is if ever I need to find it," I say as I sprint over to where the Cult had discarded my things. My morningstar I slide into its sheath. Everything else is scooped up and crammed into my satchel, including William's things. "Time to go," I say, feeling no need to shout or stress for urgency. I stand to leave. Mym comes to my side. As we make our way to the secondary egress, the chambers and tunnels behind us continue collapsing.

A week passes. Not enough time to heal, but time enough to learn. Mym and I stand outside the boarding house where William kept his room. I stare up at his window. Time passes. Mym is patient. I feel the flow of the city around me. The noise is a muddled and distant symphony. Words are spoken to me as people walk by, but they wash over me as so much rain. Some of the Patrons, certainly mine, consider what transpired as a victory. I thought little about it in the aftermath. There were important things that needed to be taken care of before I would allow myself to believe that it was over.

The artifacts needed to be scattered once more. The Stone Dagger I had shipped back to the family who claimed it as an heirloom. The Fingerbone I returned to Saint Magnus. The Key is buried once more in the gardens at Chelsea. The Cup I left at the Almshouse. The Jar I left buried. The Ring is destroyed – ending any attempt to reperform the Ritual of Solomon. Each artifact has arcane qualities, but they've been hiding in plain sight for a long time. I saw no harm in doing so again. The Diadem, however, I decided to hide. It wasn't a priority for the Cult because, in essence, they already had it. I don't know what remains of the Cult now, but knowing what the Diadem can do, I felt it better to keep it unnoticed. Museums are big places with many nooks and shelves; one box can go unnoticed - especially when it has a little help.

Victory – it feels like failure. I continue to stare up at William's window until I feel a nudge at my side.

Rumble. Puff.

I nod and lift Mym into my arms. As we step inside the building, I push the attention away from us. The three people seated in the parlor comment on the wind pushing the door open.

I use William's key to open his door. Light shines in from the window, but there is a chill in the air. I think about starting a fire, but I won't be here that long. I step over a few notes that have accumulated on the floor. Friendly messages of worry, no doubt. I set Mym down and shut the door. I glide my fingers along the fabric as I walk by his oversized chair. As I come to the armoire, I set my palms against it and then my forehead. "Dear friend and mighty warrior, you will be missed but not forgotten. I hope you have found the peace and love you so sorely missed." I step back and reach into my bag for the small crystal orb William had kept as a memento of his wife.

Rumble. Puff.

I stare at the orb for a moment. "I admit, the arcane is not my best skill, but we spent the last week studying the Cult's notes. We followed the incantation as instructed."

Crackle. Puff.

"Let's find out." I walk around the room, touching the crystal orb to the chair, the table, the bed, the chest of drawers, and the armoire. I place a palm on the top of the orb and turn my hand clockwise. As I do, soft beams of light emit from the sphere in my hand. There is an iridescent shaft for each item I touched with the orb. The beams' light consumes the furniture and then retracts into the crystal. As the items vanish, I find myself staring into the orb. There's a vastness in the palm-sized sphere. I can see the orb, but I feel like I'm looking through a window into an immense warehouse.

The room is empty. I smile – it feels like the first time in several days.

Rumble. Puff.

I shake my head and laugh as I put the orb in my bag. "As always, your words of confidence bolster my resolve."

Puff. Crackle.

I pause before answering – taking in the quiet and empty room for just a moment more. "Now we move on," I turn to leave and come face to face with my Patron. I take in a sharp breath and a step back. "Charon, what is thy will?" I bow my head as those flame-lit eyes stare at me. He says nothing as a vision fills my mind.

A wooden skiff upon a river. A punter and a traveler. I hear William's voice and the story he is telling.

"She was perfect in every way. I was flush with anger, having just spent the last five minutes shouting at my uncle and him at me. She came to me on the veranda. I told her I was not good company. She said I had a wonderfully strong voice and wondered if I enjoyed singing. I told her I did enjoy singing. After such a shout, she said I should keep my throat moist. I asked if the drink she had in her hand was for me. She said," William chuckles, "she said, `what this? No, this is for me.´ I don't know why, but I laughed. And she laughed. And we spent the rest of the evening talking."

The vision blurs, and suddenly, I'm sailing over a vast ocean. The water stretches endlessly in every direction. I can feel the breeze and taste the salty air. The sea passes under me at a great speed until I fly over a new city and land. I hear musket and cannon fire and the shouting of voices, the screams of pain, but see none of it. I pass over open fields and small villages. I see a mighty river ahead.

And then I'm back in the empty room.

My Patron is gone.

Rumble. Crackle. Puff.

I smile. "We have a ship to catch."

www.ingramcontent.com/pod-product-compliance
Lightning Source LLC
Chambersburg PA
CBHW022240020726
47496CB00004B/997